This book is from
the library of...

Bernadette

The High Valley

The High Valley

JESSICA NORTH

Random House   New York

All rights reserved under International and Pan-American Copyright
Conventions. Published in the United States by Random House, Inc., New
York, and simultaneously in Canada by Random House of Canada Limited,
Toronto.

Library of Congress Cataloging in Publication Data

North, Jessica.
  The high valley.

  I. Title.
PZ4.N8579Hi [PS3564.0725]   813′.5′2   72-11460
ISBN 0-394-48103-8

Manufactured in the United States of America

FOR VERA
who taught a child to read . . .

And I shall flee from the darkness
From the stone places of silence
For my heart wants flowers to hold in my hands
Beautiful songs, beautiful flowers . . .
—Aztec poem

ONE

Yesterday the first snow fell, great feathery flakes that vanished as they touched the ground. We watched, standing together at the window of this rented cabin, while the glass in front of us, silver-framed by frost, mirrored the blaze of pine logs on the hearth.

"Winter is almost here," I said.

"Yes." His hand touched mine, but his thoughts, I knew, wandered toward a faraway country. "We must go home soon. We've been away long enough." He spoke as much to himself as to me.

"I think so too. We should be ready now." But my voice carried an assurance I did not really feel.

Just then the overcast sky brightened, pale sunlight struck the surface of the northern lake where we are staying, and Puerto Vallarta came suddenly to my mind, as vivid, as beautiful in memory as in life. In imagination I saw a flash of azure—the incredible blue of the Bay of Banderas—and beyond it rolled the Pacific, white-capped by the wind. I seemed to feel the warm sands of Yelapa Beach, and remembered that its name, in the Indian language of the coast, means "place of reunions."

Reunions. I am not yet ready for a reunion there. We have had more than our share of violence, and the scars of it have not yet healed in our minds. I still cannot think of Veronica without a quickening of my blood, a fear I refuse to call by its true name. But her ghost no longer haunts me, she does not stand behind my chair, silent and insubstantial. Her gray eyes do not watch me now, nor does Veronica control and move my hands as she did one night only a year ago. Not any more.

I try to banish all memory of Veronica, and I know I must not think of her as a spectral presence emerging from the mists that shrouded that huge, gabled house in the High Valley. Not a ghost, I tell myself, but a real woman who was helpless and terrified. I have learned only too well to understand such feelings. Yet Veronica returns when the chiming of a country church bell reminds me of Puerto Vallarta,where it all began.

I wonder if he, too, thinks of her often. One day last week I almost asked him. He was standing alone on the path that leads to the shore, gazing at the hills toward the west, and I said, "What are you thinking?"

"Look, Alison," he told me, pointing to the sky. "The mallards are going home." Then I saw the V-shaped squadron flying southward.

"Home?" For a moment the word surprised me. I am a New Englander, born sixty miles from this lake, and to me the country of pine forests and cold streams is where the mallards, the teal, and the curlew live. Their home is here, and the autumn flight is only a sojourn. But he sees it differently, of course.

"Remember the mallards in the High Valley?" he asked. "They come back a month after the rains have ended, but some years they are late." He smiled quietly. "They have a Mexican disregard for time."

The High Valley. He spoke the name I'd temporarily forced from my mind. I had allowed myself to think of Puerto Vallarta, but the High Valley, that cup of land hidden in the mountains far above the town, was the setting for the violence and malice that changed our lives and made us what we are. Suddenly I saw the black upthrusts of volcanic rock, the slashed arroyos where torrents have gouged the earth, the shafts and pits of its abandoned mines.

And soon we will return there, return to take up our lives, to watch the seasons change and wait each year for the great downpour of summer rains. We will ride together in the mountain meadow, our horses splashing through shallow brooks, and we will find the places where wild orchids bloom. The chimes in the tower are to mark our hours, and at twilight there will always be distant music—a guitar, a bamboo flute, a shepherd's harp. The High Valley is now "home."

Our homecoming must not be marred by the past, and I think it was at the moment when the mallards vanished into the darkening sky that I realized the only way to forget was by remembering. I would relive all that happened—all of it—one last time, and then have done with the past forever . . .

"Please fasten your seat belts and observe the no smoking rule. We are now approaching Puerto Vallarta."

When the stewardess spoke, I involuntarily braced myself, a little nervous about the landing, which, I supposed, would come in five minutes. I was twenty-five years old, a child of the space age, but I'd seldom traveled by plane and still felt uncertain of the takeoffs and landings. My father, years ago, had insisted that these were moments of mortal peril. But of course, he suffered motion sickness in the air and so became the arch enemy of aviation. "If God had meant for man to fly," he said, "he would have given him a stronger digestion."

My mother, Helene, was exactly the opposite, forever dashing to catch a flight for New York or Hollywood or anywhere else her overly optimistic theatrical agent chose to send her in futile search of a role. She never took me with her, of course. I didn't board planes, I *met* them—helping Helene with her hatboxes and make-up case, getting quickly out of the way if an airline publicity man chose to photograph Helene's voluptuous figure and kittenish face.

So this was my first long plane trip, and flying, I'd discovered today, made the world astonishingly small. New York in the early morning, Mexico City at noon for a rush through customs and a quick change of planes. Now, only an hour later, Puerto Vallarta on the Pacific Coast. The other passengers, chattering and laughing, seemed to take such speed for granted.

The two seats between me and the window were occupied by a fat American woman in a droopy flowered hat and her pudgy preteen daughter. Both flaunted big plastic badges proclaiming that they were members of something called a "Happiness Tour."

The woman, ignoring the stewardess' announcement, puffed her cigarette with stabbing motions and read aloud from an airline lure folder about Puerto Vallarta.

Her daughter squealed, "Liz Taylor and Richard Burton! Yesterday's paper said they were flying down to their house there in Frank Sinatra's private plane! You'd think they'd have a private plane of their own, wouldn't you?"

"Well, they've probably lent it to somebody. Maybe we'll see them on the street. It's a tiny town," said the woman avidly. Then, surveying her own girth, she added, "They say she's not much to look at offscreen. Plump. Runs to flesh."

The fat woman's spite irritated me, and another voice, my mother's, came back—Helene's gay ripple as she described me to her admirers. "Poor Alison's nothing but bones, eyes, and elbows. I'd make her drink malteds to gain weight, but I'm afraid she'd slip through the straw and fall in!" Always "Poor Alison!" The words slid out so unthinkingly, so automatically, as she tilted her pretty curls and drew back her shoulders to emphasize that she herself was nothing but curves and soft-ness.

The plane began its swift descent, but the rushing sensa-tion in my ears did not drown out the memory of Helene's lilting voice. Ironic that it was not Helene but "Poor Alison," who in a moment would be set down in what the travel folder called "A tropical paradise for sportsmen and sun worshipers." A place whose list of celebrated visitors sounded like roll call at an Academy Awards ceremony. How Helene would have loved to be near them!

The Beautiful People. What was it like to be a Beautiful Person? I swallowed hard, my ears popped, and the handker-chief I twisted in my hands grew limp. After hours of buffeting in a bus, a limousine, and two planes, I felt a good deal less than beautiful. In fact, I barely qualified as a person. I was Miss Nobody going nowhere alone because she had no other place to go and no one to go with her. And furthermore, Miss Nobody didn't care at all. Rebellion surged in me. If no one needed me, well, I didn't need anyone either.

My decision to quit my job on one day's notice, give up my apartment, close my small savings account, and fly off to Mexico had been so impulsive—almost panicky—and every-thing had happened so fast that somehow I had left my own identity behind. My passport claimed that I was Alison Mallo-ry, born in Old Bridge, Massachusetts. I was five feet, seven inches tall. ("Don't worry about it," Helene used to say, smiling up at me. "In flats or sandals you're no taller than I am.") The passport alleged that my eyes were gray, although my driver's license insisted they were blue. At any rate, they were extraordinarily large and I had two of them, and besides, who cared? The surprised-looking girl in the photograph dis-played my features, lips fuller than I would have chosen; and the long brushed-back hair, so pale that it blended into the light background, was certainly mine. Hair the color of new cornsilk. ("Don't worry, dear. It'll darken to honey-blond as you grow older." It hadn't.)

I was, I supposed, the only fugitive on the aircraft. The other passengers were going toward something. The entwined couple across the aisle whom I'd nicknamed "the honeymooners" traveled toward the beginning of a new life together. The fat woman and her daughter moved, they hoped, toward celebrities and a glimpse of glamour. The red-necked man in the seat ahead who'd twice tried to strike up conversations with me was on a girl-hunt.

But I was not consciously going toward anything. I was running away. Running from things I couldn't bear to think about. Gripping the seat belt, I blinked hard and rapidly, vowing to myself that there would be no more useless tears.

Puerto Vallarta, a town I knew little about, was an accidental destination. Margaret Webber, widow of a physician, lived there in retirement. Every Christmas her card said; "Please come for a visit." Now I was doing it—but not a visit, an escape. And because, not for the first time in my life, I needed Margaret badly.

"I'm on an adventure," I told myself silently but firmly and for the hundredth time.

Then, in the last seconds before landing, I decided to play The Game, a secret left over from childhood, a kind of instant fortunetelling. I closed my eyes and listened intently, pretending that the first thing I heard, the next words, the next sound would tell me what lay ahead.

There was silence except for the rush of air breaking against the plane like surf, then, just as the wheels touched the runway, the man across the aisle spoke clearly to the woman beside him. "Journey's end, darling."

Journey's end. Those should be the mystic words, but for a moment they held no meaning for me, although they seemed disturbingly familiar. Then I remembered the Old Bridge Summer Theatre production of *Twelfth Night,* Helene poised and pretty waiting to enter as Olivia, and myself sitting on a hard bench in the wings, a teenage prompter. The boy playing the clown role sang on stage:

8

*"Trip no further, pretty sweeting;
Journeys end in lovers' meeting,
Every wise man's son doth know . . . "*

As the plane rolled to a halt, I opened my eyes, glancing at my hand which for more than a month had seemed unfamiliar without the engagement ring I'd worn so long. *Journeys end in lovers' meeting.* Not likely. The Game was not working well today. I felt annoyed with myself for having played it. Silly and childish, part of the self I'd left behind, part of the outwardly practical and punctual girl who, underneath, believed in too many romantic daydreams.

"Pardon me, please!" The fat woman cast me an irritated scowl as she and her daughter bulldozed past me into the packed aisle. Lowering a well-padded shoulder, she rammed herself through the confusion of flight bags, cameras, and sun hats. New acquaintances, met on board the plane, called hurried good-byes to each other, while I waited until the aircraft was almost empty.

I started toward the exit, the journey had ended. I had arrived, suddenly confused, bewildered, and sure that everything I had done in the last few days was madness. I made my way down a short flight of steel steps, felt the sun strike me. Then I looked up and found I had entered a new world.

Color. A sky so blue that I caught my breath. Huge pearl clouds heaped upon each other, and below them shone the green of tropical forest. And flowers—vermilion, purple, orange flowers that seemed not to bloom but to blaze. A flight of gulls sailed overhead, their white wing tips flashing silver. All of it was unreal. Somehow I had stepped into a painting by Gauguin.

And there was music. Guitars and a marimba and a dark young man in a flowered shirt singing "La Golondrina." Did they always do this? Did musicians welcome every plane, or was some celebrated Beautiful Person arriving or departing? It didn't matter. Even if by accident they were welcoming *me.*

9

Although the runways were broad and new, the terminal building sleekly modern, I found myself in the midst of what seemed to be a village fair. Vendors hawked flowers and fruit, laces and scarves, some voices hoarse, others shrill, but their cries were strangely melodic. Two little girls, starchy in white confirmation dresses, gazed at me with almond eyes. Porters, vacationers, hucksters, children, and musicians ignored the ropes and marked boundaries to overflow onto the tarmac in a heady confusion of colors, smells, and languages.

As I walked toward the terminal, I realized I carried the plaid cloth coat that only this morning the sleet of New York had pierced. I had lived so long with grays and browns, had seen light only when filtered through smoke and exhaust fumes, that now everything from the brilliance of the poppies to the transparency of the air astonished me and left me giddy.

Inside, the terminal was cool and uncrowded except for the pushing group at the luggage counter. I did not join them. I was in no hurry and no one waited to meet me, since I hadn't known my arrival time when I'd sent the telegram to Margaret Webber. Sitting on a comfortable leather couch, I relaxed, my eyes wandering toward souvenir shops displaying gay shawls and gossamer mantillas. Then, as I glanced down a corridor, I saw the two Beautiful People approaching.

The woman was a golden blonde, her burnished hair cascading over bare shoulders so loosely, carelessly, and naturally that its perfect fall simply couldn't be natural. She moved like a queen, proud, erect, and confident, tall even in flat sandals. Her sleeveless white shift was skillfully cut to reveal the curves of a slender figure and skin glowingly tanned by tropic sun. A film star? A television personality? The men at the counter turned their heads as she passed, and even the male of the honeymoon couple gave a long second glance.

It was hard to imagine a situation in which she would not have commanded every eye—and she knew it. But today she had major competition, for the man escorting her was even more dramatic than she was. His long, easy strides were accented by the clinking of silver spurs. The tightly fitted suede trousers gleamed with two rows of silver buttons and more silver shone from the handle of a pistol strapped to his hip, while the short jacket over his linen shirt flashed with braid and embroidery.

His sombrero, its broad brim rolled both in front and back, gave the impression of a Mexican highwayman or a Pancho Villa, and one might have expected a swarthy face and bristling mustachios. He did have a mustache, but it was pencil-thin and light brown, the same color as the forelock showing under the sombrero. He couldn't be Mexican, I thought. He must be a fair-complexioned, hazel-eyed American dressed in an exotic costume. Yet never, except in antique Spanish portraits, had I seen such sharply chiseled features, a thin, aquiline nose that gave him a patrician appearance but somehow suggested coldness—perhaps even cruelty. A long, narrow scar, deeply etched on his left cheek and vanishing under his collar, suggested some episode of violence. Like the blond beauty beside him, he was poised and in command, but unlike her, he appeared unaware of the attention he drew.

The couple paused a few yards from me, waiting for a porter, who struggled with a heavy suitcase, and then I realized that the woman's face was flushed with anger.

"I want to know just one thing!" Her throaty voice rang through the terminal. "How much longer? That's simple enough, isn't it?"

His face tightened, but he spoke softly in Spanish, words I couldn't hear. If the reply was meant to soothe her, it failed. Her green eyes widened, her cheeks flared with rage, and suddenly she swung her arm.

I gasped as I saw the slap coming, but he saw it too, and his hand darted out, catching her wrist just as it reached his shoulder. He gripped her and for a second that seemed an eternity the two were frozen, her face a mask of silent rage, his fixed in a mocking smile.

"Siempre la dama perfecta, Karen." The ironic voice

would have sliced steel, and this time I understood the Spanish.

"Damn you!" She spat the words. "Veronica should have poisoned you. Veronica . . . " His grip must have tightened, for she gave a startled cry of pain that cut off her words.

"Enough of that!" He spoke in slightly accented English, and the tone was still razorlike. "I told you not to say her name."

He released her, and the arm fell limply to her side. "Good-bye," she said. "Good-bye and go to hell."

"Not good-bye, Karen." Sweeping off his sombrero, he bowed formally, tauntingly. *"Hasta la vista."*

Turning away, she gestured to the baggage man, who had been watching the scene, fascinated. Then she moved toward the exit for departing passengers, the proud head high, her steps deliberately slow and controlled.

I thought he was going to follow her. He seemed to start forward, seemed about to call. Then he checked himself. For only an instant I saw his face stripped of insolence, its features stricken—a naked look of longing so private that I, an intruder, lowered my eyes.

He strode past me, then hesitated and suddenly glanced my way, startled. For less than a second his look held mine, then he murmured, *"Buenas tardes,"* went swiftly toward the terminal doors, and was gone.

I heard the fat woman's voice, loud and excited. "He just *has* to be a movie star! I'm sure I've seen him in *something.*"

As I claimed my suitcase, I realized how every detail of the brief but vivid scene had stamped itself upon my memory. I would never forget the man's insolent smile, the silver-handled pistol, even the clink of his spurs. And the woman's taut, lovely face, the tilt of her head. Karen. That was her name. Only later would I remember that another name had been spoken. A name that would mean far more to me. Veronica . . .

. . .

I stretched myself comfortably in a woven chair in Margaret Webber's sunny patio. I'd showered, unpacked, and now my feet were propped on a rattan footstool. A tall limeade, the glass frosty, stood at my elbow.

Margaret lay on a hammock that was suspended between two flowering pepper trees. I had not seen her in four years, not since her last trip to the United States, but she was unchanged. The gray-flecked hair, cropped short and tightly curling to frame a scrubbed New England face, was dearly familiar, and her warm laughter remained as motherly as it had seemed in my childhood.

"You're sure you wouldn't like some gin in that drink?" she asked.

"No, thanks. After all that's happened today, it would go straight to my head. I feel as though I've changed worlds, landed on another planet."

"Alison, I can't tell you how good it is to have you here!" The warmth of her smile was like a handclasp. "How many times have I said that in the last hour?"

"Never mind. I love hearing it, I love to feel welcome."

"Not just welcome, dear," she said quietly. "You're at home, you know."

A hummingbird hovered near the trumpet vine, a flash of emerald against golden blossoms. I could hear the calls of tropical birds I couldn't identify, and the air was sweet with the perfume of roses. Margaret, as she'd written me, had "gone native" in a zany but delightful way. She was barefoot, wore a shapeless Mother Hubbard spangled with floral designs, and she had topped off the costume with jingling silver bracelets and coral beads. Her former neighbors in Old Bridge would have said she was "all decked out for a Halloween party," and she would have enjoyed the joke.

The starchy Yankees of Old Bridge had always been scandalized by two women of the town—Margaret and my mother. But the men, at least, forgave Helene for being theatrical and stage-struck because she was pretty and helpless-looking. Besides, she flattered them outrageously. Margaret's outspoken honesty and fierce independence were harder to tolerate. She wore what she liked, did what she wanted, said what she thought.

"Tell me about the town," I said. "I've heard it's filled with millionaires and movie stars."

She chuckled. "I wouldn't recognize a movie star. Except I did once meet that nice Mr. Burton and his wife." I tried not to smile. Who but Margaret would describe the famed couple that way? She had liked them and that was all that mattered. Fame did not impress her. "I imagine I know everybody in town except the tourists. Some are millionaires, some others have a hard time scraping by from week to week. Everyone goes his own way, and I like that."

There was a pause. I sipped my drink, realizing we had momentarily run out of small talk. She studied me, wanting to ask questions, yet determined not to be tactless.

"You're wondering why I came so suddenly, aren't you, Margaret?"

"Well, yes. I might as well admit it. The last time you wrote it was about setting a date for a wedding. I have a present wrapped and waiting in the hall closet. I was going to mail it as soon as you sent word."

"You can unwrap it and put it to use," I said, as lightly as I could. "Donald broke our engagement last month. I'm a woman scorned, and I'll admit that for a few days I felt like one of hell's furies. But not now." Avoiding her shrewd eyes, I tried to shrug my shoulders casually. "The two years with Donald are just so much lost time. That's all."

I knew how hollow the lie sounded. Those years had meant everything, and could not so easily be erased from my life.

"I'm glad you're not moping, and I'm glad you're here where you belong," she said, accepting what I had told her too quickly. "You're well out of it, Alison. When it takes a couple two years to decide about getting married, there's something lacking. Not enough fire, I suspect."

I murmured agreement, knowing she was wrong. There had been fire, all right. But we faced a problem few young lovers have to solve. Donald had been blinded in an auto accident that left him completely sightless, unable to distinguish darkness from sunshine. We'd met because I was a teaching assistant at Bradford Center for the Blind, a private school for adults not far from New York City.

Donald, at the time of his arrival, had shown the worst symptoms of being what we tactfully called "an emotional case" in staff meetings. While finishing his last year of law school he'd lost his sight, and with it, he felt, his future. It was useless to point out to him that law is a profession in which the blind have enjoyed great success. Alternately defiant and despairing, Donald Nelson came to Bradford after leaving two larger institutions, and like several other "emotional cases," he became my responsibility, one of a group nicknamed "Alison's barbarians" by staff members.

I was not a trained psychologist, and when I'd taken the position at Bradford, I hadn't even known that the Braille alphabet has sixty-three characters, much less what they meant. My sketchy knowledge was instinctive and practical, learned on the job and during long evenings of study. Maybe the "barbarians" sensed my insecurity, my struggle to learn along with them, and sympathized with me.

One of the first things Donald said to me was a blunt comment. "Miss Mallory, you don't really know what you're doing half the time, do you?"

"Less than half," I answered sharply. "But I'm trying hard. And that's more than I can say for you, Mr. Nelson."

Suddenly he laughed, the first time he'd done this at Bradford. "Thanks for snapping at me. At least there's one person who doesn't smother me with sympathy."

He had summed up the hardest problem: how to be sympathetic but not smothering. Adults who suddenly find themselves sightless face many problems and struggles, but such mechanical tasks as learning Braille are the least of their difficulties. The great challenge is the battle to regain confidence and self-respect, to overcome fear of being a perpetual burden to others and an object of pity. Somehow, inexperienced though I was, I seemed able to help them in this battle until they reached the point where specialists could take over.

It had been this way with Donald—but during the process we had fallen in love. Not a wild, desperate love, not the secret Romeo and Juliet dreams of my girlhood. We were, I told myself, too mature and sensible for that. But we had other things: the mutual need of two lonely people, respect, affection, and tenderness.

Then one night the secure little world I thought we were building together collapsed.

In the sunshine of Margaret's patio, I remembered the snow outside my apartment window that night. I remembered how Donald took my hand and tried to tell me as painlessly and tactfully as possible that there would be no marriage, no future for us. At first I couldn't comprehend what he was saying. Then, when I realized this was the end, I suppose I should have behaved like one of the "civilized" heroines in the brittle comedies Helene loved to appear in. But I couldn't. "Why are you doing this?" I demanded, my voice breaking as I fought to hold back tears. "What have I done? Why?"

"Because you don't want to be my wife, Alison. You want me to be a child, forever dependent on you. You feel safe with me, but love has to mean more than safety. If I could see you, you'd run away, hide yourself."

"That's not true!"

"But it is." The dark glasses were fixed on my face, and for a second I felt that the sightless eyes behind them were looking into the very depths of my self. "I have my blindness, Alison. And you have yours, too."

Now I pushed the bitter memory of that scene from my mind and struggled to concentrate on what Margaret was saying. Something about a wonderful vacation and a good rest.

"I've worried about you, dear," she continued. "The work you do is important. But your letters always make me feel that it's—well, too much of your life." She frowned. "When you write, it sounds like news from a girl in a convent. There's a wide world outside that school, you know."

"It *is* a convent," I answered. "And I've leaped over the wall. I quit." She had taken the news about my break-up with Donald so matter-of-factly that I knew she had expected it. But now she was astonished.

"Well! But you always . . . "

"I quit, resigned, walked off. And I'm not going back."

"Then this can be a long vacation. Good!"

Not as long as I'd like, I thought, remembering the thinness of my checkbook. "Margaret, if it's not too much trouble," I said, "I will have some gin in this drink now."

Juana, Margaret's dark Indian maid whose eyes were like amethysts, served us supper at eight o'clock, a time that seemed a little late for me and early for Margaret, who followed a Mexican schedule.

The house clung to a steep hillside, no two rooms on exactly the same level, and the small dining room overlooked the walled patio to command a magnificent view of the Pacific, now shimmering in cool moonlight. The tall windows had screens and louvred Barbados shutters, but no glass. "No need for it," said Margaret. "When there's a west wind and rain at the same time, I just draw the draperies—they're waterproof. And if rain wets the tile floor, what's the difference?"

"I hardly know if I'm indoors or out," I told her. A giant philodendron, the largest I'd ever seen, gave a jungle effect to one corner of the room, and vines climbed to the rough-hewn beams supporting the roof.

"This red snapper's delicious, isn't it?" she said. "I caught it myself yesterday morning. The pineapple's from my own garden and so are the limes."

"Do you fish often?"

"Not so often as when Ed was living. I go out about once a week. And I still sail now and then."

It had been the Webbers' love of fishing that brought them to Puerto Vallarta the first time, a dozen years ago, and they had returned for several winter vacations. Then Dr. Webber and my father, who were close friends, were drowned together in a boating accident off Cape May. It was a terrible blow to Margaret, yet she found strength to comfort and console me, while Helene alternated between hysterical grief and enthusiastic plans for enlarging the Old Bridge Summer Theatre, of which she was already owner and female star.

Margaret then shook off her former life entirely and moved to Puerto Vallarta, returning to Old Bridge only once—when Helene died suddenly and I again needed Margaret's motherly strength. Even after this Mexican village became world-famous for its beauty, I never understood what kept her in such a remote place. Now, after only a few hours, I realized she had always belonged here.

At the end of the meal Juana served spicy coffee flavored with Kahlúa and orange peel. Margaret switched off the light, leaving only the two small candles on the table burning. "Not very romantic with no males present, but I like to look at the moonlight on the bay."

We sat in the dimness, feeling the peace of the quiet ocean, while a gentle offshore breeze freshened the warm night.

"Your mentioning males and romance reminds me of something I saw today." I said, and then described the couple at the airport. "Do you know them?"

"A woman named Karen? No. She sounds like a tourist. How old was the man?"

I wasn't sure. "Maybe thirty-five. He didn't look Mexican, not with that brown hair and fair skin."

Margaret's deep laughter resounded in the room. "Oh,

Alison dear! I could introduce you to four blond, blue-eyed Mexicans tomorrow, and you'd swear they were Swedish or Dutch."

"I suppose every country has immigrants. But aren't Mexicans a mixture of Spanish and Indian blood?"

"Most are. But there are Irish and French and German families who've been in this country for generations. Then you have the pure Spaniards, and believe me, they consider themselves special! Their ancestors had built cathedrals and lived in palaces in New Spain when the American Pilgrims were chopping trees for log cabins. And they're not shy about reminding you of the fact, either! Don't let blondness fool you. Your romantic-looking man is probably as Mexican as a nopal cactus."

"He must be a professional horseman."

"Not likely. All that suede and silver you described is a *charro* costume. There was a riding exhibition here this morning. The *charros* are too aristocratic to be professional. It's a gentleman's sport. Lord knows, they cut dashing figures."

It was a quaint word to apply to a man nowadays, I thought. "Dashing." Did I know even one man who could be called dashing? I was acquainted with a few who were handsome, others one might describe as attractive or interesting. But there were no Lochinvars riding the gray streets of northern cities, and the words "dashing figure" suggested only a commuter panting to catch a train.

"But you don't know who he is?" I felt oddly disappointed. "He had a scar on his left cheek. Not like a dueling scar but—"

"Oh, that must have been Carlos Romano. He has a ranch, one of those huge haciendas back in the mountains. I've met him, and we have some mutual acquaintances. We're not friends, of course." She smiled, adding, "He's more interested in lovely young blondes than in elderly widows."

"The blonde at the airport today was glamorous enough."

Margaret looked thoughtful. "I wonder if it could have

been his wife. She left him a few years ago. Maybe she's come back."

"Left him? They were divorced?"

"No, not divorced. She just deserted him. There was a lot of talk at the time. The Mexicans said you should expect that from an American wife—she was an American, you see. I don't know much about it. Gossip's a poisonous thing in a small town. It's best not to hear it."

"Of course." But at the moment a little gossip was exactly what I wanted. The woman, Karen, had worn no wedding ring, and I felt certain she was not a prodigal wife who had returned only to leave again.

"Don Carlos is a dramatic type, certainly," said Margaret, looking at me with eyes that were too shrewd.

"Arrogant might be a better word," I answered. "Not a very likable character."

"Well, there are other men here who are. When word gets around that I have a beautiful *gringa* staying with me, there'll be so many serenades that we won't get a wink of sleep."

"Serenades? Don't tell me that Latin lovers really sing below balconies! I thought that was only in old movies on television. Jeanette MacDonald and Nelson Eddy and a donkey!"

"Of course there are serenades. Mr. Cooley—he's a widower who lives here—had me serenaded for my saint's day. The most ungodly caterwauling band you ever heard. Every hound in the neighborhood howled all night."

"Saint's day? You're not a Catholic."

"No, but everybody here has a saint's day. It means two birthday parties instead of one." Margaret smiled and her voice softened. "It was sweet of Herb Cooley to hire that band. A pity they couldn't play on key."

I went to my room early, thinking I'd fall asleep at once. And I did, only to awaken an hour later, my mind still filled with the speed of the trip and the newness of my surroundings.

I tried to relax, listening to the breakers wash the beach below. The breeze had strengthened, and now it rustled the draperies and brought with it the salt tang of the ocean.

Putting on a robe, I went to the balcony outside the window. The house stood on the edge of the old town, near the cluster of tile-and-thatch buildings that had comprised the fishing village before it became famous. It was a simple, comfortable house, its high ceilings equipped with hanging fans that turned lazily during the hot hours—a modest home compared to the new South Seas mansions I'd glimpsed from the taxi. But its stone walls blended into the hillside and even the tile roof, weathered by wind and rain, seemed part of the land.

From the balcony I looked at the Moorish dome of a church silhouetted against a clear sky, and I heard the sound of music, not a serenade, but the playing of a dance band at a hotel farther down the beach where flares blazed to light a fiesta. Going inside, I tried to concentrate on the only book I had with me, *Advanced Conversational Spanish,* but felt too restless to follow a complicated dialogue in the future perfect tense.

The house was silent as I tiptoed downstairs to search the bookcase for a cheerful, undemanding novel. Moonlight streamed through every window, its pale illumination giving an aura of unreality to such common objects as tables and chairs, investing them with strangeness. Fumbling in the dimness, I switched on the tiny desk lamp in the living room.

Margaret was apparently not a reader of fiction, so I selected Madame Calderon de la Barca's *Life in Mexico.* Hesitating, I listened to the unfamiliar sounds of the night. In the patio a nocturnal bird repeated an eerily human call, a cry as lonely as a whippoorwill's, and it seemed to ask, "Who are you? Who are you?" Wind sighed in the palms and pepper trees. Then a different sound, harder and firmer, the hoof-beats of an approaching horse galloping on the road outside, iron shoes ringing on cobblestones. The living-room windows faced the inner patio, so I could not see the unknown rider plunging through the moonlight, but I stood perfectly still, filled with a sense of expectancy, an unaccountable assurance that the horseman would halt at the gate. He was here now, hoofbeats resounding, and my breath came rapidly. Then he passed without pausing, and the hammer strokes of iron on stone died away in the night.

I reached to turn off the lamp, and it was then I saw Margaret's leather-bound engagement diary lying on the desk, open to today's date.

I have never considered myself superstitious, never believed that one heard voices from a mysterious Beyond—much less did I think that phantoms had power to control lives in some unknown way. But long afterward, when I knew so much more, I would remember that first night, the words I saw on that page, and no matter how stubbornly I have told myself that it was only an uncanny coincidence, I have never been sure.

It was my own name that caught my eye. Margaret had scrawled in capital letters: ALISON COMES TODAY. Then I glanced at the bottom of the page where small black type announced in Spanish that this was February 4, that thirty-five days of the year had already passed and three hundred thirty were still to come. And that today was the saint's day of Veronica.

The airport flashed into my mind, the taut, furious face of the woman called Karen, and then her words, "Veronica should have poisoned you . . . "

Veronica—a lovely and uncommon name. Who could she be and why had she inspired that taunt about poison?

From the patio came the unknown night-bird's plaintive call: "Who are you? Who are you?"

"Where shall I go? Where shall I go?
Could your house perhaps be the place
of the fleshless?
Or perhaps inside heaven?"
—Aztec poem

TWO

The next days passed swiftly. I joined Margaret in her morning swims, basking in the blue water, and lost my northern pallor as I lay on a mat spread on golden sand. She gave me a blue straw hat with a sewn-on scarf that formed a chignon to hold my hair. "And here are some good sunglasses. Don't venture out without these and the hat," she warned me. "The breeze makes the sun deceptive. It's powerful!"

I explored the winding streets and was fascinated by the gay native market, where an old man with snow-white hair and the unlined face of a St. Francis offered polished mangos, great slices of papaya, and pomegranates. He gravely complimented my Spanish, and even the purchase of one banana inspired him to elaborate, antique courtesies.

"I hope the señorita enjoys this beautiful morning . . . Please take my most sincere greetings to the Señora Margarita . . . A thousand thanks, señorita. Go with God . . ."

Before I realized, a week had passed—a week of church bells and guitars, of yellow sunshine and vermilion sunsets.

"How I love it all," I said to Margaret as we finished breakfast in the patio. "Every minute!"

"You should have come long ago!" Then her expression became serious. "I'm worried, Alison."

"Why?"

"You've been in every shop in town, admired everything, and hardly bought a picture postcard. That's not normal vacation behavior. Are you short of money?" She was not prying; her concern was honest.

"I'm not short because I haven't spent anything. Soon I have to think about the future, and right now my future looks—well, rather blank. There's the matter of earning my living."

"Earning your living?" She frowned at me, puzzled. "Why, I thought you worked at that center for the blind just because you wanted to. I mean, your father's money must . . . "

"What money?" My cup clattered on the saucer. "The rich Mallorys of Old Bridge! Have you any idea what Helene spent even when Dad was alive? Those useless trips to Hollywood! Subsidizing that summer theatre so she could play the leading roles. And after Dad died—Margaret, you couldn't believe what happened."

"I can believe it," she said dryly. "People wrote me how she was trying to buy her way onto Broadway."

"There was nothing I could do to stop her. Nothing!" My voice quivered, but I couldn't control it. "When I begged her not to be so foolish, she'd just laugh. You remember that lovely laugh? And she'd say 'Jealousy doesn't become you, Alison.' By the time she died, everything was gone."

We sat in silence for a moment while her wise, kind eyes studied me. Then she said, "Jealousy didn't become Helene, either."

"I don't understand."

"You've seen the wild poinsettias on the hillside above the house. When they first start growing they're awkward, gangling plants, not very attractive. Then they burst into blossom and there's nothing so glorious on the hill. But the poinsettias themselves don't realize this, of course."

"Margaret, please."

"Yes, Helene was jealous. She saw the flowering begin, and tried to deny it." Margaret sighed and shook her head slowly. "Anyway, I think you ought to stay in Mexico awhile. The pace is slow here and you need time."

"I can't live off you, Margaret. You know that."

"Swallow that foolish Mallory pride for once, Alison! It's not easy to find work in this country. There are legal problems and the pay is miserable." She stopped, midsentence, and stared thoughtfully at her juice glass.

"What is it?"

"Probably nothing at all. But I just remembered something. I wonder . . . " She said nothing more except that she had an idea, a possibility so remote that there was no point in raising false hopes. And I, not being as good a mind reader as she was, remained puzzled.

Later we had some easy work to do. Margaret owned a small but charming house near the town plaza, and the rent from it formed an important part of her income. "It's not as roomy as this house, but a lot fancier. Air conditioning and a birdbath of a swimming pool." New tenants, a couple from Mexico City, were arriving today, and we spent an hour taking inventory, counting dishes, glasses, and linens.

"They'll be here at least three months," she said. "I hope the house will still be standing. I've never rented to people with children before."

As we were leaving, a sleek white Cadillac, gigantic in the narrow street, halted in front of the house. It was the new tenants, a German businessman named Heiden and his wife, plus a uniformed Mexican nanny shepherding two small boys who, mercifully, had inherited the wife's thin, aristocratic features and not the husband's square jaw. Margaret explained something about the air conditioning, wished them a happy sojourn, and then we walked to the plaza.

"Those boys look like destructive little devils," she said

gloomily. "Mexican women are loving mothers but they do spoil their children."

"Mexican?" I was startled. "I thought she was German, too."

Margaret chuckled. "There you go again, fooled by a light complexion! Of course she's Mexican." As we approached the taxi stand she said, "You go along and do what you like. I have an errand."

"Can I help?"

"No. Go and enjoy yourself." She climbed into an ancient taxi, and after two or three tubercular coughs, it finally wheezed away.

That evening she said casually, "I met some old acquaintances and we're invited to a cocktail party tomorrow. Very high society and I suppose it'll be deadly dull. But we'll survive."

Something in her tone aroused my suspicions. Could she be playing Cupid, wangling an invitation to a party where I'd meet what she'd call "a nice young man your own age"? It was quite out of character for Margaret to do such a thing, but her mysterious errand in the afternoon indicated that she was up to something. Twice during supper she was on the point of saying what it was, I thought, and then changed her mind.

I wondered again the next day when she made a careful inspection of the way I dressed. "That long peasant cotton is perfect for you." She beamed. "Blue is exactly your color!" Before we left she added, "Don't forget your hat and scarf."

"Hat? But I wasn't going to wear one."

"Oh, yes, you are. The Millers have a huge house, but they entertain on what they call the sun deck. There's never enough shade. They seem to have no qualms about broiling their guests alive."

The taxi we took from the plaza struggled up a road that seemed almost perpendicular, and I had a pessimistic feeling that at any moment the driver would invite us to get out and push. Palms and blossoming trees screened the anonymous walls of houses on both sides, but I caught glimpses of thatched roofs and gardens ablaze with parrot flowers and frangipani. Then we stopped at a wildly modern house jutting over the edge of a sheer cliff.

Margaret saw my surprised look. "A bit much for a Mexican fishing village," she said, raising an eyebrow. "Well, you asked about our millionaires. Here's where one of them lives—in expensive discomfort."

A gardener in a white cotton shirt and bloomerlike trousers opened the gate for us, and we followed a flagstone walk past a swimming pool to the house. A maid ushered us through a vast living room and down a hall. "How can anyone live like this?" Margaret asked in a low voice. "When I come here—and it isn't often—I feel I'm on exhibit at a World's Fair pavilion. Nothing but plate glass and steel beams and too much money."

About twenty chattering guests were scattered over a sundeck the size of a tennis court. The view was breathtaking—a panorama of sky, mountains, and ocean that gave a feeling of being on shipboard near a craggy shore. The guests, people of all ages dressed in chic sports clothes, paid no attention to the playing of a *mariachi* band in one corner or the competing music of a dance combo on a raised platform. Waiters, costumed like chorus singers in *Carmen*, circulated with trays of drinks and canapés.

"Maggie, my darlin'!" A huge bear of a man with a sun-flushed face lumbered toward us, clasped Margaret in an enthusiastic and alcoholic embrace, then, without waiting to learn my name, hugged me the same way. It proved to be our host, Harry Miller, an oilman from Texas. His wife, who seemed to have no name but "Sweetie," shouted an over-hearty "Howdy, y'all."

I was presented to the guests, all the introductions so rapid and confusing that I caught not a single name. Harry Miller suddenly blew a police whistle, summoning a waiter to give us drinks.

"Oh, Alison," said Margaret, pulling me. "Come over here. There's someone you have to meet." She led me to a small table that had a sun umbrella planted in its middle. And sure enough, there was the "nice young man your own age." He sat alone, a sandy-haired American whose khaki shorts and plain shirt made him an alien in this flamboyant coterie.

"Roger!" exclaimed Margaret. "So you're back in Puerto Vallarta. How good to see you." The performance was so skillful that if I hadn't already decided she was engineering something, I would have thought her surprise genuine.

He rose, smiling, and shook her outstretched hand. "Hello, Mrs. Webber. Yes, I'm back for a few days."

"Roger, this is my niece, Alison. Well, not really my niece, but she should have been. Alison, this is Dr. Blair."

He invited us, a bit awkwardly, to join him, but no sooner were we seated than Maggie was up and away, tossing off the improbable excuse that she wanted the cook's recipe for mango chutney.

We made a few unsuccessful stabs at conversation, but Dr. Blair was naturally shy and I felt reticent after having been shanghaied to the table. "Do you have a medical practice in the United States?" I asked.

"I'm not a physician," he said. "I'm a veterinarian. My job is here in Mexico with the Alliance for Progress."

"How interesting." My voice must have conveyed far more interest than I felt, for suddenly his shyness vanished, the honest, freckled face began to glow as he launched into descriptions of the mountain ranches. We had somehow arrived at the subject of hoof-and-mouth disease when I glanced toward the entrance to the sun deck. The *charro* from the airport was standing there.

He was not wearing the spangled horseman's outfit, but a white linen suit whose severe, almost formal cut made the other male guests in their flowered and striped casuals look like popinjays. Our host and hostess rushed to greet him, but this time the bear hug Mr. Miller lavished on both sexes was omitted. I could hear nothing they said, but the Millers were obviously aflutter. A social catch. They must have hoped he'd appear.

Roger Blair's voice penetrated my consciousness. "Now what do you think about that?" he asked. "I'd really like your opinion, Miss Mallory."

I was caught without the least idea of what his question had been. "Your calling me Miss Mallory seems very formal, Roger," I said, giving what I hoped was a winning smile. "My name is Alison, you know."

"Well, yes. Yes, of course. Alison." He was sufficiently distracted to forget what he'd asked. Then he said, "Look. Don Carlos is here. A red-letter day for the Millers."

"So that's Don Carlos," I replied. "Margaret mentioned him."

"Yes, that's the great man." He grinned, making fun, I felt, not of Don Carlos but of those too impressed by him. "The Conde Romano."

"A count? I didn't think Mexico had nobility."

"The title's Spanish, not Mexican. The family's been in this country about four hundred years. Ever since the conquest. But they're still more Spanish than the Alhambra. Don Carlos doesn't use the title, he calls himself Señor Romano. But people like the Millers know about it."

"Wouldn't it take more than a count to get the Millers so excited?"

"He *is* more. He was once a fairly famous bullfighter and he's the best horseman I've ever watched. Olympic class." A wistful note crept into Roger's voice. "That, plus a lot of money, ought to be enough for one man. But he's also owner, or at least part-owner, of the High Valley."

"What's the High Valley?"

"El Valle Alto. It's a ranch in the mountains about sixty miles from here. A ranch so beautiful I'd give my right arm to own one tenth of it." Roger Blair's voice had become dreamy. He was no longer a dedicated young veterinarian, he was a farm boy yearning for land of his own.

"There's a stone aqueduct with colonial arches that brings water down the mountainside. And two houses, almost castles. They even have a bell tower, the only real carillon I know of in Mexico. Sometimes when I'm working in that country, I hear the bells ring Angelus, miles away."

A waiter interrupted with fresh drinks, and then an attractive middle-aged couple joined us, partly to chat, partly to escape the sun in the shade of the umbrella. The crowd on the deck had more than doubled and I lost track of Margaret, but twice I glimpsed Carlos Romano's white jacket. The couple at our table drifted away. Then, to my amazement, Margaret appeared at my side escorted by Don Carlos. When she introduced us her expression was triumphant.

"*Mucho gusto, señorita,*" he murmured as he touched my hand. "*Me encanta.*"

My memory of him was so vivid that I almost said, "We've met before," but a nod in an airport is not really a meeting. Don Carlos and Roger Blair exchanged greetings in Spanish, but were quickly interrupted by Margaret.

"Roger, I hate putting you to work," she said brightly, "but Sweetie Miller's poodle has tossed its chopped sirloin twice today, and the poor dear's frantic. Would you be an angel and come with me?"

Before Roger Blair knew what had happened, he was being led away, and I was left alone with Carlos Romano. Margaret, I decided, had taken leave of her senses. Don Carlos was anything but "a nice young man your own age," and certainly had nothing in common with me. There was an awkward silence, made even more uncomfortable by the fact that he seemed to be studying me.

"The Señora Webber has been telling me about your work in the United States," he said.

"Oh, has she?"

"I found it fascinating. I want to hear more."

Fascinating, indeed! Was Latin gallantry always so obvious? Yet, despite the exaggeration, his tone had such sincerity that I was at a loss to answer. Another silence, then, vaguely indicating the musicians and the horde of waiters, I said, "It's an elaborate party, isn't it?"

"A boring party given by dull people for other dull people." He dismissed the matter with a shrug which indicated total indifference.

"Then why did you come?"

"To meet you, Miss Mallory."

"To meet *me*?"

"Señor Miller, whom I do not know well, telephoned me yesterday afternoon and told me about you. So I came to talk with you." He smiled at my confusion. "But we cannot speak here, we will be interrupted. Come. I know a quieter place."

He rose abruptly, took my arm, and propelled me across the deck to a flight of steps. A moment later I found myself in a shady garden with stone benches and a tiny waterfall.

"Sit down, please. We will talk here." He spoke courteously and casually, but I realized that Carlos Romano was accustomed to giving commands. When he said "Sit down," it was a polite order rather than an invitation. Taking out a silver case, he offered me a cigarette, and when I refused, he nodded. "You are right. Smoking is bad for the lungs. It makes the breath short. When I worked with the bulls in the *corrida*, I never smoked. Now I only ride, so it is not so important." He flicked a lighter, touched it to the cigarette. "Finding you in Puerto Vallarta is most fortunate. Señora Webber tells me you are not returning to the school where you taught in the United States."

"No, I'm not."

"Good. Then I am hiring you. You are the person I need." His firmness implied that everything was settled and it was pointless for me to ask questions.

"Hiring me for what?"

"As a teacher for the blind. Did not Señora Webber tell you about my mother?"

"No one told me anything," I answered, completely bewildered.

"Forgive me, I thought you knew." Rising, he stood at the edge of the pool formed by the waterfall and stared down at its rippling surface. He spoke quietly, but there was controlled tension in his voice. "Last year was an unlucky time for my family. There was an accident. My small son was trapped in a burning building. My mother, the Señora de Romano, is a woman of great courage. She rushed in and saved the boy. His burns were painful, but after a long time in a hospital he has now returned home. My mother was not so fortunate. The smoke and the heat . . . "

He returned to the bench, crushed out the cigarette with unnecessary force. "Her sight is lost. The doctors say it is hopeless. A terrible thing."

I had heard these words often in the past. "Hopeless . . . tragic . . . terrible . . . " But I had never seen grief curbed by so tight a checkrein. His face, for all it revealed, might have been carved from flint.

"Please don't be offended," I told him, "but you are exaggerating."

"Exaggerating?" His eyes widened in surprise and I detected a flash of anger in them.

"Blindness is a handicap. It isn't the end of life, and it needn't be the end of happiness. Tens of thousands of blind people enjoy full and useful lives. Your mother needs help and sympathy, but you must stop thinking of her as a tragic figure. It's so easy for people to dramatize the problem of blindness, especially when the blind person is someone they love. You mustn't fall into this trap! It helps no one. Least of all, your mother."

"I think I understand," he said slowly. Then a smile played at the corners of his mouth. "And I see that you are a young lady who expresses her opinions strongly."

I felt color rising to my cheeks. My words, because I knew they were true and necessary, had poured out in a torrent. Perhaps he was not accustomed to women who spoke emphatically.

"Tell me, señorita," he said, leaning close, really too close, to me. "Do you think I am a man given to too much pity?"

For a moment I couldn't answer. I looked into his face—the hawklike nose, the slightly mocking smile that did not reach his eyes, and the harsh, cruel line of the scar on his left cheek. I felt I had spoken like an utter fool. Pity? Not a shred of it! Involuntarily I drew back a little, and as I did, his sardonic smile broadened.

"Most people exaggerate handicaps," I said awkwardly. "It's only natural."

"Perhaps I am not as natural as you assume."

"Really, I . . . " But he had turned away, giving a gesture of dismissal.

"*Está bien.* When can you begin? I do not know what is a fair salary. We will find out, and I will pay it."

"Please! You decide things so fast, Don Carlos." I felt dismay, as though I had somehow been kidnapped. "Your mother should go to a good institution."

"She will not do that. The señora is a stubborn lady."

Although I had studied Spanish in high school and college and had recently worked with both Cuban and Puerto Rican students, I found myself saying, "Besides, there's the problem of Spanish. Your mother needs help in her native language."

"My own opinion exactly. My mother is a native of Pennsylvania."

"Pennsylvania? Then you must be . . . "

"Half *gringo?*" He chuckled. "No. The señora is my stepmother. But she is the only mother I ever knew, so that makes no difference. Besides, we tried a Mexican teacher. The señora did not care for her."

33

"Nevertheless, I . . . " Why was I stumbling this way? Groping for reasons to avoid accepting what seemed an ideal position? A good salary, living in a beautiful and exotic place. Only one elderly lady to worry about, not a dozen cases of maladjustment. Still I resisted. "There wouldn't be enough for me to do. At first your mother could work only a few hours a week. I wouldn't earn a full-time salary."

"Ah, the Yankee conscience," he said with irritating solemnity. "To make you feel less guilty, you might help my son with his English." He shrugged his shoulders as if it were a matter of no importance. "How soon can you come to the High Valley?"

"But I haven't agreed."

He checked his watch. "I am flying back this afternoon as soon as the mechanic has my plane ready. That does not give you enough time. But a jeep from the ranch will be in Puerto Vallarta day after tomorrow. The driver will call for you at Señora Webber's. About noon." He stood up, ready to return to the party.

"Just a moment! I haven't accepted, you know."

"True," he said lightly. "Nor have you said you would not. You have all day tomorrow to decide. If the answer is no, then tell the driver you are not coming."

Never had I seen anything so self-confident as his smile. He was positive I would accept, had not the faintest doubt. Was it because I was a woman, and women automatically said yes to Carlos Romano, especially when he chose to turn on the full dazzle of his personality? It was an annoying suspicion, almost enough to make one refuse just for the sake of denting his assurance. But would a refusal matter to him? No, this man was impervious.

"I'll think about it," I said, rising. "I can't promise."

"I wonder why not." His solemnity had returned. "My offer is a good one. I must have offended you in some way. You worry about the job because you worry about the employer. Is that it?"

My cheeks were suddenly flushed, for he had spoken the exact truth. The whole world apparently found Carlos Romano attractive and admirable, but although I could not explain it, he somehow frightened me and put me to flight. Was that why Margaret had told me nothing about this interview in advance? Had she suspected I would try to evade it? Illogically, Donald's hurtful words came back to me: *If I could see, you'd run from me, hide yourself from me.*

"I've no reason to worry about you at all, Don Carlos," I said, hoping my tone carried the proper coolness.

"Perhaps I used the wrong word. Often my English fails me," he replied carelessly.

We started toward the sun deck, he humming the song that the musicians above were playing. The party had not broken up; it was now double in size. There were a hundred guests milling about, some of them dancing. We reached the top step when I saw Carlos Romano tense, halt abruptly. His chin lifted and his shoulders stiffened. I tried to follow his gaze, but in the shifting crowd, could not tell at whom he was looking.

"Pardon me, Señorita Mallory," he said. "Too many people. I do not like mobs, so I will leave without thanking my host. He will not be surprised. My rudeness is well know."

He went quickly down the steps, but paused midway to say in a different tone, "Please come, señorita. You are needed at the High Valley."

"I promise to think about it. And now good-bye."

His smile came again, confident and winning. At that second I was ready to say yes, of course I would accept, of course I would come. But what he said next made me hesitate. For I had heard both the tone and the words before, when they were spoken in the airport to the woman called Karen.

"Not good-bye, señorita. *Hasta la vista.*"

THREE

Doom, I supposed, lurked around the next bend in the winding road. The only question was: What form would it take? Another cow charging in front of the jeep from nowhere, as one had done a few miles back? Or would we smash into a boulder that had rolled down the mountain slope? This had almost happened ten minutes ago. Maybe the road, gouged from the flinty walls of the canyons, would simply end at the brink of a precipice like the cliff on my right. It all seemed quite possible.

The gnomelike Indian driver, who bore the incredible name Primitivo, hummed cheerfully as he sped around blind curves while a rosary and a St. Christopher medal, taped to the sun shield, swung like pendulums. He was far too polite to chuckle at my nervousness, but whenever I gasped, the corners of his dark lips twitched a little.

At least we were taking the scenic route to Eternity. The crags and summits gleamed in the sun with breath-taking magnificence, and we had climbed from tropical jungle into high, rugged country dotted with oaks and hawthorns. On my right, when I dared look down, I saw a frothing stream, a spate of white water hundreds of feet below, twisting on the canyon floor. Gradually I began to relax, and my quick intakes of breath were less signs of fright than tributes to the wild beauty of the land.

Primitivo had arrived at Margaret's more than two hours late. I had decided, with mixed feelings of relief and disappointment, that Don Carlos had changed his mind. "Nonsense," said Margaret. "His driver's running on Mexican time. The man will be a punctual two hours tardy." And she guessed correctly.

The ancient jeep groaned under bags of cement, a nail keg, salt blocks for cows, and coils of barbed wire. In a woven cage a young and evil-eyed falcon perched, gazing angrily with a reptilian stare. My luggage was added to the collection, and after a quick good-bye to Margaret, we were dashing, rattling, and bumping through town.

Toward what destination? A beautiful, hidden valley—that much I knew. But Margaret's friends, despite a slight acquaintance with Don Carlos, provided scant information. I learned that years ago he had made a youthful marriage to "some woman from Mexico City" and it had ended unhappily. His second wife, an American woman none of Margaret's friends had met, had caused a scandal, "hushed up of course," by abandoning both her husband and young son. Most people assumed it was for some other man. Not a pretty story.

My hope that Primitivo would tell me about the people at the High Valley proved futile. He understood my questions, but I could make little of his answers, which were machine-gun fire in a language half Spanish, half some Indian dialect packed with tongue-spraining consonants. The supplies in the jeep, I learned, had been ordered by Señor Jaime Romano, who managed the ranch—Don Carlos' half brother, whom several people in Puerto Vallarta had mentioned vaguely.

The falcon was being taken to "the old lady." I assumed

he meant Leonora Romano, the blind woman with whom I was to work. But no, the "old one" was Don Carlos' grandmother. The struggle with the dialect became too much and I finally stopped questioning him.

The little man sat on a thick straw cushion, a burro pad, so he could see over the wheel. His white bloomerlike trousers, floppy white shirt, and huge sombrero reminded me of a circus costume, but there was nothing comical about the revolver strapped to his hip.

Several times along the road I noticed small wooden crosses with a few stones piled nearby. Charming, I thought. Some prayer or blessing for travelers. As we approached one, I asked Primitivo, "*Qué es?*"

I didn't fully understand his words, but there was no mistaking his meaning when he drew a finger across his neck in a gesture of throat-slitting, pointed to the cliff rim, then said, "Others just dropped dead," and crossed himself. So the crosses were death markers for wayfarers who had perished in one manner or another on this road. Their charm evaporated.

Primitivo pounded on the horn as a flock of goats skittered across the road and vanished up the slope among the rocks. A moment later he stopped the jeep, making a sign to me that meant our halt would be brief.

A tiny shrine had been carved into the mountain. He approached it reverently, carrying a bunch of marigoldlike blossoms that had been on the seat beside him. I climbed out too, grateful for a chance to stretch my legs. We had left Puerto Vallarta's perpetual summer behind, and in the mountains had found springtime, daffodil weather. I took off Margaret's sun hat and scarf and removed the tinted glasses. A fresh breeze felt gloriously cool as I shook my hair loose, letting it tumble over my shoulders.

Primitivo finished his prayer, and rising, turned from the shrine. When he saw me, he gasped and his head jerked back in astonishment. "*Dios!*" Then, after a second's hesitation, he smiled and nodded, seeming to have made an important discovery. "*Ay! La cuñada!*" The smile broadened to a friendly grin as we returned to the jeep. In my pocket dictionary I found that *cuñada* meant exactly what I knew it meant: sister-in-law. He had mistaken me for someone else, but I had no chance to correct him, for now he chattered full speed. Whatever resemblance I bore to some unknown woman had to lie in the pale color of my hair and perhaps my eyes, for he had noticed nothing until I took off the glasses, hat, and scarf.

We drove on through the fading afternoon, the road now so tortuous that even daredevil Primitivo had to slacken our pace. Then he pointed straight ahead, exclaiming. The shoulder of a mountain blocked the way completely. I saw an ancient, deeply rutted road climbing toward the crest.

But Primitivo, ignoring this trail, went confidently forward, driving us through a tangle of oaks and underbrush, then wheeled sharply to the left. A huge hole gaped in the side of the mountain, and we plunged into its pitch-darkness.

A cave? No, when he flicked on the headlights, I realized we had entered an abandoned mine tunnel. "*Vía corta al valle,*" he exclaimed, and this time I understood his words. We were taking a shortcut to the valley, not going over the mountain but through it. The people of the valley had put this huge worn-out mine to practical use.

I heard water dripping and could see dark trickles running down the high walls as the chill dampness raised gooseflesh on my arms. At times the tunnel would widen where black side passages jutted off, and there were several great chambers with pillars of rock left standing to hold up unimaginable tons of earth and stone above us. Catacombs—miles of them. An army could vanish into the labyrinth of this hollow mountain and never be found. The sense of entombment made me uneasy, but I couldn't be frightened when Primitivo hummed and whistled so cheerfully.

We turned right, and ahead I saw the flicker of torches. In a moment we had overtaken a group of pedestrians, a dozen men, women, and children also on their way to the High

Valley, also using the shortcut. When Primitivo halted the jeep, I had a panicky feeling that we were being attacked by a bandit tribe. They swarmed over the vehicle, squeezing into every space, seizing every handhold. A small boy wailed when his toe struck barbed wire. Two tiny children in white bloomers fought to sit on my lap, and both finally found room there. They stared up at me with big brown eyes, smiling shyly, while everyone laughed and chattered as they extinguished their torches and blew out candles. A gnarled old man, jammed between my suitcase and the salt blocks, played a harmonica, inspiring Primitivo and then the others to burst into song as we started forward again. When we emerged from the long tunnel, our passengers departed as quickly as they had scrambled aboard, leaping off to hurry down a path through a grove of hawthorns and jacaranda.

Suddenly I caught my breath and felt my pulse beat faster. The High Valley, emblazoned by sunset, stretched before me. "Wait," I told Primitivo, and stepped from the jeep to stand gazing at the vast panorama below.

I had no sense of distance, except that it was great. Mountain palisades walled the valley on every side, cliffs and escarpments of green, pink, and ebony rock broken by sloping mountain meadows. The valley floor rolled gently, crisscrossed by two streams and by wandering stone fences. But the mountains encroached upon the gentler land, invaded it with upthrusts of lava, dark pinnacles and spires. To the east were orchards and forest, and beyond them, silhouetted against the darkening sky, rose the yellow-tile dome of an ancient church surrounded by a village.

My eyes widened then as looking northward I saw an incongruous building utterly at odds with the landscape: a huge early-nineteenth-century house with gables, mansard roofs, and two fanciful square towers, one taller than the other, rising to sharp peaks. Even in New England such a lofty, antique structure with its friezes and cornices and half a dozen brick chimneys would have been a surprising curiosity.

But here, in the mountain wilderness of Mexico, the building was astounding.

"*La casa grande,*" said Primitivo proudly.

Beyond "the main house," perhaps half a mile farther and separated by a stream, stood another house, a Spanish or Moorish style castle-fortress with high windows and pointed battlements. Though far away and obscured by trees, it conveyed a forbidding majesty, a reminder that even this serene valley had over the centuries seen pillage and revolution.

"The old one's house," Primitivo said, and added other Indian words I couldn't translate. This stone stronghold, then, was the home of Don Carlos' grandmother.

As we returned to the jeep, I knew why Roger Blair had spoken of this valley with such love and envy. Don Carlos called it "a ranch," but it was more than that—a hidden kingdom, a secret and beautiful world.

We drove down an incline past ruins of what had once been mining buildings, the road running beside a great aqueduct whose Roman arches had been hewn from the mountain. The gravel road then merged with a cobblestone drive lined with eucalyptus trees. As we halted in front of the house, the overwhelming sense of loveliness I'd felt only a few moments before vanished. "*La casa grande,*" with its strange peaks and gables, loomed before us, even more enormous than I had thought. And far more somber. Although sunset was fading rapidly, not a welcoming light glowed behind the slitted shutters. The long veranda stretched bare of furniture. No one, I felt, ever sat on this rambling porch; no one enjoyed the shade or listened to the rustle of its ivy.

The air was filled with the harsh, grating cries of grackles, hundreds upon hundreds of black birds flapping and swarming about the towers and chimneys, circling, then swooping to perch in the eucalyptus and quarrel raucously among the branches of live oaks shrouded in Spanish moss.

Primitivo honked the horn, got out, and began to gather

my luggage, while I climbed reluctantly from the jeep and hesitated in the shadow of the tall trees flanking the entrance steps. Then I heard a horse approaching at a brisk trot, and turning toward the sound, I saw a rider on a roan stallion, his back toward the diminished light, his face obscured by the broad brim of a sombrero. Yet it was easy to recognize the proud but easy posture of Don Carlos, riding not in fancy dress but in leather work clothes and boots. Primitivo doffed his hat and waited respectfully.

As he swung down from the saddle, I moved forward, saying, "Good evening."

When the rider turned to me, I realized my mistake. Not Don Carlos, but a darker man who resembled him physically but not facially. For a second he stared at me as though frozen, thunderstruck. Then, "My God, you've come back!"

"Come back? I don't understand."

With swift strides he advanced upon me and seized my arm in a hard grip. The look of astonishment had changed to naked anger. "What kind of game is this?" he demanded. "Who are you? I want the truth!"

For a second I was so startled and frightened that I couldn't speak. Then outrage overcame all other feelings. "Let go of my arm, please. And don't shout at me. This is insufferable!"

I could hardly believe that the cold, contemptuous voice was my own. It was sheer acting, to cover my alarm and confusion. Releasing me, he stepped back, and we stood glaring at each other, an unflinching pair of antagonists. I forced my eyes to meet his, determined not to give way.

I realized this was Jaime Romano, the younger half-brother of Don Carlos. Younger? He did not look it. The rugged face, bronzed by sun and wind, might have been slashed from the mountain rock and was gypsy-brown. A fall of jet-black hair brushed the high forehead above heavy brows arching deep-set eyes—arresting eyes, cold blue in the dark face. His resemblance to Don Carlos, except in stature, was slight, and if this man had strode through the Puerto Vallarta airport, no one would have mistaken him for a film star, but they would certainly have kept out of his way.

Turning away, he exchanged rapid words with Primitivo. I understood "sister-in-law" and "the Señora Margarita of Puerto Vallarta." Jaime Romano glanced at me, his lips twisted in a scornful smile. "So you are being passed off as Carlos' sister-in-law. A childish and quite unnecessary deception."

"I have no idea what you're talking about. Primitivo is confused and mistaken," I answered. "Will you kindly inform Don Carlos that Miss Mallory has arrived? He is expecting me."

"His lordship, Don Carlos, the Conde Romano, has flown off on some mission of vast importance. Perhaps an elegant little riding exhibition." The initial rage had now become sarcastic courtesy. "I was not told of your expected arrival. But I will have Primitivo show you to Carlos' rooms. I hope you will not find the night too lonely."

"*His rooms!*" The aloof poise I'd assumed deserted me, and I blazed with anger. "Of all the rude insolence! Are you suggesting that I am here to—" I stopped short, pulling myself together as I saw he enjoyed my fury and had deliberately baited me. Brushing past him, I mounted the steps of the veranda, chin high, although my hands trembled. There must be someone in this enormous house who was at least civil, if not welcoming.

Dim light now glowed behind the stained-glass panes of the door. I searched in vain for a bell or knocker, and then Jaime Romano was beside me, flinging open the door, removing his sombrero in an ironic salute. "My house is your house, señorita."

Ignoring him, I entered a huge, shadowy hall where a curving staircase wound upward on my right. On the opposite side were closed double doors. Light came through the archway ahead, but as I started toward it, a chandelier flashed on, and the hall, though far from bright, was illuminated. A wispy gray-haired woman in a drab cotton housedress leaned over the banister at the top of the stairs.

Jaime Romano called to her. "Miss Evans, will you come down, please? We have an unexpected guest, a friend of Carlos."

"Oh, I thought I heard someone." Miss Evans fluttered down the stairs, sparrowlike.

"Good evening. I'm Alison Mallory. Don Carlos Romano was expecting me today. I'm a therapist and teacher for the blind." I glanced toward Jaime Romano. "Don Carlos hired me to help his mother. That information doesn't seem to be known here yet."

"We were expecting you. Carlos told us this morning, but he wasn't quite certain you'd come." She smiled vaguely and with little warmth, a smile that touched her colorless lips but did not affect the mistrustful eyes behind steel-rimmed glasses. Miss Evans appeared a good deal less than delighted by my arrival.

"Teacher for the blind?" Jaime Romano's tone was dry and doubting. "He told you this after I'd left for the dam, Miss Evans?"

"He could hardly have told us before, Jaime. You were gone before dawn." Miss Evans was on the defensive, afraid of this man. And who could blame her? She continued nervously, "I told the housekeeper to change the bed in the room Señora Castro had. At least, I *think* I told her. Spanish is so very difficult!"

"While English is so very easy, no?" Jaime Romano's remark stopped just short of outright rudeness. His own English, although as fluent as his brother's, had a slightly bookish sound and a Spanish lilt.

Miss Evans pretended not to hear him. "Señora Castro's room is a bit small, but I hope you'll like it."

Jaime Romano interrupted her. "She *should* like it. After all, I now realize she drove Señora Castro out."

"I've driven no one out," I retorted. "I was asked to come here. Persuaded, in fact."

He paid no attention. A sudden gleam had come into the cool blue eyes. "You are right, Miss Evans. That room is much too small. I think the Octagon is more appropriate for Carlos' friend."

"The Octagon?" Miss Evans seemed alarmed. "But should you? Isn't that where—I mean . . . " Her voice trailed off as she searched for some objection to what he had decided. "It's been closed so long. There are personal things in it."

"At last count, Miss Evans, five maids worked in this house. We can spare three or four to get it ready at once." He jerked a bell cord, went to the archway, and shouted orders toward the rear of the house. Within seconds, three girls in embroidered blouses and long cotton skirts covered by big aprons had rushed into the hall.

"I wouldn't be any help," Miss Evans murmured. "If you'll excuse me . . . " She faded up the stairs, an uneasy exit, pausing once to peer furtively back at me, a brief, sharp glance that blended hostility with suspicion, and she looked away the instant she realized I saw her.

"This way, señorita." Primitivo, the three maids, and I followed Jaime Romano through the sliding wooden doors. One weak, unshaded light bulb did little to combat the gloom of the baronial living room filled with bulky pieces of furniture shrouded in dust covers. There was an immense stone fireplace, the hearth heaped not with logs but with a bouquet of withered flowers in a brass bowl. A life-sized portrait hung above the mantel, and in the dimness I mistook it for a Velasquez copy or the work of another Spanish court painter.

"My late father, Don Victor," said Jaime Romano in a flat voice, "as you have doubtless been informed in advance."

He took a candle from the mantel, lighted it, and handed it to Primitivo, who now led us down a long corridor. I saw electric wall switches, but no one touched them, and felt a strange sensation of being transported back in time—a medieval dwarf with a candle, then a tall figure in black leather whose neckerchief in silhouette seemed like the collar of a cape; the maids' skirts rustled behind me and the floor, beneath worn carpet, creaked as our strange procession moved through the deep shadows. At last we reached a narrow arched door, where Primitivo halted, drawing a ring with many over-sized keys from his pocket.

"The electrical generator for this part of the house no longer serves," said Jaime Romano. "But I believe women find candlelight flattering."

I set my lips in a tight line and made no reply. No matter how uncomfortable he made me, I had no intention of trading insults. Nor would I leave this place until I had had my hour of reckoning with Don Carlos.

The air was stale in the apartment they called the Octagon, yet I caught a subtle fragrance of lingering perfume, a faint scent of lavender. The maids scurried about, opening windows and shutters to let in a flood of moonlight and the freshness of a mountain breeze. Oil lamps soon gave a flickering yellow light that mixed with the pale-rose tones of a Coleman lantern disguised with a cranberry-glass shade. I found I was in a spacious, pleasantly cluttered bedroom, divided from a sitting room by colonnades and an arch of lacy wrought iron.

The fourposter bed had a gaily striped canopy and a butterfly quilt. Near it stood an old-fashioned china cabinet with etched glass doors, now used as a bookcase. As the maids bustled about changing linen and putting towels in the bathroom, I realized that the apartment's personality derived from the fact that someone *lived* here—framed photographs and prints, pressed flowers under the glass on the bedside table, stationery, pens, and drawing pencils in the pigeonholes of a drop-front desk. The maids removed zippered clothing bags from a big wardrobe chest.

I felt Jaime Romano's watchful eyes on me, scrutinizing my reactions, a brooding gaze of resentment and doubt.

Glancing at my watch, I said, "Perhaps I should meet Señora Romano, since it's still early."

"My mother does not choose to receive you tonight."

And just how, I wanted to ask, had he acquired this information? But his tone forbade contradiction, unless I wanted an open battle on the spot.

"*Qué pasa aquí?*" A stocky, pockmarked man almost as coffee-colored as Primitivo had glided silently into the room. He was not so tall as Jaime Romano but far broader and heavier.

I couldn't catch every word of the rapid exchange in Spanish between them—an argument about opening these rooms. Jaime Romano ended it almost at once, saying, "I give the orders here, Nacho. Get out."

The man started to leave, then stopped, staring at me in surprise. "*Buenas noches, señorita.*" His gravelly voice was hesitant, uncertain.

"You are in the way here, Nacho. Go."

He left them, moving noiselessly, lithe despite his bulk. "Nacho. My brother's flunky," said Jaime Romano. "But perhaps you have met before? In Puerto Vallarta or Mexico City?" He intended the question as a taunt, but it was meaningless to me.

"No." I said. "He seems courteous. I always remember good manners."

"We keep Spanish hours in this house. A maid will bring your supper tray later. And do not take any moonlight strolls. The watchdogs are loose now and they do not like strangers."

Like dog, like master, I thought, but again kept an angry silence. Turning from him, I went to the sitting room, hoping my back conveyed lofty disdain but afraid I was flouncing out like a furious child. I sat stiffly in a chair and waited until I heard the hall door open and close twice. Then, cautiously, I rose and went to the colonnades. A maid was still there, fluffing pillows as she finished the bedmaking, and to my surprise Jaime Romano lingered, standing near the door in profile to me, gazing at a picture that was hidden from me by its deep frame of gold leaf. He clenched his fist at his side, and there was such intensity in his face that I thought for a second he was about to smash the glass of the picture.

Then he did a bewildering thing. The hand, now open, lifted slowly, and although he did not bow his head, he made the sign of the cross with the gentleness of a benediction. Unaware of my having seen him, he left the room, vanishing into the blackness of the corridor.

In my surprise at this unexpected gesture, I hardly heard the maid as she told me in careful Spanish that my room was now ready and she would soon bring my supper.

"*Gracias,*" I said. "What is your name?" The girl was small and doll-like. Her braided hair, tied in big loops with pink yarn, framed a sweetly innocent round face.

She curtsied, giving a shy smile. "I am called Ramona, your servant."

Together we moved toward the door, and I paused to look at the painting that had so deeply moved Jaime Romano. But it was neither a painting nor a photograph. The heavy gilt frame held a square of linen yellowed by time and edged in fine lace. Somehow imprinted on it was a blurred image of the face of Christ in agony, crowned by thorns, bloodstained. Perhaps if hung in some ancient church, it might have had sacred meaning and even a savage beauty. But not here, not in this cheerful, soft room.

"What is it?" I asked Ramona, who was standing beside me. My voice seemed a whisper.

Ramona's large, liquid eyes regarded me with surprise, puzzled at my ignorance. "Oh, my lady," she said in a tone of awe. "It is the countenance of Our Lord. His face, as it appeared by a miracle. That is the handkerchief of Veronica."

"I don't understand. Tell me about it."

"When Our Lord was crowned with thorns and was dragging his cross toward Calvary, a beautiful woman stepped from the watching crowd and knelt beside Him. She was very brave, not afraid of the Roman soldiers, and she wiped Our Lord's brow with her handkerchief. A miracle happened! His face appeared on the cloth."

Ramona stepped close to me, reverence and almost fear in her voice. "The old Conde gave that handkerchief to Luis' mother. Do you think it could be the true one, my lady? The one the saint touched Our Lord with?"

"It's very old," I said. "Very beautiful."

"I thought it might be the true handkerchief because sometimes Luis' mother would stand looking at it. And her face was so strange then. "

"Strange, Ramona? How?"

"I think"—Ramona's voice fell to a whisper—"I think she was afraid."

Half an hour later, when Ramona returned with my supper tray, I had changed my dress for a housecoat and done my best to wash away the dust of the mountain road. My hope for a shower had been dashed when I turned on the hot-water tap. No matter how long I let it run, it remained cold enough to turn my hand blue. Straight from an icy mountain spring, I supposed, and added this to the list of insults and irritations Jaime Romano should answer for.

In the sitting room Ramona put my tray on a marble table and drew up a chair for me. I was famished, and the steaming avocado soup, pungent tamales, and frothy hot chocolate could not have been more welcome. A yellow rose nodded in a silver vase—Ramona's thoughtful touch. I seemed to have found at least one friend in this hostile house.

"I want to talk with you, Ramona," I said. "Do you understand my Spanish?"

"Yes, my lady."

"Good. Please sit down."

"Thank you, my lady." But she appeared shocked at this extraordinary suggestion and remained standing.

"Who is the North American lady, the Señorita Evans?"

"I am not sure. She came only two months ago when the Señora Romano returned from the hospital in Mexico City. I believe she is an old friend, and she reads aloud and talks to Doña Leonora in English."

Miss Evans, I decided, was a paid companion. An old acquaintance, too, for she referred to both the Romano sons by their first names. Yet her servile attitude marked her as an employee, and not too sure of her position.

"Tell me, Ramona, who lived in these rooms before?"

She looked so astonished that for a moment I thought my Spanish had not been clear. Then she said, "But you must know, my lady! These were the rooms of your sister."

"My sister?" I was dumfounded. The cup of chocolate, halfway to my lips, nearly splashed over.

"Your sister. Doña Veronica."

"I have no sister! What gave you such a notion?"

"Primitivo. He said he did not recognize you in Puerto Vallarta. He was told only to meet a North American lady at a certain address. Then, on the mountain, he thought he saw a ghost. We laughed at him, because you do not really resemble Doña Veronica except as a sister. You have her eyes and her beautiful hair. But otherwise . . . " She stopped speaking, and lowering her eyes, blushed deeply. Ramona, not accustomed to such conversations with her employers or their guests, found this an ordeal.

"Only one thing more, Ramona. What happened to the Señora Veronica?"

"She went away."

"Where?"

"No one knows. She went away almost three years ago." Ramona hesitated, trying to remember. "Yes, nearly three years. Just a few months before the old Conde, Don Victor, died. The housekeeper says Don Victor died of grief and shame because his daughter-in-law left his household."

"Do you think so?"

Ramona, troubled, shook her head slowly. "No. He was a

very old man with an illness of the heart. But he was saddened, as we all were, that she was gone. Doña Veronica, they tell me, left letters saying she would not come back, but the old Conde did not believe this. He ordered these rooms to be kept for her. And they have been—until now."

"Please tell the others here that I am not her sister. I am a teacher, come to help the Señora Romano."

She nodded, a little sadly, I thought, then moved quickly across the room. "I should close the windows, my lady. The mist is in the air tonight."

This was true—wisps of mountain fog drifted outside. A dozen questions in my mind demanded answers, but I realized I would learn no more from Ramona until we were better acquainted.

"Shall I draw the curtains?"

"Not yet, thank you. The mist and the moonlight are lovely against the glass."

"I will heat water for your bath."

I followed her into the bathroom, wondering how she would accomplish this miracle. Ramona opened a tall cupboard in the corner, and inside stood a metal tank with a tiny furnace at its base. She took a paper-wrapped package from a drawer, put it inside the furnace, then touched it with a burning match. A second later flames roared up, fed by wood shavings that had been soaked in kerosene.

"The water will be ready in a little moment only, by the time you have finished supper." She curtsied again, "*Hasta mañana,*" then was gone, moving quickly, anxious, I supposed, to avoid further questioning.

I sat down at the table, bewildered by the events of the day. But some mysteries were now solved. I resembled Veronica, Carlos Romano's wife who "went away," but the resemblance was superficial. The Conde's wife must have been a very beautiful woman, and I smiled a bit ruefully remembering Ramona's embarrassment when she said, "You have her eyes and her beautiful hair. But otherwise . . . " Yes. Quite otherwise.

My mind leaped back to two meetings. The Puerto Vallarta airport, Carlos Romano turning back in surprise when he saw me, clearly because I reminded him of his wife. But during our interview at the party he noticed no resemblance. The reason was simple: a pair of darkly tinted glasses, a sun hat, and a scarf which covered my hair. Exactly the same thing happened to Primitivo. Jaime Romano had believed for a second that I was Veronica, but this had been in twilight standing several yards away, and he had quickly realized his mistake.

Could so slight a resemblance, a complete coincidence, have caused his resentment of me? He seemed to feel that I was part of some conspiracy, some plot against him—a notion so preposterous that I could not accept it. Yet why had he lodged me in Veronica's rooms? It was a taunt, a challenge of some sort, directed both at his brother and at me. Perhaps it would mean something to Don Carlos, but I found the whole thing unfathomable.

I pushed aside the supper tray, feeling too weary and confused to think more about Jaime Romano, who detested me. Why should I care about his opinions? Or about Don Carlos? Or Miss Evans, a woman who obviously resented me at sight. And this house, although my rooms were now friendly despite the uncertain lamplight, was a gloomy prison, a monstrosity which marred a glorious landscape. I didn't have to stay, I could leave tomorrow. And I suspected I might do just that.

I rose abruptly from my chair, then gasped as I caught a glimpse of a face outside the nearest window. It vanished instantly into the whiteness of the mist, but although I had seen it only from the corner of my vision and discerned no features, there was not the least chance I had been mistaken. For a second I was paralyzed by astonishment and alarm, then

I rushed to the window, quickly closing the draperies, thankful they were made of heavy handwoven cloth through which no one could see.

To my dismay there was no means to lock the door to the corridor. Primitivo must have taken the key with him. There had once been a bolt—I could see the marks plainly—but the broken wood near the screw holes showed it had been torn from the door violently. When? Who had once forced his way into this room?

I improvised with a chair under the doorknob, then sat on the edge of the bed, forcing myself to be calm. The face could have been that of a curious servant, one who wanted to see "Veronica's sister."

"Stop these jitters!" I told myself sharply. I had much to be annoyed about, but surely nothing to fear. It was even possible that Jaime Romano had sent someone to my window deliberately to frighten me. Well, he would not succeed with such a childish trick.

I filled the big sunken tub with warm water, confident that a relaxing bath was the world's best tranquilizer. Later, when the bell of the clock in the village softly chimed ten, I was in bed, propped by pillows, studying a cheerful if useless passage about night-clubbing in *Advanced Conversational Spanish.* The warm tub had succeeded. Before long I dozed over the book and at last fell asleep with it in my hands.

I am not sure how long I slept nor do I know what awakened me. Surely it could not have been the thin, terrified cry I heard a few seconds after I had opened my eyes.

The scream was so faint that I was not certain I had really heard it, until it was repeated, seeming to come from the direction of the sitting room. When the frightened cry sounded again, I hurriedly put on my robe and slippers.

I had noticed in the sitting room that one section of wall did not quite match the rest of the room, had supposed it was a sealed-up door and thought no more about it. Now I realized that the sound, which had changed to a muffled sobbing,

54

came from whatever room had once been connected to this one.

The sobbing rose to a wail. "Mama, Mama!"

Heedless of anything except that terrified cry for help, I unlocked the tall French window and stepped onto a narrow porch, part of the veranda. Blinded by enveloping mist, I groped my way along the wall, turning sharply where the Octagon and the wing containing it jutted from the main structure of the house. The window of the next room was not locked, and as I pushed it open the child's sobbing seemed to engulf me.

I stood in a broad, lofty chamber, with almost no furniture except a tall wooden wardrobe, a bureau, and a bed on which a small body writhed in a nightmare. A dim night light burned on the bureau and, thankfully, it was electric. I found a wall switch and a chandelier filled the room with light. Hurrying to the bed, I shook the shoulder of the tormented little boy as gently as I could. Two large almond eyes snapped open, bewildered. For a moment he gazed at me fearfully, then flung himself into my arms, still weeping, but quietly now.

I held the frail body close. "There, dear! It's all right. Only a dream." I struggled to remember even one Spanish word, and at last could whisper, *"Está bien, mi niño. Un sueño malo, nada más. "*

At last the thin shoulders ceased their trembling. The child lay back on the pillow, gazing at me gravely as I brushed the light brown hair back from his white forehead. The small hands clasped mine. He was, I supposed, about nine years old, but his eyes had a strange, adult wisdom.

"Tía?" he asked, both fear and hope in his voice. *"Mi tía?"*

I was not his aunt, his *tía*, of course, and I realized now that this child was Don Carlos' son—and Veronica's. The mother, I thought bitterly, who "went away."

"Why do you think I'm your aunt?"

It took him a moment to understand my Spanish, then he

said, "Primitivo told the servants that my mama's sister had arrived. I wondered why you did not come to see me." His face puckered, and I expected more tears, but he held them back. "So I listened outside your window. You told Ramona you were not my mother's sister." He swallowed hard, refusing to cry. "Then you are not my aunt after all?" His hands gripped mine more tightly, as he waited, still hopeful, silently pleading with me to deny my words to Ramona.

"Would you like me to be your aunt?"

"Oh, yes! Now that Señora Castro is gone, I need someone. I liked the señora well enough, but an aunt like you would be much better."

Now it was my turn to hold back tears. I, too, as a child had awakened alone in the night, terrified, crying for a mother who was so seldom with me. I had often pretended that Margaret was my aunt, that I would soon go to live with her, and I had even told neighbors this story.

"What are you called, Nephew?" I asked, smiling.

"Luis. But I am really Victor Luis Carlos Romano y Landón," he said proudly.

"Such a long name!"

"Yes. My great-grandmother says the 'Landón' is not important. It was only my mother's name and I am supposed to forget it." A stubborn note crept into his voice. "I think I will not forget, but you must not tell my great-grandmother."

"I promise not to."

"Did I cry loudly in my sleep? Is that why you came?"

"Oh, very loudly," I told him, making a joke of it. "I thought you'd wake everyone in the house. Maybe all the people in the village, too."

"Please, *Tía*—" He was fearful again. "You must not say this to my Uncle Jaime. Please!"

"Very well. It is our secret. But why not tell him?"

"He would make fun of me. He would say I was not *macho*."

Macho. Although I knew little enough about Mexico, I'd already learned to detest that word and the mentality it implied: super-maleness, toughness, the kind of swaggering masculinity that is the mark of a bully.

"I must be very *macho,*" Luis was saying. "Some day I will be Conde, like my father, so my uncle must not laugh at me. You understand, *Tía?*"

"Yes," I answered grimly. "I understand very well." Jaime Romano would one day hear from me about the concealed shame that haunted this child.

"Who takes care of you, Nephew?"

"I take care of myself. I am nine years old. Of course, when I was in the hospital in Mexico City, the nurses took care of me."

"Were you there a long time?"

"A very long time. From last spring until almost Christmas." Throwing back the blanket, he pulled up the legs of his pajamas. "Look, *Tía.* I have a new skin. The doctor in Mexico City gave it to me."

The thin legs were mottled with scars of skin grafting. Luis had been cruelly burned in the fire that also destroyed Leonora Romano's vision. This child had endured physical pain I could hardly imagine, but the doctor in Mexico City had been kind and wise enough to make Luis feel that he bore not defacing scars but a "new skin" he had earned proudly through pain.

More than an hour passed before I left him sleeping peacefully. He had learned to pronounce my name in English, not easy, because "Alison" has not one vowel sound found in Spanish. I was exhausted by all that had happened, tired by the struggle of communicating in a language not my own, but still I lay awake, thinking about this sad and beautiful child, Luis, and turning over in my mind one of the last things he had said before sleep came to him.

"Ramona told you a lie," he whispered, glancing uneasily toward the window, as though afraid of being overheard.

"Maybe she just made a mistake about something," I said carefully.

"No. She told you my mother went away." Kneeling on the bed, he spoke close to my ear. "My mother is . . . dead."

"Luis, how do you know this?"

"I know." The future Conde Romano set his determined little jaw and would say nothing more. Nor did he shed more tears.

Now I turned uneasily in the big fourposter bed, once shared, I supposed, by Carlos Romano and the wife who "went away." Or had she? Luis was an imaginative child. Perhaps he told me only something that came to him in his nightmare. Yet I wondered. Until sleep came at last, I gazed into the dimness at the dark square on the opposite wall, at the handkerchief of Veronica. But it gave no answer, and all was silent except the creaking of the old house and the sigh of the wind swirling the mountain mist of the High Valley.

"If in one day I leave,
In one night pass into the mysterious regions,
. . . Remember me . . . "
—Aztec poem

FOUR

At a quarter to seven the pealing of bells awakened me—a dozen bell voices, some deep and mellow, others crystalline and tinkling. Daily reveille in the High Valley, a folk song rung from a bell tower.

Despite what must have been a troubled sleep, I rose with an exhilarated feeling that somehow the world was mine today. Slipping into my robe, I swished back the draperies and let morning brilliance pour into the rooms. The mist had vanished, leaving behind dew to sparkle on the broad lawns and twinkle in the Spanish moss. Half a dozen horsemen, Mexican *vaqueros,* rode along a trail beyond a low stone fence, and seeing me at the window, they waved. When I returned the greeting, one spurred his horse to perform a sashaying dance.

I recalled bright May mornings in New England, although here palms spread broad fronds among the live oaks and the orange blossoms of Chinese hat lent tropical flamboyance to the scene.

59

Hearing a soft tap at the door, I almost called "Come in," before I realized that a chair still barricaded the entrance. I removed it, embarrassed by my fears of last night. Foolish, too. Had I really believed that a fragile chair could block any determined intruder? A pitiful precaution.

Ramona, a fresh ruffly apron over her blue cotton skirt, bobbed into the room, wishing me a good morning. "From the Señorita Evans," she said, handing me a note, then went to the bath to set the water heater blazing. Miss Evans, using purple ink on lavender paper, wrote a ladylike hand.

My dear Miss Mallory,

   Wouldn't it be nice if you took your continental breakfast with me? The maid who brings your tray can guide you to my room.

   If you are indisposed after yesterday's travel, I understand perfectly.

Hoping to see you,
Ethel Evans

Continental breakfast? It sounded like a hotel. And Miss Evans was probably more curious than cordial.

Half an hour later Ramona, bearing a tray, led me along the corridor we had followed last night, which with its closed doors and dark service stairs was hardly less dismal by day. We crossed the enormous living room whose slitted shutters admitted only the narrowest stripes of sunshine, and I nodded good morning to the fierce portrait of the late Conde Victor Romano.

Miss Evans greeted me in her second-floor room. "Dear Miss Mallory! How *nice* of you to join me." The smile, like the enthusiasm in her voice, was a bit overacted. She spoke to Ramona in English. "Put the tray over there." When the maid shook her head in confusion, the command was repeated in a louder tone, as though volume could bridge the language gap. "Oh dear, they'll never understand!" By then Ramona had seen Miss Evans' own tray on an onyx-topped table in the window alcove, and quite sensibly she set mine opposite it.

"You see! If one speaks very loudly they eventually comprehend."

Miss Evans, still as fluttering as she had been last night, had changed radically in appearance. She wore an exquisite robe of brocaded Thai silk, a golden fabric whose folds engulfed her. Gorgeous, except the sleeves were too long and the hem, where it had been taken up, was not quite even. The effect was further flawed by cheap felt slippers.

The room was no less surprising than the expensive robe. It was a hodgepodge of styles and periods, Oriental, French Empire, and Italian furniture combined with Mexican silver bowls and very old Dresden figurines. Every piece was lovely in itself, but in concert they gave the impression of an overstocked antique shop.

"Do you like my room?" There was coy pride in her question. "It's much like my old home near Gettysburg."

"So many exquisite things," I murmured. If Miss Evans had ever lived in such surroundings, it must have been long ago. Her whole manner proclaimed genteel poverty, and the badly altered robe had to be a gift from a larger woman.

"Do sit down, Miss Mallory. Isn't the view lovely?" She sighed then, her face clouding. "But sometimes looking at so much beauty saddens me a little when I think that poor Leonora will never see any of this again."

There was no possible reply to this bit of false sympathy and saccharine sentimentality. But Miss Evans, intent on chattering, did not notice my silence. "Leonora and I have known each other almost all our lives. We'd lost touch in the last few years. But she was such a woman of action that I forgave her not writing. When I learned about this tragedy, I came at once. Poor Leonora's so helpless now. Pathetic. I try to make things easier, but there's not much one *can* do, is there?"

"Quite the contrary. There's everything."

"But the complete helplessness . . . "

"Let me tell you something, Miss Evans," I said rather

sharply. "Three years ago in my own apartment I learned to cook a complete five-course dinner blindfolded. Yes, I had some nicks on my fingers and burns on my hands. It was slow, difficult, and frustrating. But I learned. That's one example out of a thousand."

"Such determination," she said. "How very unusual."

Anyone who worked with Leonora Romano would find a dangerous, subtle opponent in Miss Evans, who was bent upon making Leonora forever dependent. I changed the subject. "Will Don Carlos return today?"

"I wouldn't know. He left in such a rush, just time to mention you and to make sure all of Señora Castro's things had been cleared out of the house."

"Who is Señora Castro?"

"A dreadful woman some institution in Mexico City sent here. Jaime made the arrangements." She sniffed haughtily.

"Do you mean there was a teacher here until night before last?" I could hardly believe what I had heard.

"Yes. But not teaching. Snooping and interfering." Mild, innocuous Miss Evans lowered her voice to the buzzing tone of gossip, and at the same time unconsciously raised her true, malicious colors. "She thought she was going to manage the whole place. Trying to make Leonora do things the poor creature couldn't possibly do. Leonora didn't care for her at all."

"Why not?"

"They just weren't compatible. But the worst thing was the sneering look on Señora Castro's face when Leonora fumbled or dropped something. "

And how, I wondered, had Leonora Romano *seen* that sneer? Through Miss Evans' eyes, no doubt.

"And she took to pampering little Luis. She was with him every spare minute. A fine way to turn a weak boy into a sissy!" She leaned forward, eyes glowing. "Then, my dear, she turned out to be a thief."

"A thief?"

"Leonora had a cameo locket set with tiny rubies. Last week she asked for it, and it was gone from her jewel box! Well, a few days later it was found in Señora Castro's room. She'd tucked it under her handkerchiefs!"

"What a surprising story, Miss Evans."

"Isn't it?" Detecting a doubt in my remark, she retreated into her helpless-but-sweet disguise, brushing imaginary crumbs from her robe. "Don Carlos behaved like a perfect gentleman, so kind. He had the locket removed, of course, but didn't openly accuse her. Just sent her away. We didn't tell Leonora about the theft. Much too upsetting! I said Señora Castro was suddenly called back to the city, and pretended to find the locket caught in a shawl Leonora had worn with it. The poor woman has enough to bear without adding to her troubles."

The diffident voice carried a threat. Silently she was saying, "Don't *you* tell Señora Romano, if you know what's good for you!" In fact, the entire conversation now struck me as nothing except veiled threats. "Don't interfere . . . Don't come between me and my dear Leonora . . . Stay away from Luis . . . Or you'll be sorry!"

I rose abruptly. "I've imposed on you too long, Miss Evans. When will I meet Señora Romano?"

"Leonora? Well, we have this little continental breakfast now at seven-thirty, then there's the real breakfast between ten and eleven. Then at three o'clock—"

"I know the dining schedule," I said impatiently. "When may I talk with the lady?"

Her smile brightened. "I'll send a note to your room. But don't expect her to receive you too quickly. If she's in one of her solitary moods, it may go on for days."

"Let me know as soon as possible."

At the door Miss Evans said, "If Leonora doesn't care to meet you, don't be disappointed. This is a difficult household, and terribly isolated. A talented girl like you must have so many opportunities."

"Thank you. Please send word soon."

As I descended the broad stairs, I wondered what sort of game Miss Evans was playing. Her objective, beyond doubt, was to make me leave as soon as possible. Perhaps she hoped to delay my meeting Leonora Romano while she convinced the lady that I was an undesirable character. Or maybe to gain time while Jaime Romano caused me so much discomfort that I would go voluntarily and eagerly. But why? I could see no reason.

Was there any truth in her story of the stolen locket? No. The blind are constant victims of petty thieves. It is so easy for a housekeeper or cleaning woman to make off with seldom-used articles. I knew of countless such cases. But hiding precious jewelry under a few handkerchiefs was utterly improbable. The maids who did personal laundry would open Señora Castro's bureau two or three times a week. Besides, the accused thief had to be a professional woman of excellent character or no institution would have sent her here. Miss Evans' report was a malicious lie, and I had no doubt of it.

On the veranda the sunlight was now a golden yellow, and a falcon sailed across the cloudless sky. I followed the veranda around the house, passing closed shutters, coming to my own rooms, where the porch narrowed and six sides of the Octagon angled from the main building. Farther, and around another corner, the windows of Luis' room were open, and I waved to a barefoot maid, not Ramona, who was making his bed.

When I turned another corner and came to a short flight of steps, the whole atmosphere changed. I was back in the Mexico I'd known in Puerto Vallarta. The huge house faced south, and from the front, one saw only gables, the taller and lesser towers, wooden arches, friezes, and balconies. But behind this lay a Mexican patio, ten times as large as Margaret's. In the center a roofed well was shaded by lime trees and by fern-leafed pecans. On my right and left stone walls with broad gates stood so weighted with bougainvillaea that they seemed made of nothing but blossoms and leaves.

Another building enclosed the far side, a one-story structure of pink stone and adobe. Wooden posts upheld the tile roof of its long, shady porch. A charming, earth-warm building. Was it the servants' quarters? If so, the servants lived more gracefully than their masters.

I heard a shout beside me, and a pair of thin arms encircled my waist. "Tía Alison!" cried Luis, almost giving my name its English sound. A spate of words poured out.

"Slowly, slowly, Luis!" I ruffled his brown hair. "Remember my bad Spanish."

"You speak a little strangely," he agreed. "But I understand you, *Tía.*"

I had supposed that "Aunt Alison" would be demoted in his affections today, that he had given me his love and trust last night only because I had rescued him from a nightmare. A child's heart can be fickle. But now, as he hugged me, I felt this was not so with Luis.

He stepped back and with great effort said in English, "'Mary 'ad a leetle lamb. Eet's fleece was wyte ez snow.'"

"Very good! Who taught you that?" I asked in clear English.

He answered in Spanish, "My grandmother," but then struggled proudly through "Leetle Boy Blue" and "Leetle Chack 'Orner."

"Do you know what the words mean?"

"Yes. My grandmother speaks to me in English. I have learned some, but it is hard." Luis pointed toward the peacock. "I don't like him. He used to chase me when I was little."

"Who lives there?" I asked, indicating the house across the patio.

"Uncle Jaime. Come, *Tía.*" He tugged at my hand. "I'll show you his rifles and his ivory-handled pistol. He isn't there now."

"Then we can't go in, Luis."

"Why not? It's my house, too." He saw my doubtful look and added, "All the High Valley is mine. Uncle Jaime helps me take care of it until I'm bigger. But my grandfather told me everything was mine. The servants say so, too."

"Just the same, we don't go into people's rooms without asking." I didn't understand what he meant by "mine," and I had no chance to ask, because the smile had suddenly vanished from his face and the child's sad eyes looked up at me gravely. "Luis, what's wrong?"

"Are you going away?" he asked. "Señora Castro went away."

I longed to take him in my arms and promise I would not leave. He needed this desperately, but I could give him no promise. "Do you miss her very much?"

"No. But I would have, if you had not come last night."

A decision had to be made at once. This child must not form a strong attachment to me only to be disillusioned by my leaving him. At the same time, I knew I *wanted* to stay. Not only because Luis needed me and had touched me deeply. It was the High Valley itself, so beautiful, so magnificent that its mile-high grandeur dwarfed my past life, made all that had happened to me before seem small and constricted. One could draw strength from these mountains, warmth from this land.

An idea came to me. "I hope to meet your grandmother soon, Luis," I said.

"Do you? I'll take you to her now, if you like."

As he led me up the hall staircase, I imagined Miss Evans' consternation. Alone, she might delay me forever, but she could hardly keep out Leonora Romano's grandson.

We crossed a gallery, then another passage, more steps. A maze, I thought, and slowly it dawned on me that we were going to the tower. Odd that a blind woman would choose to live in the highest, most inaccessible part of the house. We reached the entrance. Its gilt doors were appropriate to open upon a royal chamber, and before I could knock, Luis had flung them open, darting into the room beyond. *"Abuelita! Abuelita!"* he shouted.

"Say 'Grandmother,' Luis." A weary voice spoke the words automatically.

The tower room was far larger than I had supposed, and its brilliance dazzled me after the dim stairs. Sunshine flooded through Gothic windows on three sides. In the fourth wall were doors, presumably of closets and bath, and still another stairway leading to the attic above.

Leonora Romano was slumped in a big upholstered chair, her head crowned by a mane of short, thick white hair. Behind her, comb and hairbrush in hand, hovered Miss Evans, gaping at me in astonishment and reproach. Señora Romano leaned forward, offering her cheek for Luis' quick kiss.

"Grandmother, I 'av brung—"

"Brought, Luis."

"Brought a mans—no, a ladies who—" In despair he reverted to chattering in Spanish.

The señora listened a moment, then interrupted him sharply. "Miss Mallory?" Her head lifted, the tired, drooping woman in the chair, realizing a stranger was present, became Leonora Romano, queen mother of the High Valley, shoulders erect, chin high, a figure of force and dominance.

She did not wear dark glasses, but her left eye was covered by a black patch. The right eye, sightless but clear and unscarred, seemed to search the room, and it reflected the same cold blue of her son Jaime's eyes.

"Good morning, I'm Alison Mallory." I moved closer to her. "I hope I'm not interrupting."

"Oh dear," murmured Miss Evans, "I forgot to send word. I was doing Leonora's hair and there hasn't been time."

Señora Romano seemed not to hear the papery whisper. "The housekeeper told me you arrived early yesterday evening. I wondered why you hadn't introduced yourself. I sat up late." A querulous note stole into the commanding voice, the plaint of neglect, a symptom I knew so well in my students. Now she was no longer formidable.

My confidence rose as I felt professional, sure of my

ground. "You're almost inaccessible, Señora Romano. I've been trying to meet you since seven o'clock last night."

"Don't call me 'Señora,'" she said impatiently. "We're speaking English. Besides, it reminds me of the ridiculous people who called me 'Condesa' when Victor was alive. I am Mrs. Romano. Fancy titles are better for my mother-in-law. She laps them up. I don't need them."

Easy to see where Jaime Romano acquired his bluntness. But I liked this woman's lack of nonsense. Ungracious, perhaps. Yet direct and honest.

Miss Evans launched into rambling excuses why I had not been brought here earlier, until Leonora Romano cut her off. "Sometimes I think your tongue should be hinged in the middle so both ends could flap at once," she said with a sigh. Then, more sharply, "I'm tired of having things kept from me."

Miss Evans flinched visibly.

"Will you ask me to sit down, please?" I inquired. "It's rather awkward standing here like this."

"And how am I supposed to know you're standing, Miss Mallory?" she snapped.

"Oh, but you *do* know. You're very perceptive. When you speak to Luis, you lower your head. When you speak to me, you lift it."

I hoped I saw the ghost of a smile cross her face. "Maybe two perceptive women are present," she said grudgingly. "Sit down, Miss Mallory. And Ethel and Luis, go somewhere. I'll speak with Miss Mallory alone."

Luis again brushed her cheek with a kiss, then skipped out. Ethel Evans departed without a glance in my direction.

When Leonora Romano had first become aware of my presence, she had assumed an air of aristocracy and majesty. On closer view, this did not change. But the components were different—she was still a queen, but the queen of some sturdy nomad tribe. Her face and hands were those of an outdoors woman who had not lived a pampered life. The resolute mouth reminded me of a portrait that used to hang at home in Old Bridge of an ancestor of mine, a woman who had taught school, helped plow fields, and fought Indians with a flintlock musket. Leonora Romano's body was still strong despite telltale hints of extra flesh that so often mark the recently blinded—too much time in a chair, too little exercise.

"Carlos didn't tell me much about you," she said. "No one tells me anything these days. Who are you?"

I gave a brief biography, concentrating on my professional qualifications.

When I had finished, she smiled faintly. "You omitted some things. For instance you have blond hair, not quite what we used to call ash-blond, but very light yellow. Your eyes are large and blue-gray. You have full lips, are tall and slender. In an unusual way, you're a very attractive woman."

"Miss Evans flattered me far too much," I replied, startled.

"Not Ethel. Candelaria, who's been my housekeeper for twenty years. Also, you look rather like Veronica Romano." Frowning, she leaned closer. "Is that why Carlos hired you? Do you know each other rather well?"

I answered calmly, although my cheeks flared with anger. "I met him once, a professional interview, and I'm positive he's unaware of any fancied resemblance to Luis' mother. But the coincidence has already caused unpleasantness. If you have any doubts about me, ask a driver to take me back to Puerto Vallarta as soon as possible. I suggest this is the wisest course."

For an instant she was confused, taken aback, then she chuckled. "Well done, Miss Mallory, you sound absolutely poised. But you're seething inside, aren't you? I can tell. For years I had to hide my temper. Now I'm old. People are afraid of me, and I needn't pretend any more."

"Politeness isn't pretense. It's kindness," I answered. "And kindness is in short supply in this house."

She hesitated, then rubbed her deep temples with her

palms, perplexity written on her face. At last some conflict within her seemed to resolve itself, and she spoke quietly. "Let's not have a foolish misunderstanding. Señora Castro— I'm sure you've heard of her—is mysteriously summoned to Mexico City. We didn't much like each other, but I'm astonished she didn't say good-bye to me or give any explanation. Odd, isn't it?"

"I agree."

"Then, yesterday morning, Carlos tells me in great haste that he has miraculously found a qualified woman to replace Señora Castro. As if people with such training were as common as chili peppers! You arrive and turn out to be a type that Carlos, by two unlucky marriages, has shown himself attracted to. Now what am I to think, Miss Mallory? Do you wonder I asked you a blunt question?" A thin, bitter smile came to her lips. "You might say I am out of my sight, but not quite out of my mind."

"I had better begin at the beginning," I said slowly, trying to put my confused thoughts in some order. Then I told her in detail of my interview with Don Carlos, of Primitivo's surprise on the mountain, and the hostile reception from Jaime Romano. I reported it unemotionally, omitting only my meeting with Luis and Ethel Evans' trumped-up story of the theft. Leonora Romano was shrewd enough to learn about that in her own good time. "Don Carlos did not miraculously find a replacement for Señora Castro. I must have been the immediate cause of her—" I hesitated—"being sent away. He hired me while she was still here. But of course, I didn't know this at the time."

She nodded thoughtfully when I had finished, then smiled—an open smile, with only a touch of weariness. "How good to hear the truth for a change! Neither of us understands all this, but some day we will, Miss Mallory. I want you to stay, but on one condition."

"And that is?"

"You are to be employed by me," she said firmly. "Not by Carlos or Jaime or the ranch. You need give no reports about my progress or lack of it, and are not responsible to anyone except myself. Is that clear and acceptable?"

"More than acceptable. In fact, it's the only way I would continue here."

"Splendid. Maybe you can do me some good. But maybe I'm too old and too tired to learn new things. Maybe for the first time I'm really defeated."

"Don't believe it!" I said warmly. "I think you're a fighter, Mrs. Romano. Are you?"

"Yes." The answer was unequivocal. "We're going to get along famously. We're both fighters, Miss Mallory!"

We had *desayuno*, the midmorning meal, together. Candelaria, a stout Indian woman with jet braids dangling below her waist, served us and helped Leonora, all the while eyeing me like a suspicious watchdog.

When the blind woman began to tell me about herself, the pent-up story she had longed to share flowed freely. She had come to the High Valley thirty-seven years ago, she said. The wife of an American mining engineer. "Not really an engineer. Henry was more of a prospector, a wildcatter with a nose for ore. I was the one who studied the books. I'm a good mineralogist and geologist, Miss Mallory. At least I used to be."

Smallpox had ravaged the valley that year, and a hundred people perished, among them the Conde Victor's wife and Leonora's husband. The newborn baby, Carlos, contracted the disease and had a close brush with death. "I nursed him through it. There weren't any doctors, there wasn't even a road. Just a trail. And it took three days on horseback to reach Puerto Vallarta.

"The next year Victor married me—in spite of his mother. She would have killed me to prevent it and maybe she even tried. I've never been sure. But I was beautiful in those days.

Besides, Victor's first wife had already given him an heir in Carlos just before she died, so what did it matter if Victor's second wife was a penniless *gringa?*

"But I knew how to use the brains God gave me. The Romanos, for all their pride, were land-poor. The silver mines had run out. *I* was the one who learned that where there's silver, there's usually lead and sometimes mercury. I started the mines working and made the High Valley rich again. And I did it alone!"

The Romanos, I thought, were not the only proud ones. Leonora held her head high as she recalled her triumph. "I gave Victor a fortune, and with Jaime, I gave him a second strong son. Sons are important in this country, Miss Mallory. So important that when Carlos' first wife proved barren, he divorced her with my husband's blessing. And that's why Victor thought the earth centered around Carlos' second wife, Veronica. She bore him what he wanted most in the world—a grandson. Luis."

She ceased speaking abruptly, as though some forbidden subject had been mentioned, and turned her head slightly away, so I could see only the unreadable lined cheek and the black eye patch.

"Are you satisfied with your rooms in the Octagon?" she asked.

"Yes. But I wonder what Don Carlos will think. Surely I'm intruding."

She laughed dryly. "Whatever he thinks, he'll say nothing. I suppose Jaime put you there as some sort of sour joke on Carlos. His sense of humor mystifies me at times. But if you're contented, you might as well stay in the Octagon."

"Perhaps something could be done to provide it with electricity."

"Electricity? Oh, yes. Jaime said something about the generator. I'll see it's taken care of, Miss Mallory. Heaven knows it's a problem keeping up this preposterous house."

"Preposterous?"

"Of course. Look on the wall above the desk."

I saw a framed yellowing photograph, a picture of a house resembling this one but much smaller.

"That's Dove Cote," she told me. "Where I lived as a child in Pennsylvania, a place I loved. How I wish that photo had never been taken!" She gestured at the room around her. "This expensive museum was built because of that picture. I've cursed it, I can tell you."

"But surely this house is much older than the photograph."

"No. The foundations and rear walls go back four hundred years, when the first Romano rode into the High Valley with his Spanish cavalry. When I came here, there was nothing but ruins where this house stands now."

"Yet it seems so old."

"It was built old. Parts of it came from antique mansions all over this country and the United States. We were spending a year in Europe, and before we left, Victor secretly gave that picture to an architect and told him to create the same thing but five times as large. A surprise for me! When we returned, it was already half finished. I pretended to be pleased, and over the years I've become used to the place." Her features softened as she thought of the Conde Victor's colossal but misguided gesture for the new wife who had restored his fortune.

"He didn't like the name Dove Cote, of course. Too peaceful for Victor. He had the name 'Falcon's Nest' etched in the glass over the door. *El Nido del Halcón.* I've never used the name, but it suited him. He was a falcon himself."

And so are you, I thought, and so are both his sons. "A rather grand present," I said. "A house like your family's home."

Again her laughter came dry and mirthless. "Dove Cote was never my family's home. My father was an artist, and he died young and poor. My mother became housekeeper at Dove Cote to make a living for herself and me. Victor never knew that, never asked. He took it for granted my people had once been rich. Rich, ha!" The eye patch moved slowly from left to right, as though she could still survey the spacious room, the vast acres of the High Valley beyond the windows. "A housekeeper's daughter, La Condesa de Romano! Cattle, mines, land, and a house that could swallow the place where my mother worked for Ethel Evans' family! Life plays strange jokes, doesn't it?"

Ethel Evans' family. The joke was not strange; it was cruel. These two women might have been girlhood friends, but one had been the daughter of the house, the other the daughter of the housekeeper. I could neither like nor trust Miss Evans, but now I pitied her. How could she help resenting the shift of fortunes? She always said, "Poor Leonora." Now I knew it was "Poor Ethel" as well.

Before leaving, I suggested that Leonora needed exercise and the two of us should go riding tomorrow morning. The idea confounded her only for a second, then she said, "Do you really think I could?"

"With the right horse you could win a steeplechase," I assured her. Riding, because she would be accompanied and mounted on a well-trained horse, would be an easy beginning for her reentry into the outside world.

"I much prefer you to Señora Castro," she said. "With her, all the talk was about learning Braille. I'm far more interested in horses. But it didn't occur to me that I could ever ride again."

"Don't be too hopeful. I'll do more than talk about Braille when the time comes," I warned her. "We'll read together, but you'll do all the work."

"Of course I'll do all the work," she said. "That's been the story of my life, Miss Mallory." But there was no self-pity in her voice, only a dry irony that reminded me of her son, Jaime. The two were far more alike than I had first believed.

·   ·   ·

At noon I sat on the veranda outside the Octagon writing a letter to Margaret, telling her how beautiful the High Valley was and that I planned to stay for a while, "an indefinite time." Although I wrote nothing of the strangeness of the household I had joined, my pen halted several times while I considered the peculiar world around me.

Riches and near-poverty. Don Carlos flew his own plane, but the carpets in his home were frayed and shabby with age. A dozen servants, yet one wing of the house lacked electricity because of a burned-out generator. Handsome blooded horses, but I'd seen no motor vehicles except the ancient jeep Primitivo drove.

And it was a household rife with smoldering antagonism, with the unconcealed resentment in Jaime Romano's voice when he spoke of Don Carlos, Leonora's bitterness about her mother-in-law who lived in the fortress house across the stream a mile away. Then the covert malice of Ethel Evans. Smoldering, yes. Did it ever blaze and erupt? Had these hatreds forced Veronica to go away?

I heard the tread of boots on the veranda. Jaime Romano, followed by a workman carrying a coil of electric wire and a tool kit, approached, his bronzed face hostile as ever.

"Good morning," I said, determined to be civil.

He ignored the greeting. "My mother tells me you are to stay for a while. She wants electricity in the Octagon." Obviously *he* did not care if I spent my life in total darkness.

"You're repairing the generator?"

"It's beyond repair and a new one is too expensive. I am making temporary arrangements."

He placed just enough stress on "temporary" to assure me that I would be out of this house soon. Before I could answer he and the workman had gone into the Octagon.

Far away I caught the faint drone of an engine, then saw a moving speck in the sky. Don Carlos was returning, and while I hardly thought of him as a friend, it would be a relief to have someone in the house to control the insolent character who was now giving instructions to the workman in the room behind me.

"Tía Alison!" a voice called. "Look at me!" Luis was about fifty yards away astride the big roan stallion his uncle had ridden the night before. The roan, I thought, must be gentler than he looked if Luis was permitted to ride him.

The child looked so tiny and so proud in the man-sized saddle, that I clapped my hands and shouted, *"Bravo! Bravo, Luis! Ole!"*

At that second the drone of the airplane engine became a roar as it zoomed low. The horse reared, and I was suddenly knocked against the railing when Jaime Romano plunged past me, vaulting it, shouting, *"Yaqui! Alto!"*

He was too late. The frightened roan was already charging away, Luis screaming, clinging wildly to its neck. Another horse and rider raced from behind the patio wall, running in pursuit, streaking to head off the runaway before he reached a grove of live oaks at the edge of the meadow. The branches, I thought in panic, imagining Luis swept from the roan's back, hurled against the tree trunks.

Then the bolting roan changed direction, began to circle back, and a moment later the second horseman was beside him, seizing the dangling reins. I gripped the railing, frozen with fear, sure that both horses would stumble, both riders would be thrown and Luis crushed beneath the massive bodies and flailing hoofs of the animals. But then the roan broke his stride, slowed, and snorting and lathered, permitted himself to be led back to the house.

Luis, quaking, was lifted down by his uncle. "Good work, Marcos," said Jaime Romano. "And good luck, too. I will remember this. Now take Yaqui to the stable. Dry him well."

Jaime carried the trembling Luis to the veranda and sat him down roughly in a chair. "Why did you do this foolish thing, Nephew?" he demanded. There was no sympathy in his voice, only controlled anger. "Answer me!"

"You said I could ride Yaqui." Luis gasped out the words.

"In the corral. Only in the corral!"

"The gate was open," the boy sobbed. "And I wanted to show Tía Alison." Springing from the chair, Luis ran to me and buried his face in my skirt, trying to stifle the sound of weeping.

"So it's 'Aunt Alison' already?" Jaime Romano's hard hands were clenched. "You work fast, señorita."

I knelt beside Luis, holding him tightly. "It's all right, darling. You were very strong to hold on the way you did. Brave, too. I'm so proud of you! Most boys would have been thrown off."

Jaime towered above us, saying nothing until Luis had become quiet, then he took command. "Luis, you are forbidden to mount Yaqui ever again. Now go to the stable and have Marcos saddle a horse for you. Not your pony. Take the pinto and ride to the airstrip to meet your father."

Luis clung to me, face averted. "Nephew, do as I say."

I started to protest, but the boy was already moving away in obedience to that unyielding voice. Slowly I rose and faced Jaime Romano. "Is this necessary? Must you punish that frightened boy so?"

"This is a country of horsemen. Luis must ride again at once, and have no time to think of fear or to remember it."

"At least I hope the horse will be less skittish than that roan!"

"Yaqui is not skittish. But the sound of that crop duster makes him nervous. Even I have trouble controlling him when my brother treats us to an aerial display. Do not complain to me. Speak to Luis' father about flying the crop duster so low." The crop duster? So that was how he referred to his brother's plane. Another hostile thrust.

I still thought he was too harsh with Luis, but would have held my temper if he had not added, "Miss Mallory, all of this is none of your business."

Then my anger flashed. "A frightened, neglected child is *everyone's* business!"

"Frightened? Naturally a runaway horse is frightening."

"Not only that. Luis . . . " I was cornered, unable to speak of the nightmare and the lonely, isolated bedroom without breaking my promise. Still, anger goaded me on. "Luis is sensitive, something quite beyond your understanding, I gather. Who takes care of him? Who gives him the least love or attention? No one, as far as I can see!"

"Perhaps you think he needs a kind stepmother," he said coldly.

"Your remark is so ridiculous that it doesn't bother me at all," I snapped back. "Maybe he needs an uncle he's not afraid of."

"Afraid? What do you mean?" he demanded.

"You know very well, and I'm not continuing this argument."

A puzzled expression, a look of doubt crossed his dark face, and the blue eyes beneath the thick brows studied me keenly, as though he could peer into my mind to confirm or deny some suspicion. The intensity of his gaze disconcerted me, and involuntarily I drew back, strangely awkward and uncomfortable. He confused me, alarmed me, and the only thing I wanted was to get away from him. "Was there something more you wished to say to me, señorita?" The question, asked in a surprisingly gentle tone, only added to my distraction.

"No . . . " I started to leave, then, trying to regain lost dignity, I said, "I need a key for my door. The bolt is broken, too."

I squared my shoulders, prepared to answer some taunt about whom I wished to lock in or out. Instead he merely nodded. Then, stepping close to me, he looked down into my face. "We have quarreled, señorita, you and I. I cannot expect you to accept my advice."

I felt the veranda rail press hard against my body as I pulled myself away from his closeness.

"If you are the good, sincere woman you seemed just

now, the woman my mother seems to believe you are, then I advise you to leave this place. For your own sake." He paused, and I looked away from him, not understanding, unable to answer. Then his voice hardened. "But if you are what I think you may be, then stay. You will deserve what will happen to you. *Adiós, señorita.*"

Then he was gone, moving rapidly down the veranda toward the patio with long, confident strides.

"I come to your window at night,
I call your name from the shadows.
Hear me, hear me! Do not turn me away . . . "
—Mexican serenade

FIVE

I did not see Don Carlos that day. Ramona told me that after landing he had gone directly to "the other house" to see his grandmother, whom she spoke of in an awed tone as "the Excelentísima." A duchess? I was not quite sure about the terms and degrees and titles of nobility, but I thought that was what she meant.

In midafternoon Luis and I had a picnic under the eucalyptus trees in front of the house. He was stiff and sore, but otherwise no worse from the morning runaway. A cloud of gold and black butterflies fluttered near us, and somewhere beyond the stone wall a guitar was strummed while a man sang in a high, youthful tenor.

"That is Marcos," Luis said. "He is the one who helped me today when Yaqui misbehaved."

"What's he singing about?" I asked, unable to catch the words.

"About love. I'll tell you a secret, *Tía.*" He lowered his

voice. "Marcos is in love with Ramona. It makes him silly sometimes. Were you ever in love, *Tía?*"

I hesitated, expecting to feel the pain which had become familiar to me in the last weeks. Instead there was only regret, a sense of having lost something precious and familiar, some object dear to me, one I would always remember but nevertheless could live without. "I thought I was once, Luis. Now it seems like a long time ago."

"Did it make you silly?"

"No, not silly. Just . . . mistaken, I think."

"I will never be in love—except with my grandmother and you."

"And your great-grandmother," I added in a half-question.

"Yes," he answered doubtfully. "And I think I still love Señorita Gomez. She was my nurse when I broke my ankle."

"You broke your ankle?"

"Yes. I had this big swing. Oh, very big. Under a eucalyptus tree near the old barn. One day the rope snapped. Lucky I wasn't swinging very high. Grandmother said I might have broken my foolish neck."

His young life seemed replete with accidents. A broken swing, the fire, and just today the narrow escape with Yaqui. I could almost have believed him marked for ill luck, but none of these mishaps, except the fire, had serious consequences.

Luis and I then began a game, I speaking to him in English and he answering in a mixture of language we called "Spanglish." Since it was fun, not a lesson, he seized eagerly on every word. Then his ears, keener than mine, first caught the sound of carriage wheels on the cobblestone drive. "Look! My great-grandmother's *calandria.*"

An open black carriage, iron-rimmed wheels grinding the drive, approached slowly, drawn by a skeletal sway-backed gray horse—a picture from an earlier century. As it came nearer, I saw brass coach lamps with broken lenses, red leather upholstery pierced by protruding springs, and two remarkable human figures. The coachman was a child, not much older or larger than Luis, though he sat draped in the livery of a full-grown man, a crimson uniform whose heavy gold epaulettes made his shoulders droop like the sagging back of the horse. Small eyes peered out from under the glossy brim of a tall fur-and-leather hat which must have been stuffed with paper or rags, otherwise it would have come down over his face like a candle snuffer.

An ancient woman, swathed in black shawls and veils, hunched in the carriage behind him, shielding herself from the sun with a torn black umbrella.

"Your great-grandmother?" I asked Luis.

"Oh, no. It is her *dueña.*"

Dueña? A chaperone? A governess? Luis' great-grandmother, to say the least, must be a little old to have a nursemaid whose usual duty was guarding the innocence of unmarried maidens.

Leaning from the carriage and shading her eyes with a gnarled hand, the old woman saw us. "*Alto!*" she screamed at the driver with the shrill, ear-piercing screech of a harpy. The carriage halted, the boy leaped down, holding up the trailing red coat with both hands to avoid tripping on it. Luis ran to help, and the two children assisted the *dueña* from her seat.

She hobbled toward me, umbrella in one hand, a cane as twisted as her own fingers in the other. Rheumy eyes stared at me from a web of wrinkles, eyes that were the only living things in the dead-white face, reminding one of two flies newly caught in a spider's web.

"You are the lady teacher staying here?" she shouted, standing not three steps from me.

"Yes."

"What?" She leaned forward, clasping the cane under her arm and cupping a hand to her left ear.

"Yes!" I shouted back, realizing she was deaf. She gestured to the coach boy, who, coat trailing, went to the carriage and returned with an ear trumpet made of tortoise shell.

"Yes!" I shouted again.

Taking a deep breath, she then cried out a memorized speech. "My lady the Excelentísima Ana Luisa Sollano de Romano requests the presences of her beloved Luis and your esteemed self at her house, the Villa Plata, which is also your house. You will be received at your house at two o'clock tomorrow afternoon. This invitation to the Villa Plata, your house, is extended with the greatest cordiality and my lady's most affectionate, gracious, and warmest regards for the health of your person and your soul."

She paused, taking a deep breath, trying to remember something more, then shrilled at Luis, "She says you are to appear in her presence only in civilized Christian attire. Not like the disgraceful ruffian you were last week. Remember that, you little devil!"

Since this was a royal command, she awaited no reply, but returned to the carriage, balancing herself carefully, wobbling a little. With the umbrella held high, she gave the impression of an uncertain tightrope walker. The boy clambered to his high seat, flicked the reins and clucked to the horse, which, after more flicks and much pleading, plodded back the way it had come. The rear of the carriage was emblazoned with a shield, a crest of nobility that was rusting away.

"Two o'clock," I said. "Does that mean we are to eat with your great-grandmother?"

"Yes," he replied sadly. "And I must wear a necktie."

"Who is the boy driving the carriage?"

"Oh, he is Jesús María Smith. An Englishman."

"Smith? But he is darker than Marcos or Ramona."

"His grandfather was brought here to drive the carriage long, long ago. My great-grandmother says it is always fashionable to have an English coachman." Luis stood up. "Excuse me, *Tía*. I must go now to Padre Olivera's house in the village. Three afternoons a week I go for my lessons."

"Padre Olivera? Is it a catechism class?"

"No. Arithmetic and history and things. My great-grandmother teaches me about religion. You know, how all the martyrs had their feet roasted and were tortured and burned to death . . . "

That night two bright electric lamps burned in the Octagon, connected by extension cords run through the wall to Luis' room. Jaime Romano had more than kept his word about a key. Not only had the bolt been replaced, but a modern spring lock gleamed on the door and its key lay on my bedside table.

The bells had chimed rosary more than an hour before, and now the valley lay bathed in cloudy moonlight, wisps of mountain fog crowning the trees with a shimmering silver like angels' hair, while the night-blooming jasmine Ramona called "sweet-by-night" perfumed the evening. As I stood at the open window, spellbound by the scene, it seemed impossible that any violence could ever disturb the valley's infinite peace. The panic I had known only this morning—the huge, bolting horse with its tiny rider—seemed to have happened long ago. Now only the moonlight and the silver-touched land were real.

Leaving the window open, I went to the desk to finish a list of reminders for tomorrow. I would find out which horse would be suitable for Leonora Romano's first ride since her accident. Did Leonora have a cane? I hadn't noticed one in her room. For Luis, I noted, "Children's books in English."

My glance fell upon a thin packet of documents, my passport, visa, and a few other personal papers. Careless of me to have left them out this way. I considered locking them in my suitcase, then noticed that a small mahogany cabinet in the corner had a key emerging from its lock. It was a lovely piece of furniture, and as I knelt to open its door, I rubbed my fingers over the smooth richness of the wood. Inside were three shelves, the bottom one empty, the upper two containing some albums and notebooks.

Taking one of the albums near the lamp, I opened it idly.

A large color photograph filled the first page, a pretty young woman holding a child in her arms, madonna-like. At first she meant nothing to me, then realization came. This was Veronica. The child, perhaps two years old, was Luis.

Why did anyone think I resembled her? Yes, her hair was almost the color of mine and she, too, wore it brushed back and loose, falling over her shoulders. Certainly our eyes were alike. But there all similarity ceased. Veronica's features were much softer than mine, and there was an ethereal quality about her, a combination of sweetness and fragility.

Yet everyone seized upon our similarities and not our differences. Slowly the answer dawned on me. Veronica, gone three years, remained in the thoughts of all those in the High Valley. They lived with her memory, wondered about her, worried about her. Although we were really so different, my coming here had rekindled imaginations and recollections.

In the photo, Veronica smiled down at Luis, a look of love and tenderness, so beautiful and so painful in the light of what had happened that I quickly turned the page.

Scores of pictures of the High Valley and its inhabitants. Leonora, Jaime, Carlos, the late Conde Victor whose hawk's face shone with pride as he lifted little Luis high in the air as though to proclaim, "Look, world! This is my grandson!"

I knew these faces, but not these expressions, not these personalities, for the album brimmed with happiness and love. Only a few years ago. How these people, this house, had changed. God knows they had had enough tragedy in their lives, but still . . . On the last page Jaime Romano smiled at the camera. Dressed in a boldly embroidered shirt and fringed trousers, he was dancing with a little girl at a village fiesta, carefree and youthful. The rugged face showed strength and determination even then, but there was no anger in it, no bitterness.

Quickly I returned the album to its place, feeling I had intruded upon other people's lives. I put my own papers carefully on the bottom shelf, locked the cabinet, and slipped the key into the pocket of my robe.

I glanced at my watch. Luis would be in bed by now, but perhaps not asleep. The album had touched me deeply, and someone, not a servant, should say good night to the child, someone should give him back a trifle of the love he had lost.

On the veranda the mist was thickening, not the blanket of last night, but smoky patches of cloud shot with moonlight. And tonight Luis' window was locked, the draperies closed. I moved toward the patio, remembering a door leading to a corridor in the adjoining wing of the house.

The patio gleamed faintly iridescent, transformed by night, while the curtained windows of Jaime Romano's quarters shone as bright rectangles of yellow. The shadow of a figure crossed one window, then the next, then, turning, moved slowly back again. A man pacing back and forth, restless. Planning and scheming? Or only a lonely man in a lonely room? Impossible to know, impossible to fathom anything about Don Carlos' brooding, angry half brother.

The outer door of the north wing was not locked, but it creaked an alarm as I slipped into the dim hall, going cautiously toward a turning where a light burned. But when I reached the corner, I halted in surprise.

A thick straw mat lay spread on the floor across Luis' doorway, and on it, a blanket beside him, sat Marcos, the young rider who had overtaken Yaqui today, his brown fingers working nimbly as he braided leather thongs.

"*Buenas noches, señorita.*" He rose politely, but did not smile. "You have lost your way?"

"No. I was going to say good night to Luis."

"He is asleep."

"Then I won't disturb him."

Marcos nodded in agreement, his amber eyes, long-lashed and limpid, regarding me with curiosity.

"Do you always sleep here, Marcos?"

"No. This is the first time."

He offered no more, and plainly my questioning was unwelcome. After bidding him good night, I started back toward the Octagon.

Now there were no lights in the building across the patio, and mist had all but blotted out the moon. Groping my way, I reached the veranda, where light, blurred by the smoky whiteness, shone from my open window. I had moved only a few steps when I heard, somewhere ahead of me in the stillness, a sharp *click*—louder than a light switch, more metallic than the snapping of fingers. Despite obscuring mist, I could see that the veranda lay deserted, and no one stood near it. Pressing against the wall, I moved on, cautious, alert, yet not really afraid, although I was quite sure the sound had come from my rooms. Easy enough for someone to have entered the Octagon through the open window. I almost expected to surprise Ethel Evans there. She might very well search my room; she was the prying type.

But there was no one. Everything remained as I had left it. Fastening the window behind me, I decided that the click had come from elsewhere and there was some natural explanation.

Tired, yet not at all sleepy, I searched the bookshelves for something to read. Veronica's books—I tried to banish the smiling photographs from my mind.

Most of the volumes were in English, only a few in Spanish. She had enjoyed poetry and drama, and I found collections of plays familiar to me from childhood when Helene pored over possible scripts for the summer theater. The poetry was old-fashioned, much of it sentimental, and in this I felt a kinship with Veronica.

I turned off the sitting-room lamp and moved the other lamp to the bedside table, noticing again Veronica's collection of pressed flowers under the glass, a quaint display of fading blossoms. I wondered if she and Luis, very small then, might have searched the meadows together to find one wild rose, one calla lily, one begonia, for no two flowers were alike.

An hour later my eyes wandered over the pages of *Selected Poems of Robert Browning.* Questions and indefinable anxieties loomed in my mind, making it impossible for me to concentrate on the printed words.

Every sound startled me—the sighing of the house, the ivy outside rustling as a breeze swept the High Valley of mist, the lonely howl of a wolf on the far mountain slope. The island of light around me seemed so small, a tiny circle rimmed by shadows, and beyond them the dark house in the midst of a wild land blanketed by night. The draperies were closed tightly, yet I felt watched, a sensation that unknown eyes gazed at me.

A dozen times I glanced quickly into the shadows, certain that something had moved, shifted. I had a troubled, uneasy feeling that was more like fear than anticipation, as though I knew someone was about to tap at the door or on the glass of the window and whisper my name.

I forced my eyes back to the poems. With a sharp intake of breath, I read the lines:

> *Beautiful Evelyn Hope is dead!*
> *Sit and watch by her side an hour.*
> *That is her book-shelf, this is her bed;*
> *She plucked that piece of geranium flower,*
> *Beginning to die, too, in the glass . . .*

And the words spoke to me, spoke like a voice I had expected from the shadows beyond the light of my lamp. Words I had known last night, knowledge I had suppressed all day. Now, softly in the quiet room, I spoke the truth aloud: "Veronica, you are dead."

The book slipped from my hands. Trembling, I sat straight and stiff in the bed—Veronica's bed—near her bookshelves, beside her fading flowers.

89

Luis had told me last night but I had not believed him, since he gave no reason. Now the reason shouted itself in my mind. He knew his mother had not "gone away" because he knew she loved him. Only six years old when she vanished, yet he was sure—just as I was certain that the woman in the album whose soft face glowed with mother love would never have left her child behind. She might have been driven from the High Valley by forces unknown to me, but even in flight she would have taken her son with her.

Why had not the others in the house realized this? I knew from the books she chose and treasured, from the sadness in Ramona's voice when she spoke of her, and above all from the photographs, that Veronica had never been a heartless, unnatural mother. Didn't Leonora realize this? Didn't Don Carlos and Jaime? Of course they did! Yet they pretended ignorance of her death. And even as I decided this, some instinct warned me that I, too, must pretend. For a while I must appear blind to the obvious. Pretense was the powerful undercurrent I had felt in this house, but had not, until now, been able to give a name.

Rising swiftly, I went to the small cabinet, unlocked it, and looked once more at the first photograph, knowing it did not lie to me. Then, as I closed the door, I saw the scratch near the keyhole—tiny and raw, newly gouged into the wood. I remembered touching the mahogany, examining its grain and texture. The mark had not been here earlier tonight. Someone had made it while I had been trying to say good night to Luis, someone watching through the open window who had seen me leave, then entered to work hastily, perhaps with a knife, trying to pry the door catch. The click I'd heard—what could have made that sound?

My eyes scanned the room with new sharpness, and a moment later I stood at the door to the hallway, turning the handle of the new spring lock. It was still hard to twist. The door swung open silently onto the dark corridor, then I pulled it shut. The lock, upon closing, snapped into its hasp. The click I had heard. There was no mistaking it—someone had been in this room and left as I returned. Someone searching—but for what? Veronica's possessions had been un-molested for three years. What had changed? Only that I was here.

I slid the bolt home and rechecked the catches of the windows. Beyond the glass, moonlight smiled in the High Valley. The mist had vanished except where it whitely shrouded the fence and orchard. A night so lovely, so serene that who could know it was haunted, that it had concealed some menace, something that had destroyed the girl who once slept in this room?

I heard the voice of a nocturnal bird, the same bird I had listened to the first night at Margaret's house, and now I knew it was called a nightjar. But then its eerily human cry had been "Who are you?"

Now it seemed to repeat "Veronica . . . Veronica . . . ?" An invitation. A futile summons that the woman who "went away" could never answer. Still, lonely and seeking, the night birds asked again.

"Veronica . . . ? Veronica . . . ?"

"The witch had a house filled with black birds . . . "
    —Mexican folk ballad

SIX

Spring-fresh morning flooded the meadows and cliffs of the High Valley with light, and when I awoke the Octagon, swept clean of shadows, seemed outwardly not to have changed. But for me the two rooms would not be the same again: Veronica's memory was here.

As I prepared for the day ahead, as Ramona served my breakfast, I realized more and more how this cheerful, welcoming apartment would be haunted by a pale, bittersweet ghost. I felt no fear, no uneasiness. Only a sense of being close to the unfortunate woman who had lived here before me. It was as though Veronica and I had made an unspoken pact. We would have been friends, I thought. We *are* friends, united by something I did not understand. And I knew I would learn more.

After Ramona had taken my breakfast tray, there came a soft tap at the door and Nacho, Don Carlos' tall, pockmarked servant, came gliding into the room bearing a brief, elaborately courteous note from his master. Would I give Don Carlos the "inestimable pleasure" of speaking with him at eleven o'clock in his apartment?

"In which wing is his apartment?"

"I will come here and guide you, señorita," he said, bowing.

Nacho departed, his soft sandals making no sound. He was the only servant I had met here that I did not like. There was oiliness in his perfect courtesy and the hooded eyes studied me too keenly.

If I saw Don Carlos at eleven, I would still have more than an hour to devote to Leonora's first attempt at riding, ample time. But as matters turned out, I did not work with her that morning. I was on my way to the stable to select horses when Ethel Evans intercepted me.

"I have bad news, Miss Mallory," she said smugly. "Poor Leonora has a migraine. She asked me to tell you she'll have to postpone any try at riding until tomorrow at least."

I was not surprised. It is not unusual for the blind, during the first steps toward reeducation, to become "ill" when facing a new challenge. Miss Evans appeared annoyed when I took the delay in stride.

"I'm so sorry," I said. "Give her my sympathy. I'll talk with her later today when she feels better."

"Today? Oh, she couldn't possibly!"

"Miss Evans, now that she doesn't have to ride, her migraine will vanish rapidly. You may count on that."

She gave me a reproachful look, and the tightening of her lips announced that I was a cold, unfeeling creature. I continued on to the stable to make arrangements for tomorrow. Leonora had lost a minor skirmish with her own confidence, but my faith in her eventual victory was unshaken.

I felt less sure of myself when I stood inside the big whitewashed stable, gazing in bewilderment at half a dozen horses and twice that number of empty stalls whose equine tenants had been taken to the pastures that morning. The stableboy hosing down the stone floor looked at me blankly when I said in careful Spanish, "I will need a very gentle horse for the Señora Romano tomorrow morning."

His reply spurted out in an utterly incomprehensible language. I repeated my question; he gargled another answer. I tried sign language and gestures. Nothing worked.

"Good morning, Señorita Mallory," said a voice behind me. "Are you taking lessons in the Tarascan Indian tongue?"

I had not heard Jaime Romano enter. He was leaning lazily against a doorpost, and I supposed he had spent several minutes enjoying my frustration.

"No. I'm looking for an interpreter," I said stiffly. "I imagine you'll do very well."

"This boy is from a mountain village. He speaks little Spanish, but understands some of it. Even gringo Spanish."

I raised an eyebrow at the words "gringo Spanish," but held my tongue.

"Have no worry, señorita. I have already taken care of your problem."

"What problem?"

"Your horses, naturally. You want a horse for my mother, another for yourself. I suspect Luis will go with you, and he will ride his pony."

"And just how did you know about my plans?"

"I make it my business to keep track of what you're doing, señorita." He smiled, but there was some implied warning in his tone. "By the way, you will stay within sight of the house."

"Indeed?"

"Yes. When you wish to ride farther away, tell me a day ahead. I will go with you or Marcos will go. If we are both busy, then none of you go. Am I clear?"

"I understand your words perfectly. Your English is clear, even your Mexican English."

"*Touché.*" The wry smile returned to his lips. "When riding alone, go anywhere you like. It is nothing to me." Dismissing this matter, he strode to one of the stalls. "This is Estrella," he said, letting a beautiful black filly nuzzle his hand. "She is for my mother. Well trained but with a proud spirit."

I gazed at Estrella with misgivings. She was far bigger and younger than the gentle, rather elderly horse I had hoped to find. And her "proud spirit" didn't encourage me. "I think not," I told him. "She's beautiful, of course. But isn't there an older mare? A more gentle horse?"

"I have chosen this one."

The words were flat and final. His choices, I thought angrily, were God-given judgments. For a moment we stared cool defiance at each other. His blue eyes beneath the jet brows were unyielding, hard to face, and I spoke quickly, afraid I would give way. "This plan for riding is my responsibility. If there should be an accident, I would—"

"I have considered the chance of accidents." The strength of his voice silenced me. "When I heard of this riding idea last night, I thought it was crazy, *loco*. I was going to forbid it. Then I realized I was mistaken. Now you, señorita, are going to admit you are wrong." He moved closer to me. The anger had faded but the dark face was still cold and demanding. "I want the riding to succeed because it will give my mother confidence. This is important to me. I begin to believe your intentions are good and so are your ideas. But you do not know my mother! She was a horsewoman, señorita. A great horsewoman!"

"Yes, but that was before—" I started to protest, but he gestured impatiently for me to be quiet.

"What would she say if we mount her on such an animal as you suggest? She would call it a nag, a plow horse. She would sense we were afraid for her, know we thought she was capable of nothing better. I will see her thrown from the horse before I will let her pride be hurt, señorita. Understand that now!"

I looked away, unable to meet his gaze. Hurt pride? My own was smarting painfully. I remembered Dr. Thatcher, an elderly teacher at Bradford Center, who once told me, "There are no special cases among the blind, because *every* case is special." Jaime Romano has just retaught me this lesson.

At last I managed to look at him squarely. "I was completely wrong. I apologize for questioning your choice."

An expression of astonishment came over his face. He had been prepared for anything except my complete surrender in the argument. "How strange," he said.

"What?"

"That you and I should agree on something." Glancing at his watch, he turned away, moving toward Estrella's stall. "At what time?"

"Not today," I said. "Let's hope for nine o'clock tomorrow morning." I told him about Leonora's sudden "migraine," explaining that it was nothing to worry about. "I'll see her later. After Luis and I have lunch with your grandmother."

"My grandmother? Then the Dowager Empress has summoned you to her exalted presence?"

His voice was laden with the same bitter irony he used when he spoke of his half brother, Don Carlos. Did this brooding man who paced his room far into the night hate all his family? It seemed quite possible. Everyone except Leonora, I decided.

"It's very gracious of her to invite me," I said carefully.

"I am happy you are properly honored. But watch your step, señorita. My grandmother devours young women like you. Chews them up, bones and all. Enjoy your lunch." With that he was gone, and a moment later I heard Yaqui's hoofs on the cobbles of the drive as he rode away.

At eleven o'clock sharp Nacho ushered me into the suite Carlos Romano occupied on the second floor of the east wing.

"Don Carlos will be with you in a moment only," he said, and left me to wait in a baronial room which seemed to be a personal hall of fame dedicated to its occupant. There were

97

scattered pieces of bulky Spanish furniture, and the only new carpet I'd seen in the house. But one really noticed nothing except the mementos of triumph covering the walls. Framed bullfight posters, bold type and blazing color, were mixed with enlarged photographs, some of Carlos Romano, others of Latin matadors and celebrities who had scrawled admiring autographs to "Carlos" and "El Conde."

I inspected two pairs of mounted horns, razor-sharp, reminiscent of bloody victories, I supposed. The dates on the posters revealed that his career as a *torero* had spanned about eight years, ending a little less than a decade ago. He had fought in half a dozen Latin American countries and in Spain. An impressive collection, although he seemed not to have been a star in the larger cities and capitals.

A line of silver trophies on the mantle testified to his ability as a horseman, as did several equestrian medals displayed in a glass case. But who, I wondered, ever came to admire these things? Did any visitor ever stand on the pristine-white carpet? No one had spoken of receiving guests in the High Valley. Hospitality would be impossible in this armed camp.

French windows opened to a balcony, and below it, oddly near the house, I saw smoke-blackened ruins, a roofless stone building that I assumed was the burned barn.

"Yes, Miss Mallory," said Don Carlos, who had entered without my hearing him. "That is where our tragedy took place."

"Good morning. I thought that might have been the barn. It's so near the house, I'm surprised the fire didn't spread."

"The stone walls contained it. The building was intended as a chapel but never finished. My half brother had a roof put on it and used it for storage—an unfortunate decision. Do sit down, Miss Mallory."

As I moved toward a chair beside a large desk, he noticed my glance at one pair of the menacing horns, and said, "A rough fellow, that one. I have him to thank for this." He ran a finger down the scar on his cheek. "Do you enjoy the *corrida*, Miss Mallory?"

"I've never seen a bullfight except in films. It must be a very exciting sport."

"Sport?" He regarded me coolly. "The *corrida* is not a sport. It is life and death—a drama impossible to explain to a person of another culture."

Life for the matador, certain death for the bull, I thought. No, I would never understand it.

Don Carlos was, as always, impeccably dressed, the velvet jacket perfectly tailored for his broad shoulders and slender hips, the silk ascot exactly right for a gentleman enjoying a leisurely morning.

How utterly different the brothers were! Jaime, half American, so darkly Latin, no trace of his northern heritage except the surprising blue of his eyes. While Carlos, the pure-blooded Spaniard, was brown-haired and hazel-eyed. Both had been born and reared in the High Valley, yet they were of different worlds. Suavity contrasted to bluntness, polish to roughness.

"I spoke with my mother about you last night," he said, smiling faintly. "You made a most favorable impression."

"I think we'll do well together."

"Then I congratulate myself on my choice." The compliment, nicely emphasized by his nod and smile, remained formal and distant. "I understand that Jaime, for reasons unknown, has housed you in the Octagon. Would you prefer to change? We have many unoccupied rooms."

"Thank you. I'm very happy where I am."

"I see," he murmured thoughtfully. "Very well. You know by now that Luis' mother lived there. It is still cluttered with personal possessions. Nacho will remove those promptly."

For a moment he studied me, while I awaited the inevitable comment about my resemblance to Veronica. But no such remark came. He said, "I apologize for not having been here to welcome you personally. Are there questions you would like to ask? About the routine of the household? Or other matters?"

Somehow sensing I was being tested, I shook my head. "No. Everything is fine."

"Excellent." He started to rise, to terminate the interview, then added, "I have neglected one matter, a stupid formality. Since you are employed here, the government obliges me to check your passport and visa. Will you give them to Nacho? I will return them as soon as I have recorded the numbers."

"Of course."

Then, suddenly, came the flashing smile I remembered from Puerto Vallarta. "I am a wretched employer, Señorita Mallory. I really know nothing about you except your profession."

"There's little else to know." The sudden change, the unexpected shift to warmth and friendliness made me uneasy.

"You must have a family. Tell me about them."

"We're New Englanders. My father never had a career, only hobbies. My mother was an actress, but not a very successful one, I'm afraid."

"Not successful? Yet she must have been a beautiful woman to judge from her daughter." His tone was light, bantering, but it brought color to my cheeks.

"Yes, she was beautiful. I look nothing like her. And you are much too flattering, Don Carlos."

He chuckled. "Ah, but I enjoy flattering you, Miss Mallory. It is a pleasure to see you blush and then become a bit angry, no? Most women are pleased when compliments are paid them. You seem annoyed. Some day I will learn why you are this way. Now tell me about this place you come from. New England. I have never been there."

Twenty minutes later, when I finally escaped from Don Carlos, I felt as though I had just stepped down from the witness box after having been skillfully cross-examined by a wily attorney. He had learned the entire outline of my life, while I knew nothing more about him. Except how carefully he chose his words. Veronica was never called by name, nor mentioned as "my wife" or "my former wife." She was always "Luis' mother."

I hurried to the Octagon, locked its door behind me, drew the draperies, and began a quick search, determined to learn whatever possible about Veronica before her possessions were removed. Now I felt I was neither prying nor intruding. Anything I might find could prove important, perhaps not to me, but to Luis and Leonora Romano.

The photo albums had no more to tell me. I had hoped the notebooks and loose papers beside them might be diaries, but the first page, crowded with Veronica's girlish penmanship, began: *"Ser o no ser? Esta es la pregunta!"* Hamlet's famous "To be or not to be" translated into Spanish as an exercise. I found the "All the world is a stage" speech and Portia's plea for mercy. None of the papers revealed anything except that Veronica had struggled hard to master Spanish and she was a sensitive woman who loved literature.

A cardboard letter file proved equally disappointing. No one, except a few shopkeepers in Mexico City and Puerto Vallarta, ever wrote to Veronica—or at least she kept no personal letters. There were several receipted bills, quite ordinary, although one from a silver shop caught my eye. "One man's belt buckle, monogramed J.R." Jaime Romano, no doubt. A gift she had given her brother-in-law just before she "went away."

Nothing more. The servants had removed the zippered clothing bags from the wardrobe and cleared the dresser two nights ago. Don Carlos could decide for himself what other things were "personal." When Nacho knocked at my door, I gave him the albums and papers, along with a separate envelope containing my passport and tourist visa. I parted with my own documents reluctantly, feeling defenseless without them.

"*Gracias,*" he said, unsmiling. "Until this afternoon, then."

He left before I could ask him what this meant. In Spanish such a farewell suggested he would see me this afternoon. Or did he mean it would take that long to copy a few numbers?

I paced slowly back and forth in the bedroom, troubled by the notion that in my rapid search of Veronica's papers, I had missed something. The receipts, the exercise books, the carefully treasured photographs were ordinary and innocent-appearing. Yet I could not banish the idea that they contained a message for me, as though a distant voice was speaking and I could not quite hear the words. Some day I would know, I told myself. Some day I would understand.

An hour later I found Luis dressed in a sort of Lord Fauntleroy suit he had long ago outgrown, and I helped him in the struggle to knot the floppy bow tie.

"I look silly," he complained as we started for the Villa Plata to have lunch with his great-grandmother. "I hope none of the village boys see me."

He need not have worried. The path we followed, a shortcut, was deserted, and we were concealed on both sides by masses of poppies and shoulder-high sunflowers. I felt like Alice in a Wonderland of yellow-orange. Emerging from the field of flowers, we crossed an ancient stone bridge guarded by four life-sized Biblical figures carved in marble.

"The four Gospels," said Luis. "Mateo, Marcos, Lucas, and Juan."

Willows lined the west bank of the stream spanned by this bridge, and beyond them, on slightly higher ground, stood jacarandas, the battlements of Villa Plata towering above them. We passed through great gates of wrought iron and found ourselves in a flagstoned courtyard. There, sitting rigidly upright in a lacquered wheelchair, was the Excelentísima Ana Luisa.

The scene lay in tableau, motionless except for the breeze fluttering the fringe of the wheelchair's canopy. The *dueña*, hunched on a rusted iron bench, seemed asleep. So was the coach boy, who had changed his crimson livery for a white jacket and now crouched cross-legged on the flagstones behind his mistress' chair, a straw fly-whisk in his lap.

The Excelentísima, turned slightly away from us, did not observe our arrival. She stared at something in the treetops beyond the courtyard, then, suddenly extending an arm encased in a leather gauntlet, she whistled shrilly. With a rush of wings a great peregrine falcon swooped from the jacarandas and glided to the old lady's wrist. She tickled the bird's speckled plumage with a feather, the while making faint clucking noises.

"Buenas tardes," said Luis timidly.

The woman and the hawk slowly turned their heads, and I felt myself pierced by two pairs of beady, unblinking eyes. A snap of Ana Luisa's fingers brought the coach boy to his feet, then a flick of her hand, flashing with jewels, commanded him to bring two rickety wicker stools for us. When I greeted her in Spanish, she stared at me disapprovingly, then interrupted.

"Let us speak English. A barbarous tongue, fit only for infidels and salesmen, but less grating than badly accented Castilian." The thin, scarlet-smeared lips twisted into a smile to show that the insult was merely a joke, that I must not, of course, take offense at her banter. But her eyes did not twinkle—they glittered coldly. "Welcome to your house, the Villa Plata, Miss Mallory."

She tilted a carmine-smudged cheek for Luis to brush with his lips in the ritual kiss expected of all Mexican children. He stepped to her right side, avoiding the falcon, while I perched uneasily on the wicker stool, convinced it would give way at any moment.

Although I knew the Excelentísima had to be well past eighty, it would have been impossible to guess her age. Painted like a Toulouse-Lautrec cancan dancer, she flaunted a facade of grotesque artificialities. Nothing about her was real: a dreadful orange wig whose streaks revealed innumerable trips to the dye vat, mascara slashes for eyebrows, and impossibly long, curling lashes glued on unevenly. The sharp teeth gleamed as white and patently false as the heavy collar of department-store pearls supporting her chin.

The black silk dress, also dye-streaked, was a seamstress' nightmare of tucks, ruffles, folds, and pleats. Dotted with jet beads, it fell to her ankles. Tortoise-shell combs edged with rhinestones held her wig more or less in place.

Gaudy though she might be, an outrage of paste and cosmetics, the Excelentísima Ana Luisa was in no way a comic figure. Rapier-thin and rapier-strong, she held her large head high, and it occurred to me that some of the most venomous serpents are also the most gaily colored.

The falcon stirred on her arm. "What a powerful bird," I said. "He's a peregrine, isn't he?"

"*She* is a peregrine. The males are smaller, good only for bringing down grouse or ducks. This beauty can tear a heron out of the sky!" She clucked proudly, and the hawk preened its feathers. "A bit old now, but still quite a predator. She'll lay talons on anything!"

"Does she have a name?"

"Ah, yes." The Excelentísima lowered her eyes demurely. "I call her Leonora."

Silence followed. There was simply nothing to say. Luis looked wretched, and the old lady did nothing to ease our discomfort. Then, thankfully, a loud snore rumbled from the *dueña*.

"Wake up!" Ana Luisa shouted, seizing a cane hooked over the arm of her chair and trying vainly to poke the sleeping woman, who was just beyond reach.

When Luis gently shook the *dueña's* shoulder, her eyes popped open. "Is it dinnertime?" she demanded.

"God alone knows why I keep that hag in my service," said the Excelentísima, gazing heavenward with the martyred expression of a saint at the stake. "She should have been sent back to Spain years ago. "

"She's Spanish?"

Ana Luisa drew herself up. "We are *all* Spanish. She came with me on the ship from Cadiz when I was brought here to marry Conde Hernán Romano, a man of unflawed character, although a step below my own rank."

How long ago, I wondered. Nearly seventy years. "The High Valley must have been quite different then," I remarked.

"Outwardly, yes." For a moment she seemed to drift into the past as she considered the changes wrought by decades. "It was richer then. Those empty shafts that dot the hills—do you know how many mine shafts there are?"

"No. Thirty perhaps?"

"Thirty? Hah! Scores of them hidden everywhere. And each one produced a fortune in its day. A hundred fortunes for ten generations of Romanos. They were strong men, Miss Mallory. Not only strong, but ruthless."

Ruthlessness seemed to be the quality she most admired, and now she silently savored remembered cruelties I could not even imagine.

"Yet the High Valley seems so peaceful now," I said, meeting her gaze and keeping my face expressionless.

"I suppose you see it as a place of honeysuckle and orchids and larks." The Excelentísima leaned toward me. "Have you ever seen a falcon seize upon a lark, señorita?" Her right hand formed itself into a claw, and the long false fingernails, lacquered blood-red, became uncannily like the talons of the hawk that gripped the leather gauntlet.

"I hope I never do see it," I said quietly. "Apparently falconry is less fascinating than I thought."

She slipped a hood over the bird's head and deftly attached leather thongs to its legs. "Take her away," she told the coach boy. Ana Luisa gently placed the hawk on a wooden perch, which the boy carried at arm's length. "Luis, go into the house and study your catechism. And take that hideous witch with you." The *dueña,* I had begun to believe, had no name.

The Excelentísima shrilled·at Luis's retreating back, "And tell the boy to bring Coca-Cola for the señorita and myself. Make sure the idiot puts straws in the bottles. Clean straws!" She turned to me and added, with no hint of apology, "Forgive my limited hospitality. Nowadays I am permitted only two servants. A senile hag and a moronic child! Of course, there's a gardener and a maid and a scrubwoman, but they count for nothing when I receive guests."

What guests? I wondered for the second time that day. Who in the world would call here?

Ana Luisa leaned toward me, glaring balefully. "This peso-pinching is part of that woman's plot against me."

No need to ask who "that woman" might be. She meant Leonora.

"She keeps me on a pauper's allowance. The plan is to force me to close Villa Plata and move into her ridiculous house. But La Gringa deceives only herself. I am not without resources!"

"I'm sure you aren't." I felt certain that the last thing on earth Leonora would want was to have the Excelentísima sharing her house, but there was no use questioning Ana Luisa's obsession.

"La Gringa, blind or not, is a scheming vulture. But she'll not pick my bones! How long would I last under her roof? Of course, they pretend it is my grandson Jaime who forces me to live like a peon. Legally he controls the money here. But Jaime is only La Gringa's cat's-paw. I am not fooled!"

"Jaime?" I exclaimed in surprise. "How does he control the money? The High Valley belongs to Don Carlos, doesn't it?"

Now it was her turn for surprise. "Haven't the servants told you? They all gossip like macaws."

"Not with me."

"They will." She leaned forward, the false eyelashes batting rapidly. "Before you hear lies, I will tell you about this impossible position. I am a victim, Señorita Mallory. And I do not take it kindly!"

For a moment Ana Luisa seemed more pathetic than fierce—a lonely, bitter old woman who longed for an audience. No doubt I had been invited here so she could pour out her troubles and complaints. All else about her was alien to me, but I could understand this need of the very old to regale others with their problems, their sufferings, their personal histories.

"I told you that Romano men were ruthless," she said, launching her story with obvious pleasure. "Also there is wildness in them, especially when they are young. That is as it should be. I despise tame young men! But my grandson Don Carlos went too far. For one thing, he had a weakness for exotic females. Blond females like yourself, señorita."

I started to protest the malice in her voice, then wisely held my tongue. This was a time to listen, not argue.

"Carlos was sent abroad for his education. Who knows how many schools expelled him? I made novenas to implore the saints that he marry young, before some outraged husband hired a *pistolero* to shoot him. Well, he *did* marry young."

"He married Veronica?"

"No, no! This was years before he met that wretched woman. He married a girl from Mexico City. She was of a good enough Spanish family, but not a distinguished one. The girl was a bore, and Carlos soon behaved more recklessly than ever. No wonder! Three years went by and she bore him no children. Not even a daughter, much less a son! When Carlos decided to divorce her, the Conde Luis was happy to pay the costs."

"He divorced her because they had no children?" This was a strange world, a world difficult for me to comprehend.

"That was not the legal reason, but it was the real one. Why not? My son the Conde Luis wanted grandchildren. Male children are important! The High Valley had to have a male heir. When Carlos got rid of this barren woman, I thanked the angels."

"You approved? But you're a Catholic."

"They were not married in the Church," she said smugly. "He was in youthful rebellion and so was the girl. They had only a civil marriage, which proves how immoral this woman was."

"What does it prove about Don Carlos, then?" I asked quietly.

"That he is a man! Men are expected to do such things."

"Then he met Veronica?" I was determined to steer the conversation toward Luis' mother."

"Years later. While he was in exile."

"Exile?"

She waved her jeweled hand. "Exile, banishment—call it what you will. Carlos was always rebellious and wild. From the time he could walk he loved the bulls and the *corrida* more than anything on earth. We admired his courage, but then—" She paused and almost shuddered. "He went away to fight in the public rings! A Romano performing in front of a paying mob. Entertaining the rabble like a circus acrobat!"

For a second I could not understand the distinction or why it was so crucial. Apparently to be a magnificent amateur was laudable, but when the son of twenty generations of Spanish nobility became a professional, he disgraced his heritage.

"A public display! And I cannot deny he did it partly for money. We had lean years in the High Valley then. Carlos thought he had no future here. I begged him, I pleaded with him not to commit this folly. It was useless."

She stared past me, eyes bewildered, the dreadful wig awry, a woman unable to comprehend the century in which she found herself. She could only gasp at a world where young noblemen stooped to public performance for pay.

Ana Luisa steeled herself and continued. "My son, the

Conde Luis, looked upon Carlos as one dead. All communication between them ceased. It was during these years he met Veronica."

"Where was she from?" I asked.

"From nowhere. She was nobody. Another *gringa*, nothing more. I doubt she even knew who her grandparents were. One day a letter came to me from Carlos. He said he had been married for some time and had an infant son named Luis, after the Conde. He longed to return and live the life he was bred for. Would I intercede for him?

"I thought it would be useless. The Conde Luis was not a forgiving man. But Carlos had enclosed a photograph of Veronica holding little Luis in her arms. That made the difference. The Conde could not deny his own grandson, his own blood."

The Excelentísima leaned back in her chair, and her hollow cheeks, already angry with rouge, burned an even deeper scarlet. "But it turned out that the Conde Luis had really forgiven nothing at all. When he died, he bequeathed the High Valley and everything in it to little Luis! And my grandson Don Jaime is executor until Luis is of age. Is it not immoral? This was never the custom. The eldest son *always* inherited the High Valley. For centuries!"

The Excelentísima lowered her voice, but her rage did not lessen. "If the Conde Luis wished to punish Carlos, he should have taken my advice. The first time Carlos appeared in a public ring, I told the Conde to hire three or four men from the city to kidnap the boy. Bring him back here, tie him to a tree, and whip him! Then forgive him completely. If my words had been heeded, we never would have seen that simpering Veronica. The High Valley would have had an heir of unmixed blood in time. And I would not be in the power of my grandson Jaime!"

"He treats you badly?" I asked.

"I am devoted to both my grandsons, naturally. But you

will soon learn that Jaime seizes upon a peso like a hawk on a pigeon. He inherits this trait from his mother, La Gringa. She always grubbed for money like a fish seller in a market."

I clicked my tongue to indicate sympathy. Ana Luisa did not want me to reply. She cared only about having a listener. My identity did not matter, nor did the fact that I, like Veronica and Leonora, was "another *gringa*, nothing more." Any audience would have served as well.

"And Veronica simply went away?" I ventured, trying to prompt her.

"Not alone, I'm sure," snapped the Excelentísima. "She had been slipping off to see some man. One of the maids reported as much to me. No doubt she found a lover of her own class."

I thought of the narrow entrance to the valley and of the dozens of observers who would be everywhere. "That must have been difficult here. Someone is always watching."

Her eyes narrowed, and there was a moment of meaningful silence which somehow implied that I had examined the ground for my own future trysts.

"Not difficult if one is determined," she said with a cynical smile. "As one of your English writers said, 'Satan finds opportunity for those works he puts forward.' Certainly she went off with a lover. It is what one expects from a woman of no breeding. I knew from the beginning that . . . "

But I was never to learn what she had known. The coach boy approached carrying a bottle of Coca-Cola in each hand. Seeing him, she turned in her chair with such violence that the fringe of the canopy shook as though struck by a whirlwind. "You have taken all day, idiot! And you have forgotten the straws again!" Spanish curses and imprecations I could not understand spewed out while the boy quailed. Exhausted at last, she glanced at the sun to determine the hour. "Lunchtime," she informed me, almost pleasantly. "Kindly push my chair to the *entrada.*" She shouted at the coach boy, "Put those bottles on the table in the dining room."

I wheeled the groaning, squeaking chair over the flag-stones. Inside the great arch of the entry, two Malacca canes hung on a hook. The Excelentísima took them and slowly rose. Although a bit arthritic, she walked quite well, her large head held high and her spine straight as a steel lance, keeping the small body erect and regal. Even the broad flight of stairs leading to the dining room did not daunt her. I realized that the wheelchair was a complete affectation and the canes hardly needed. Ana Luisa could walk when she wanted to.

It was the warmest hour of the day, yet I shivered at the chill pervading the huge house, this gloomy fortress whose dank walls were decorated by moldering tapestries depicting the victories of El Cid.

When the Excelentísima paused at a landing near the top, I gratefully stepped into a patch of sunlight entering through a heavily barred window. Outside, I saw another patio, not stone but brick, and in the center stood an upright post with a crossbar at its top.

"The punishment stake," said the Excelentísima behind me, her soft, almost whispered words echoing strangely in the great stairwell. "Flogging was done on Saturdays so the punished men could recover enough to work again on Monday."

"Long ago, I suppose."

"No. I remember those days well." I started to turn away, but now she was beside me, holding my arm in talonlike fingers. "My husband used to stand at this very window to count the lashes. You see that fire pit over there? That's where irons were heated to brand thieves who stole vegetables from the gardens or fruit from the orchards. My husband had the power of life and death here—and he used it!" Her eyes dilated and her breathing was rapid. "Under these stairs are three punishment cells with iron doors to the courtyard. Tiny, no larger than confessionals, and like ovens in the summer. The shackles are still there. Would you like to see them, Miss Mallory?"

A feeling of horror made me shudder, and I pulled my arm free of her grip. She was reveling in memories of cruelty and torture, boastful that she had once been queen of this terrorized kingdom.

"Thank God, times have changed," I said.

The glittering, pitiless eyes held my gaze hypnotically. "Times may change, but the men of the Romano family are as they always were. Falcons who bring down larks! It is in their blood." Her lips twisted into a contemptuous smile. "Shall we go to the dining room, Miss Mallory? Our lunch awaits us."

"Fear is sharp-sighted, and can see things under ground, and much more in the skies."
—Miguel de Cervantes

SEVEN

The ordeal of the next hour and a half seemed endless. Luis, as the only male present, was seated in a huge chair at the head of the refectory table. Ana Luisa was on his right, I on his left. The *dueña,* yards away from us, drowsed at the far end. On the floor in a corner the coach boy hunched, idly pulling a rope to move a rattan fan that hung from the ceiling, even though the cavernous room was cold as a dungeon.

Unexpectedly, Carlos' man Nacho appeared to serve us at table. "My grandson always lends me Nacho when people come to lunch," she said. Again I wondered, What people?

Not once did Nacho leave the room. A kitchen maid brought trays, and he served from them, quiet, lynxlike, the thin, pocked face expressionless as he listened carefully to every word we spoke.

The Excelentísima played role after role, changing personalities as the mood struck her. At one moment she became a royal yet gracious hostess, then a pious great-grandmother,

113

and at times a snarling virago upbraiding the *dueña* for chewing noisily.

During a calmer moment, she said. "I brought this china with me from Spain as part of my dowry. Service for forty guests."

"Lovely," I murmured, looking at the chipped plates, nicked saucers, and handleless cups. A beautiful silver salt cellar stood flanked by a chili-sauce bottle and a cardboard box with plastic toothpicks. The Excelentísima, I discovered, was fluent in four languages but civilized in none of them. Despite her regal air, she ate with her fingers and a spoon, never touching the fork placed beside her plate for display.

At one point in the meal she stopped eating to stare at me, directly and rudely. "Surprising," she said after a careful survey. "You are not at all as Carlos described you."

Sensing a trap, I said nothing, leaving her to continue. "He paid his respects to me last night after his journey. Carlos knows his duties as a gentleman and a grandson, even if his behavior is at times unconventional. He told me he had hired a new teacher for that woman."

"Really?"

"I knew that earlier, of course. I am informed of everything that passes in the house of La Gringa." She added slyly, "I myself have not entered there since my son's death."

I wondered if this could be true. Her manner was suddenly that of a naughty child who denies a misdeed unconvincingly because she is proud of it.

"Now why should Carlos speak of you as he did? He told me you were a shy, awkward woman. Probably not very intelligent, but bright enough to take care of La Gringa. What was the word he used? Spineless, I think."

Luis, although he could not understand all of her English, flushed deep crimson, and as I put down my fork it clattered on my plate. Nacho, standing nearby, seemed impassive but watched me closely.

"What peculiar things for him to say, when I find you so poised and witty and intelligent," the Excelentísima purred.

"Perhaps you are both given to extreme opinions," I answered rather sharply, not knowing what to believe. Surely this was a lie told to stir up discord. Yet a doubt haunted me. What sort of impression had I made on Don Carlos at our interview? Still, I had been hired. Ana Luisa must either be lying blatantly or twisting her grandson's words to cause trouble.

"Ah, but men are all alike, aren't they, my dear Miss Mallory?" The tigress suddenly turned into a kitten. "They play their own games, and we women never know what they are up to."

"Nor do we always know what women are up to," I added.

"True." She gave me a penetrating look. "Profoundly true."

"Shall I serve dessert?" inquired Nacho softly.

Over tasteless boiled pudding she cross-questioned Luis about the lives and miracles of the most obscure saints, and I was astonished at how much the boy had memorized. But his answers, whether right or wrong, drew nothing but blistering sarcasm from the old lady.

Listening, a plain and ugly truth slowly dawned on me. She did not like Luis, had not the least spark of affection in her heart for him. Nothing he could ever do or say would please her. The boy was a usurper, a child of what she hatefully called "mixed blood" who had stolen his father's birthright. Ana Luisa might condemn Don Carlos' youthful follies, might deplore his choice of women, yet he remained her grandson, the true crown prince of untainted lineage.

Luis, trying to divert attention from himself, turned to me. "Tell me, *Ti*—" He quickly stopped himself from calling me "Aunt Alison" in her presence. "Tell me, señorita, what is your saint's day?"

"I haven't any idea, Luis. I don't even know if there was a Saint Alison."

The Excelentísima sniffed. "Of course not. It is a pagan name. Perhaps we could change it to Alicia."

"I'm quite happy being Alison," I informed her. "It's a very old name. It means 'protector of the home.'"

"But if you have no saint's day, when do we give you presents and have the musicians sing *'Las Mañanitas'* for you?" he asked.

"No doubt you have a second name that is Christian?" Ana Luisa inquired, lifting her chin a notch.

"Yes. Barbara," I answered.

"Ah, Santa Barbara! She is the patroness of arsenals and powder magazines." Ana Luisa chuckled. "Rather inappropriate, Miss Mallory. You do not impress me as being explosive. Sweet and docile would be better words for you."

My eyes must have flashed, for her expression changed as she looked at me. Even so, she had no idea how close she was to a powder magazine about to be detonated. Only the fact that Luis spoke prevented me from telling her exactly what I thought of her rudeness. Docile, indeed!

"I do not like that at all," Luis protested. "The day of Santa Barbara is not until December. That is a long way off."

"Quite so," agreed the Excelentísima. "The señorita will doubtless be gone from the High Valley long before then."

Luis gave me a frightened, questioning look, and I said quickly, "If I'm not here in December, then Luis and I will have our fiesta somewhere else."

It was a ridiculous thing to have said, but I had been caught off guard. Ana Luisa's quick perception understood all the implications instantly. She glanced from Luis to me, making a silent assessment. Now, too late, I realized she had made her remark about my leaving in order to evoke a reaction. Well, I could play this game, too.

"I know so little about saint's days," I said lightly. "Let me think. I seem to remember that February fourth is the feast of—"

"San Gilberto," the Excelentísima interjected instantly.

"Really? I thought it was Santa Veronica."

"Only in certain countries. Here she is honored on Good Friday. It is the custom."

"Good Friday," I mused. "The day of death and martyr-dom? Very appropriate, isn't it?"

The Excelentísima's eyes bored into me. "In what way appropriate, señorita?"

"I don't know. It just seems so."

The name Veronica had brought an instant reaction from Nacho, who stopped removing dishes from the table and lurked near the sideboard, his back to us. No rattle of plates or silver as he waited to catch every word.

I returned the Excelentísima's malevolent stare with a bright smile. "And when is the saint's day of Leonora?"

Ana Luisa flinched. "Leonora is a barbaric corruption of some Christian name. I have no idea which one. Nor do I care."

"I find Leonora Romano an intelligent and capable wom-an," I told her quietly. "She has all the qualities that in Spanish you call *honorable*. Apparently you hate her. Why?"

The painted eyebrows lifted in surprise. "Forgive me, but is that not a rather stupid question? Why would I *not* hate her? La Gringa came here as a prospector's wife. A woman beneath my notice. Later she somehow tricked my son into marrying her." Ana Luisa's bejeweled hands tightened, the fingers drawing up, arching like claws. "For years she has tried to steal my grandson's affection—and failed. She poisoned the Con-de's mind against Carlos, hoping that her own half-breed son would some day own the High Valley. In some ways she succeeded in this. Jaime struts about like the lord of the valley. But not for long, señorita. Not for long! Why do I hate her? I repeat, why not?"

"Leonora Romano does not feel that way about you," I said.

Her thin lips curled in a sneer. "Then she is a fool."

Our exchange had taken place in English much too rapid and complicated for Luis to understand. But he had caught at least one name, for he said, "Leonora Romano is my grand-mother's name."

"She is not your grandmother! I have told you a hundred times!" The Excelentísima seemed to force herself not to seize his shoulders and shake him. "Your real grandmother died years ago when plague came to the valley. La Gringa is no relative of yours. Your grandfather's woman—nothing more!"

Luis blanched, helpless to strike back. What she said was literally true, although I had never thought of it that way. But if there were no bonds of blood kinship between Luis and Leonora, they had other ties even stronger. I would explain this to Luis, make sure that Ana Luisa did no more damage to the child's fragile sense of security. Then I saw no explanation was needed. Color had returned to his cheeks, and he lifted his head defiantly, saying nothing. Yet the outthrust lip, the set of his small shoulders gave a silent but positive reply: "My grandmother is my grandmother!"

The Excelentísima rose from her chair. When Nacho stepped forward to offer his arm, she gestured him aside. Venting her spite had given her new strength.

"Forgive me for terminating this pleasant conversation," she said, her voice like ice. "It is past the hour for my siesta."

"So kind of you to have invited me," I replied, also rising, not able to manage even a false smile of courtesy—and not caring.

"An inexpressible pleasure! By the way, I seem to remember that there *was* an obscure saint with a name rather like yours."

"Really?"

"I cannot recall the exact name, but the details of her life return to me vividly. Before her conversion she tried to become the mistress of the Marquis de Cadiz."

"A nobleman's mistress? Unusual for a saint."

"Quite so. She was an upstart, an interloper with stupid ambitions. Her death was by fire after she had been broken on the rack. A last-minute conversion made her a martyr. I doubt that made the flames less painful."

"Thank you for telling me. You're sure she wasn't Santa Veronica?"

"We are both certain she was not, Miss Mallory. As I said, her name was much like yours." Her smile was a gleam of white, sharp teeth. "Good afternoon. Our conversation has been most instructive." Turning abruptly, she left the room, not bothering with a cane.

Nacho, coming forward, bowed slightly. "I need not escort you out, señorita. Don Luis knows the way. *Buenas tardes.*"

He spoke the name "Don Luis" with no hint of irony, but none was needed. Calling a little boy "sir" was taunting enough in its mock courtesy.

Five minutes later Luis and I were again walking in the forest of poppies and sunflowers. He had taken off his necktie, unbuttoned the tight collar, and was chattering happily, quite unaffected by the scene at the Excelentísima's. He had understood little of it, and he was accustomed to her spleen. I was too preoccupied with my own thoughts to listen, but from time to time I looked at him with new understanding. This was not just another small boy, but the owner of the High Valley, of lands measured not in acres, but in miles. Not a prince, but a child-king, and when he had said "Everything here is mine," he had spoken exact truth.

And Jaime Romano, not Don Carlos, was the child-king's regent, the temporary ruler here. But at one time he must have been the crown prince. In those years before Luis was born, the years when the old Conde disowned his eldest son, Jaime must have expected to be master of the High Valley after his father's death.

What if Don Carlos had not married Veronica, and Luis had not been born? The land we now walked on, the great hills and high pastures in the distance, would have been Jaime's. What a bitter turn of fortune Luis' birth had been for his uncle. A dream of power shattered. Could such a broken dream turn to hate? Hatred toward Veronica and even toward her son?

I looked down at Luis, who half walked, half skipped beside me, swinging my hand. Who could fail to love such a gentle, affectionate child, a boy so full of warmth and love? Yet the Excelentísima despised him as a half-caste usurper, and Nacho, I felt sure, was allied with her in this. When they looked at Luis, they saw not Don Carlos' son, but Veronica's.

His long trousers and black stockings concealed the scars of burning. If something unknown and terrible had happened to Veronica, then why not to Luis? The unwanted prince, the child who had changed everything.

Just then Luis cried, "Look, Tía Alison! A falcon!"

Above our heads a peregrine hawk sailed in a slow circle, almost as though the Excelentísima, witchlike, had sent forth a familiar spirit to follow us. I tried to smile at the notion of the Wicked Witch of the Land of Oz watching while we walked through fields of poppies.

"Listen," whispered Luis.

The soft cooing of a dove came faintly to my ears. I saw the falcon soar in a wider, higher circle. Then it plunged from the sky, swooping to strike.

I did not see it fall upon the dove, yet somehow I felt the talons stabbing and clenching. The Excelentísima's hateful smile came back to me, her face avid as she spoke of the whipping post and the dungeons. Then her words: "Men of the Romano family are as they always were. Falcons who bring down larks! It is in their blood."

"Tía Alison," said Luis softly. "You are holding my hand too tightly."

"Oh, I'm sorry, Luis. I didn't realize." I bent quickly and kissed his forehead.

We continued toward home, the *casa grande*. Luis glanced over his shoulder once, perhaps to see the falcon winging toward Villa Plata, bearing its lifeless prey. Luis looked back, but I did not.

*"A weeping woman walks at night
I hear her in the darkness . . . "*
—Spanish street song

EIGHT

Our "miracle" began the following morning. At least the servants called what happened a miracle, and even my far more experienced eyes had never witnessed anything so remarkable as the change that transformed Leonora Romano.

Its prelude was her being led downstairs—awkward, hesitant, and trying to conceal her fear. Not physical fear, but dread of failure. She had dressed herself, with help from the housekeeper and Miss Evans, as for an equestrian exhibition, beautiful tooled leather boots and a split riding skirt, russet with thong embroidery.

"I might as well fall off in my finery," she muttered as we crossed the veranda.

"You look wonderful," I told her. "But the skirt's too tight."

"Must you remind me?"

"Yes, until you take off seven or eight pounds and it fits as it once did."

"I lost half that much coming down the stairs." She laughed uncertainly. "My hands are cold. I thought people got cold feet at times like this. But it's my hands."

"Now, you're not really afraid."

"A lot you know about it!"

Ethel Evans hovered in the background, not actually carrying a first-aid kit, but implying that one waited nearby. To prevent her mumbled warnings from demoralizing Leonora further, I told her bluntly not to interfere and to keep quiet. Glowering, she clamped her lips together as though they would never open again.

Luis, on the other hand, was perfect, chattering gaily about riding with his grandmother, telling her what a fine horse Estrella was, and how he envied her having such a mount. "Grandmother, some day when Estrella has a colt, may I have it for my own?"

Mario waited near the front steps with our horses and Luis' pony. Jaime Romano, who had provided me with the sort of spiritless old mare I had first requested for Leonora, sat mounted on Yaqui, and remained a little way off, silent, watchful, and scowling. Leonora stroked Estrella a moment, then said, "Let's get it over with."

With Mario's help she swung into the saddle. For a second the blind woman seemed to freeze, then she relaxed her grip on the reins. When Estrella moved slowly forward, Leonora knew instantly that something was wrong.

"Mario, are you leading her?"

"*Sí, señora.*"

"Well, don't! She can walk by herself. And by heaven, I can ride for myself, too!"

Leonora straightened in the saddle, and she, Luis, and I rode down the path. Estrella seemed to turn toward the corral by instinct, but I suspected Jaime had been working with her during the last two days.

"We're going west," said Leonora. "I can feel sun on my back." It was a simple discovery, but her face brightened, radiating a smile that said "Look, I'm outdoors again. I'm riding. I'm not afraid."

"*Abuela,* you will soon ride like my papa or Uncle Jaime," exclaimed Luis.

"Say 'Grandmother,' Luis. Speak English," she told him, but her smile became a grin.

Entering the corral, we rode in a circle, and within minutes were surrounded by silent, smiling people. Servants came from the house, workers from the stable and from the nearby orchards. They did not speak, they made no noise that might startle a horse. But their beaming faces rang with applause, and I realized that the people of the High Valley loved Leonora. She had ruled this land through love, and over the years the people learned to admire and trust her. The Excelentísima's instruments of punishment and discipline seemed a universe away.

A dozen times around the corral, then back to the *casa grande.* That was enough for the first day. So little—yet so much.

On the way back, there occurred one of those moments a teacher dreams of. Leonora suddenly halted Estrella and breathed deeply. "The *copa de oro* is in bloom," she said. "We must be near the veranda where the Octagon juts out."

"You're right."

"I planted that vine myself. I always loved the fragrance."

"It's climbed all the way up to the roof."

"So high? We'll have to put in guide wires for it, otherwise it'll block the eaves trough. I'll tell the gardeners."

Leonora Romano had come down from the seclusion of her tower, and I knew she would not return to that voluntary prison again.

In the next two weeks she astonished everyone in the household, and I was among those amazed. In dealing with the blind, you soon learn that an initial accomplishment—even a small one—may open a hundred doors. But at best the process of building confidence and independence is slow.

Leonora's case proved utterly different. Having succeeded at one rather simple thing, she became convinced that there was nothing in the world she could not master at once. Soon the tap-tapping of her cane was heard all over the house, and often her boldness was maddening.

The servants, for all their good intentions, were careless. Mops, pails, and brooms were left on stairways and in passages. Despite my pleadings and lectures, furniture in Leonora's rooms was not always returned to the exact places I had marked. There were supposed to be seven paces between Leonora's armchair and her bed. She learned the relative locations first by counting her steps and using a cane. Soon she would no longer need to count—it would be unconscious, she would *know.* No fumbling, no counting, no hesitation.

Too often the servants forgot. I suppose Leonora tripped over something at least twice a day, but I was not a witness to these tumbles. When she complained of barked shins and bruised knees, it was in tones of cheerful exasperation, never discouragement. Sometimes I had nightmarish visions of Leonora, in her overconfidence, plunging headlong down some flight of stairs. Yet there was no holding her back from activity and adventure.

Her new-found zest conveyed itself to Luis, who decided not only to master English himself, but to teach all the servants as well. Leonora and Luis demanded every minute of time and energy I had to give, and the unexplained events that had surrounded my arrival in the High Valley were forced into the background. Not that a sense of Veronica's presence ever left me for long. I could not take a volume from the bookcase without thinking: This was hers. Sometimes, looking at Luis, I would remember a photograph, and realized that he had inherited his mother's smile, her small hands, her large, clear eyes.

There were other reminders. Ramona's careful polishing did not quite obliterate the small scratch on the cabinet where an unknown intruder had tried to pick the lock. Now it held, safely I hoped, my passport and visa, which Don Carlos had returned.

And sometimes I would awaken suddenly in the darkness when a nightjar in the trees sounded the soft, clear call that to me would always be Veronica's name.

Yet the world in which Leonora, Luis, and I lived seemed secure and happy. At least three mornings a week found us on horseback, venturing a little farther each time. Most days I joined Leonora for the four-course midmorning breakfast, helping her relearn the skills of using a knife, fork, and spoon. Then another hour of work with her in the morning, and two hours in the late afternoon, sandwiching in time for Luis' English lessons.

Thankfully, Miss Evans had shouldered the task of seeing that Leonora's new housekeeping projects were carried out. Rooms untouched for a year were cleaned and put in order. A tall, dramatic statue of St. Michael that stood on a landing of Leonora's staircase was relieved of its enshrouding dust. When the servants shook out long unused blankets and linen, I felt that more than lint and dust flew away. Ghosts and memories were banished at the same time.

Jaime and Carlos Romano moved near the edge of our lives but were not part of them. They lived by the rules of an unspoken and uneasy truce. I never saw them alone together in a room, never heard more than a formal greeting when by accident they met in the patio or the stable. Carlos spent much of his time away from the valley, flying off to distant places to participate in *charreadas,* the riding exhibitions he loved, and frequently he visited the capital, where he kept an apartment. To see a tall, lovely woman called Karen? I supposed so. When he returned from these trips his step was always jaunty, the air of a conqueror.

His greetings and brief remarks to me were unfailingly friendly and casual, but I never felt at ease in his presence. The Excelentísima had done her work well. Even though I did not believe he had described me in the way she had said, a doubt remained—a doubt that caused me to turn away from his smile, to avoid being near him.

Nor did I talk with Jaime Romano until early one afternoon when the new spring sunshine of the High Valley was even brighter than usual—a yellow sunlight that would darken to gold as the hours passed. I had taken a tall glass of iced tea to the patio and was sitting in the lime tree's shade, grateful to have a few minutes to myself after a difficult morning. Leonora, in her struggle to eat with table utensils, had been irritable and trying today, exasperated by her own slowness.

"I dribble everything like a baby!" she said. "It's infuriating!"

"Be patient," I told her for the tenth time in two hours. "It takes a little time."

"Patient? Fine for *you* to say. You're not the one stabbing her own lips with a fork!"

"But I have been. When I learned to eat blindfolded, I was much slower than you."

"Rubbish. And I'll bet you peeped under the blindfold now and then, too."

"I did not. Now let's try again. Remember to touch the edge of the plate first. That gives you a directional point."

Now, lounging in the patio, I relaxed after the trials of the morning. Since it was Saturday, a line of white-clad, straw-sombreroed workers sat on the porch of Jaime Romano's office and quarters. They were foremen, some in charge of orchards, others handling cattle, horses, or crops. One by one they entered the open door of the office, and I could see Jaime, seated at a desk, counting out peso bills—weekly pay for the foremen and their crews.

Ramona came from the house, bringing two letters on a copper tray. "For you, my lady."

"Thank you, Ramona."

One envelope bore Margaret's bold handwriting and the other was stamped with the familiar imprint of Bradford Center for the Blind. Gazing at it, I was surprised to find that I

126

felt no emotion at all. A letter from another world, a world I no longer inhabited. A dozen swift pictures flashed through my mind, memories of my years there, but all strangely impersonal. I recalled Donald's handsome, rebellious face. He, like Leonora, had been desperate over the problems of a knife and fork. He had gone into a tantrum, flinging the silver on the floor and hurling his plate after it. I had longed to comfort him that day, to hold him close, letting him feel my love and caring. It had taken all the control I could summon to say quietly, "I'm sorry you did that, Mr. Nelson. You'll have to pick them up, you know. Hunting for them will waste a lot of time."

Now the incident seemed childish and unimportant. Only one more "difficult case." I felt strangely and foolishly disloyal to realize how little it meant to me now. A sudden sense of loneliness crept over me, caused by thoughts of Donald, yet really having nothing to do with him.

The flowering patio, the soft voices of the waiting workmen, the faint rainbow in the spray of the fountain—these were my real world now. Beautiful, but at this moment somehow empty, incomplete. Lifting my eyes, I saw the V-formation of mallards flying northward, homeward to summer nests. One day I, too, would have to leave the valley, go northward. Departing as I had arrived—alone. I did not want to think about it.

The letter from Bradford was a kind inquiry by the director about my future plans, and Margaret's scrawled message urged me to come soon for a weekend in Puerto Vallarta. I had just finished reading it when Jaime Romano called across the patio, "Señorita Mallory, would you come to the office, please?"

The whitewashed room was cool and seemed dim after the brilliance of the patio. The last of the workmen had gone, and Jaime Romano was standing behind a steel desk. "Yes?" I asked.

"You will have been here one month next Monday. But

we pay on Saturdays." He handed me a manila envelope and a receipt form. "Will you please count the money and sign for it."

I signed, then counted the peso notes. "This is incorrect," I said. "You've overpaid me."

"No. Extra pay is for extraordinary work."

"In that case, thank you."

"It is nothing."

I looked up at him, surprised more by this sign of appreciation than by the generosity of the bonus. "Or is it your mother I should thank?"

"I am in charge of salaries here. My mother is not involved. Besides, no thanks are necessary."

He meant to be generous and appreciative, I felt sure of that. Yet the aloofness of his manner negated what he did. I said with coolness equal to his own, "As a favor, you might give me most of this in the form of a check. I could send it to a bank in Puerto Vallarta. I don't like carrying so much cash."

"That is impossible."

"Impossible?" The flat refusal astonished me. "Why?"

"Sit down, señorita. I am tired of standing." He seated himself in the chair behind his desk, and I perched on an uncomfortable stool in front of it, a stool whose smallness and hardness guaranteed that office conversations would be brief.

"I cannot give you a check because you are employed here illegally. Checks are too easily traced."

"Illegally? I am certainly not doing anything illegal!"

"Ah, but you are, señorita. The money you just accepted brands you a dangerous criminal." The mocking tone and thin smile made it impossible to know if he was serious or not. "You have no papers permitting you to earn money in this country," he went on. "But do not be terrified and flee to the border. What we have just done is not unusual. No one will raise questions. Still, we will not advertise we are criminals by writing checks, no?"

"Then why did your brother examine my passport? He said he had to copy the number for authorities because I was working here."

Clearly he was surprised. "I know nothing of that. Perhaps Carlos merely wished to admire your photograph for a few hours."

"Now really—"

"Ask Carlos," he said, rising. "Your passport is no affair of mine."

"I'll ask him as soon as possible," I retorted. "And frankly, I don't believe this nonsense about my being paid illegally."

He shrugged his shoulders. "Believe what you like."

I was to have lunch with Leonora—an extra practice session—and when I went to her room, I found her nervous and upset. Miss Evans was offering aspirins, which Leonora indignantly refused.

"Alison, I've just had word that Enrique Vargas and his wife and some friends from Puerto Vallarta are arriving this afternoon to spend the night."

"You don't want them here?"

"I want them and I don't want them. His father was attorney for my husband, and now Enrique does legal work for Carlos. Why couldn't they come later? When I could have dinner with them and show off my new table manners! But no, they told Primitivo in town this morning that they were coming. And how many friends are they bringing? Two? A thousand?"

"Ill-mannered," sniffed Miss Evans.

"Not really," said Leonora, relenting. "It's a Mexican feeling about hospitality. They say, 'A stranger might be God.' Visitors are welcome, expected or not."

"'A stranger might be God,'" I repeated. "A beautiful thought."

Miss Evans tossed her head, indicating that if the Almighty called on her, she would want advance notice.

129

"In the old days whole families came with no warning at all. I've had a dozen unexpected guests for lunch so many times I couldn't count them."

Guests from the outer world, I thought. This was just what Leonora needed.

"If only they'd waited a month," she said, sighing. "Until my table manners become a little better."

"It's not difficult," I told her. "You don't have to have supper with them unless you want to. Join them at the table and say you're on a diet. Just take fruit juice. You're very good with a drinking glass now."

She chuckled. "You mean I hardly ever lose one and seldom knock them over. We can invite Padre Olivera, he was a friend of Enrique's father. And hire musicians from the village. Someone should take word up to the dam for Eric to come, too."

"Eric?"

"Eric Vanderlyn. He's working on the construction of the dam up at the far end of the valley. You'll meet him tonight."

A dinner party, I thought happily, with no suspicion of the violent consequences the evening would bring.

When our visitors arrived late that afternoon, it fell to me to greet them. Leonora needed rest, Miss Evans was busy with the table arrangements, and neither of the brothers was to be found.

A long black car, dusty from the Puerto Vallarta road, rolled into the drive, and I saw a chauffeur and five passengers. The chauffeur, the first to emerge from the car, was a stocky, powerful-looking man with fierce mustachios. His blue uniform was ordinary enough, but tucked in the broad belt was an automatic pistol.

Enrique Vargas, the young attorney, came next, and returned my *"Buenas tardes"* with an English "Good afternoon." A tall, stoop-shouldered man with close-set eyes, Señor Vargas was not a type to inspire much confidence. The black hair was so heavily oiled that it adhered to his scalp like a skullcap, and as he shook my hand in greeting I noticed that his fingernails were too long, too pointed, and shone with thick lacquer. I watched his reaction carefully. He must have met Veronica often. Would there be a startled second glance, perhaps a question?

"I am enchanted," he said with no surprise, no unusual stare except the quick look of appraisal Mexican men automatically give when meeting an unknown woman. "May I present my wife, Raquel." A pretty, round-faced girl still in her teens smiled shyly at me and murmured in Spanish. "And my mother, Doña Antonia?"

Doña Antonia's plump, jolly appearance belied the black mourning dress and mantilla she wore. "'Appy to meets you!" she exclaimed. "I learn speaking the inglés from my son and phonograph *discos. Qué bueno!*"

A tall, middle-aged couple, apparently Americans, emerged from the car looking dazed. "Thank God, we're over that road," said the man.

"And out of that tunnel," the woman added with a shiver.

"Dr. George Hardy and his sister, Miss Alice Hardy."

"Pleased to meet a fellow American," the doctor growled.

He was enormous. A great wattle of skin hung below what must have been a double chin, now reduced, I supposed, by dieting which seemed not to have lessened his girth otherwise. Tufts of gray sideburns jutted in front of reddish ears, and his eyebrows, stiff and wiry as brushes, gave him a look of perpetual hostility.

His sister, Alice, except for her unusual height, bore no resemblance to him. Thin, angular, and long-necked, she was far too sharp-featured and harsh-looking to be called attractive. Still, Alice Hardy had an arresting quality that compelled attention, an intensity that one sensed rather than saw.

They were vacationing in Mexico, and Enrique Vargas told me that he had lived with them for a year when he was an exchange student in the United States.

131

"I hope we're not intruding," rumbled the doctor. "I've always wanted to see one of these Mexican *ranchos*. Enrique said he had business to do here, and that gave us an excuse."

The Vargas trio, with Primitivo and Nacho helping the chauffeur carry their bags, went quickly up the steps of the veranda. But Alice Hardy lingered a moment, staring at the facade of the house.

"A strange place," she said.

"It's unusual in Mexico," I agreed.

"Yes." She shook her head slowly. "Do you ever have a feeling that you've been in some absolutely strange place before, Miss Mallory?" Her eyes did not leave the house. "Perhaps in another life?"

"Well—" I replied uncertainly. "Not any strong feeling like that."

Dr. Hardy cleared his throat. "Alice, let's get out of this sun. Come on, now."

Miss Hardy followed him, but her restless eyes scanned the veranda, the fanlight above the door, the shuttered windows.

In the entrance hall I explained that the servants would show them to their rooms and we would gather in the patio at seven o'clock for cocktails.

Before going upstairs, Enrique Vargas drew me to one side. "Don Carlos is not in, you said?"

"No. He'll return later."

"If you see him, please tell him I have important news."

"Of course. Perhaps Nacho can find him if this is an urgent matter."

"Not urgent. Just very good news he has been waiting for." The attorney's smile was almost a leer. "*Hasta las siete, señorita.*" He hurried toward his wife, who awaited him on the stairs as though afraid to take one step in this unknown place without her husband's guidance and protection.

At six-thirty, dressed for my first dinner party in the High

Valley, I left the Octagon to make a last check on arrangements for the evening. I felt gay with anticipation, a childlike delight that for once I would not be having supper from a tray alone or from a tray in Luis' room.

Pausing before a tall mirror, I turned quickly right, then left, letting the long combed cotton skirt swirl around my ankles. In the glass I saw a girl who for a surprising second seemed not to be me at all—a smiling, assured girl standing tall and confident. Foolishness, of course. But pleasant foolishness.

The servants, with extra help recruited from the village, had taken care of everything. Tall vases filled with lilies and roses of Castile perfumed the rooms. In the patio Nacho, uniformed in a maroon jacket with gold embroidery, was inspecting torches and Japanese lanterns.

Wandering back to the house, I hesitated, hearing an unfamiliar sound, a piano being played softly. The instrument was not quite in tune, but it was easy to recognize the haunting melody of Chopin's *Nocturne,* and to know that the musician played with extraordinary skill, the cadenzas flowing like rippling water. Moving toward the music, I entered a small parlor near the main living room.

An elderly priest wearing the brown robes and white knotted belt of the Dominican Order sat at a spinet. He was balding, and the fringe of white hair above his ears gave the impression of a tonsured monk—a priest in Chaucer or from a medieval tale.

"Good evening," he said, smiling. "You must be Miss Mallory."

"Yes. And you have to be Padre Olivera," I replied. "Luis talks of you so often."

"As he talks of you, too." The brown eyes in his weathered but almost unwrinkled face regarded me gravely. Then he smiled again. "I meant to call on you before, to welcome you to our valley. Something has always interfered." Padre Olivera's features radiated innocent good will, yet I felt he was studying me, and behind the cherub face there was profound shrewdness.

"Now that we meet, I can ask a question that has troubled me," he said. "Luis calls you Tía Alison, but you are not, I believe, his aunt. Not Doña Veronica's sister?"

"Of course not. Did Luis say I was?"

"Not exactly. But he calls you Tía Alison, and when I questioned him, he evaded answering. Naturally, I hear all sorts of rumors from my people."

"Luis has chosen me to be his aunt because he's a lonely child," I said. "He feels the loss of his mother very deeply. So he pretends I'm his aunt and tries not to lie to you."

"I thought as much. I shall not ask him again."

Padre Olivera's hands lay folded in the dusty lap of his cassock. Callused hands of a workman, a manual laborer, not those of a fine pianist. The hem of his robe was frayed and there were traces of mud on it, revealing his walk from the village to the house. Here was a priest who followed his vow of poverty with dedication and, I felt, was a man I could trust completely.

"I wonder if you can tell me some things I need to know, Padre," I said. "I want to learn about Luis' mother. Not because of curiosity, but if I'm to help him, I must understand."

"Doña Veronica?" For a moment he was silent, thoughtful. "I did not really know her for a long time. She was not a Catholic, although the old Conde Luis urged her to join the Church."

"But she didn't?"

He shook his head, frowning, troubled. "In the last few weeks before she left here, she came to me several times for instruction in the faith. But not because of Conde Luis."

"Then why?"

"I am not repeating gossip when I tell you she was desperately unhappy. Everyone knew this."

For a moment we sat quietly. The sunset light was fading, and long shadows crept slowly across the floor. Then Padre Olivera spoke absently, as though thinking aloud.

"Doña Veronica had not yet realized it, but there was a deeply religious impulse in her nature in spite of her background."

"And what was her background?"

"Pitiable. She had no family, she spent her childhood in foster homes and institutions. I think the High Valley offered her the first security she had ever known." He bowed his head, sighing. "And that security proved fragile in the end. I saw her the last time on the afternoon before the fiesta of San Miguel. She drove to the village that day in the small car the Conde Luis had given her. I shall never forget it. The car was white and always gleaming, she wore a white dress, and brought a great sheaf of red roses for the church. Just before she left me, she asked a surprising question."

"What was it, Padre?" I leaned forward, listening attentively.

"She said, 'Father, is it possible to tell a terrible lie by keeping silent?' I did not know what she meant, of course, but I explained that some of the worst lies in history have been told without one word being said. And she answered that she had always known this, she had not really needed to ask. Then she drove away, toward the *casa grande.*"

Lifting his head, Padre Olivera gazed at me, the brown eyes filled with sadness. "I should have taken more time with her, questioned her. But she seemed happy, not troubled. And I was so busy that day. The fiesta of San Miguel is the greatest celebration of the year here. Everyone in the valley is at the church or in the plaza most of the night. It was one of the few times when she could leave the valley with no one seeing her."

I straightened in my chair, astonished. "Are you saying that no one actually saw her go? Not one single person?"

"No one."

"But, Padre, she might never have left at all!" I protested. "There could have been an accident."

He shook his head. "No. Her car was gone, and some clothing. Not much clothing, but she left a note for Don Carlos saying she would take nothing that belonged to him. A few days later she sent another note to the Conde Luis. It was mailed in Mexico City."

"Wasn't there a search? An investigation? Surely the police were told."

"The Conde's attorney arranged a private investigation. I believe his son, Enrique, actually handled it. A wife running away is hardly a matter for the police."

"This is hard for me to accept," I told him, rising, moving restlessly across the room. "How could she leave a child she loved? And afterward she would have sent Luis a Christmas present from somewhere, or at least remembered his birthdays."

"It is difficult to understand, and I never expected such a thing. The Scriptures tell us that the human heart is utterly deceitful, so we should not be surprised by wickedness. Yet I am always taken unawares. "

Ethel Evans scurried into the room, exclaiming, "So here you are! Leonora is asking for you, Miss Mallory. The guests are in the patio. Good evening, Father Olivera."

Outside, the beauty of the night was breath-taking. Even the blazing flares and lanterns did not diminish the brilliance of huge stars shining in the clear air of the plateau. It was a night heady with jasmine and gardenias. On the *ramada* porch of the office a group of guitarists strummed softly, and for the first time I heard the haunting, sad-sweet voice of a shepherd's harp.

We were the last to arrive. Our visitors were talking animatedly with Don Carlos, and Luis stood beside his grandmother's chair, wide-eyed at the sight of guests in the house and a bit awed at attending a fiesta for grownups.

"Good evening, Padre, Señorita Mallory," said Jaime

Romano. He alone had not dressed for the party, but wore his everyday riding clothes with a bandanna knotted at his throat. I knew his failure to change was deliberate, some gesture of protest or defiance. "Señorita," he said, "may I present my friend Eric Vanderlyn?"

A flaxen-haired Dutchman in his mid-twenties clasped my hand lightly in a pressureless Mexican handshake. "How do you do? You are the young lady who performs miracles for the Señora Romano?"

I colored slightly at the enthusiasm of his praise. "No, Leonora is performing the miracles. I only try to keep her from breaking her bones in the process."

"That is not what I am told."

Jaime Romano said, "I must speak with Padre Olivera about a matter. Talk with Eric, señorita. You have much in common."

"How is that?"

"He is the most stubborn man I know."

For a moment that remark put an end to conversation with Eric Vanderlyn. We stood in silence while Nacho, gliding among the guests, served me a tall lime-flavored drink. "You're working on the new dam?" I asked.

"Yes. You must come to see the construction one day. I like the work, but we miss feminine company. There is only the cook, who weighs almost as much as Dr. Hardy there." The grin on his broad, freckled face was warm and engaging.

"Have you been in the High Valley long?"

To my surprise he answered, "Most of twenty-six years. I was born here."

"But Leonora said you were Dutch."

"My parents were. My father was an engineer and mineralogist. Doña Leonora brought him here. Together they discovered the Hidden Treasure."

"The hidden treasure?"

He chuckled. "Not Moctezuma's buried gold. The Hidden Treasure is the name of a mine. I should have said they rediscovered it, for it's one of the oldest in the valley. Silver came out of it for centuries. When there was no more silver, they abandoned it. Doña Leonora thought mercury might be there, overlooked. My father proved she was right. It was a great mine. The last for the High Valley."

"No more mines? Can you be sure?"

"There are one hundred and fifty-seven mine shafts here. Probably we stand over a tunnel at this moment—although most are farther away. Every possibility has been exhausted." Eric Vanderlyn gestured toward the group where Don Carlos, drink in hand, seemed to be telling a joke. "Carlos still has hopes, or at least he used to. A few years ago he read all my father's old books and started prospecting."

"I can't picture Don Carlos as a prospector."

"Neither could he after a few months. He still dreams of finding silver, I think. Jaime knows the future is in cattle and crops once we have irrigation. That's his dream. He'll make it come true, too, if he doesn't kill himself and all of us with work in the meantime."

"He's a determined man," I said.

"Determined?" Eric whistled softly. "When Jaime wants something, it's like the devil was driving him. He told you I was the most stubborn man he knew. Well, that means he doesn't know himself."

I glanced at Jaime Romano, who was listening intently as Padre Olivera explained something about repairing the church roof. I saw the steely set of his jaw, the disturbing eyes as hard as blue flint, and said, half to myself, "Yes, he'd stop at nothing."

"That's right," agreed Eric cheerfully, not reading my thoughts. "Better not stand in his way!"

"Tía Alison! Señor Vanderlyn!" Luis called us. "Come here. Come see what my grandmother is doing."

We went to Leonora, who sat with a handful of small stones, little larger than pebbles, in her lap. "Good evening, Alison. Is that Eric?"

"Yes, señora."

"I'm delighted we lured you down from that dam for one evening at least, Eric."

"Grandmother knows the names of all these stones I gathered," exclaimed Luis. "Don't you?"

"Well, some of them. Tell me if I'm right, Eric." Picking one up, she rubbed it gently with her fingers. "Obsidian?"

"Correct."

"This one must be cantera."

"Right again."

"I can tell by the softness. It's green cantera, isn't it?"

Eric looked puzzled. "Now how could you know that?"

She laughed. "A guess. Most of the cantera in the valley is green, although there's some pink and gray. I played the odds." Leonora, not concealing her pride, added, "It's just as Alison's been telling me. You can see a lot with your fingers once you learn how to look."

"I'm going to learn all the names, too," said Luis. "In English!"

"Good for you," Eric told him, ruffling his hair. "I'll give you a present to help you. A small magnifying glass so you can see the fine veins in the rocks."

"Oh, thank you, Don Eric!"

Carlos Romano, debonair and laughing, joined us. "I heard you talking of rocks. No more of that! Tonight we celebrate." He shouted to the musicians, "*El járabe!* Come, Señorita Alison, I will teach you one of our dances."

His arm around my waist, he swept me toward the porch. The music burst forth, loud and rhythmic, a rollicking folk tune, and I felt myself whirled this way and that, while Carlos stamped his boots to the beat of a drum, snapping his fingers like castanets. He spoke to me, but I was too confused to hear or understand. Then I began to relax, to enjoy the swirl of my skirt, the tap of my heels. Carlos moved with the grace and strength of a tiger, his body flowing and rippling with the music—a toreador, balanced and poised.

When the music ended with a flourish, the guests applauded, and Carlos said, "Now another!" But Señora Vargas, her black dress with its great flounces emphasizing her stoutness, pushed her way between us. "Mine ees dance next!" she cried, clapping her hands.

I stepped aside as the musicians began a slower tune, and saw Jaime Romano, standing apart from the others, glaring at me. Turning away, I watched Don Carlos and the señora, who seemed to shed years and pounds as she responded to the rhythm. Her face glowed with life and youth, inspired, I thought, by the handsome gallantry of her partner.

Then a hand gripped my arm, and I found Jaime Romano beside me. "We will dance," he said, not an invitation, not even a request. This was a flat command.

Before I could answer, we were dancing. The music slowed again, the demanding beat of another drum had been added, and we moved a little apart, hands clasped. His eyes were fixed on mine, the dark face unsmiling. A feeling like panic caused my blood to pound. We were not dancing together, somehow he was stalking me, and seemed compelled to do even this against his will. I was hardly aware of the stumbling awkwardness of my movements, knowing only that I was fighting against something like hypnosis, a fascination that blotted out all else, that both held and threatened me.

The music changed, a different figure of the dance, and he drew me close to him. My cheek brushed the coarsely woven wool shirt, and suddenly I wanted the music not to stop. The light but strong touch of Jaime's arm around my waist felt warm and protective. I could lean against it, sure of its security, and not fall but always be held safe.

Then, in confusion, I realized he had stopped dancing, was standing still, and at that same instant his arms dropped to his sides, letting me go. He strode away without a word or a backward glance, moving swiftly to the patio gate and vanishing into the darkness beyond.

Don Carlos and the señora, still dancing, brushed against

me. I looked around, now burning with hurt and humiliation, but no one paid attention. Luis was occupied with Eric Vanderlyn and his grandmother; the Americans, deep in conversation with the Vargas couple and Padre Olivera, had not noticed. Only Miss Evans, seated a few yards away, was aware of what had happened. She smiled sweetly and sipped her sherry.

Nearly an hour passed before we were called to dinner, and only then did Jaime Romano, his face taut and drawn, reappear. In the dining room a hundred candles gleamed on the drops of crystal chandeliers and sparkled on antique silver. Don Carlos, the senior male Romano, sat at the head of the long refectory table. I found myself with Eric Vanderlyn on my left, and since there was an unequal number of men and women, Alice Hardy on my right.

Eric proved an easy dinner companion and soon we were on a first-name basis, but Alice Hardy was difficult, almost as silent as Jaime Romano, who ate practically nothing and spoke not a word. I avoided his gaze, angry not only at him but with myself for having allowed that moment of defenseless, foolish softness. How could I have imagined for a second that he had danced with me because he wanted to? More humiliating, how could I have been such a fool as to have permitted myself that moment of unexpected affection and happiness! He had taught me a hard lesson, and one I would not soon forget.

Yet despite myself, I glanced once in his direction, hoping against my will that our eyes would meet, that he would silently ask forgiveness, offer an unspoken apology. Head slightly bowed, he stared at the tablecloth, his features set in an unmoving mask that could not quite hide the turmoil inside him. Grief was there, I knew. Grief, confusion, and as he reached for his wineglass, the gesture revealed a strange helplessness. What had happened to him while we were dancing? Suddenly I felt that he had not meant to be rude, not

141

meant to hurt me. If only he would tell me! I would understand, I would.

Stop this, I told myself sharply. Stop this dreaming! Jaime Romano meant nothing to me. I looked away, but still could not force his image from my mind, no matter how hard I tried to concentrate on what Eric Vanderlyn was saying.

"You see, I'll go back to the National University in the late fall. I'm in the graduate school of engineering there."

Alice Hardy interrupted. "I've just realized what's been bothering me."

"Bothering you, Miss Hardy?"

"I knew something was wrong. Have you counted the guests? We're thirteen at dinner. Not a lucky number!"

"Should I take my plate to the kitchen?" Eric asked. His joke drew an icy stare from Miss Hardy, but he went blithely on. "Maybe we could count Luis as only a half. Would that make it right?"

Enrique Vargas, across the table, said, "Miss Hardy is a profound student of—what is the English word?"

"The occult." Dr. Hardy, looking pained, supplied the word.

"The occult? Superstitions?"

"Not at all." Miss Hardy spoke severely, as to a rude child. "My studies involve matters beyond conventional science. One does not understand all things in the universe through scientific knowledge. Special sensitivity is needed, too. As a priest, you agree, don't you, Padre Olivera?"

"If you mean that the Mind of God is infinite beyond all science, yes," he answered carefully.

Dr. Hardy, his voice jovial but his bushy brows frowning, said, "The talent of the cook who made the sauce for this duck is also infinite beyond all praise. May I have some more, please?"

His sister refused to be diverted from her subject. "I have a keen sense of atmospheres. This house, for instance, is filled with odd currents."

"Drafty place. Always has been," remarked Leonora dryly.

Across the table Dr. Hardy now gave full attention to dissecting his duck with *mole* sauce.

"One can't dismiss the spirit world out of hand," Alice Hardy continued, a glow coming into her eyes. "There are too many unexplained cases, too much evidence."

Luis turned to Leonora. "What is the lady talking about, Grandmother?" The English words were beyond him.

Leonora, knowing the Hardys spoke no Spanish, replied in that language, "She's talking a lot of nonsense. In a moment she'll go on about ghosts, I expect."

"Ghosts!" exclaimed Luis, delighted. This was an English word he knew. "We have ghosts," he informed Miss Hardy.

"Luis!" Don Carlos' voice was sharp. "You must not speak imaginings as facts!"

"In the Hidden Treasure," Luis murmured, dropping his eyes.

"Luis is talking about an abandoned mine that the villagers claim is haunted," Eric told Alice Hardy. "At one time it was infamous for cave-ins and avalanches. Many men died there, so a legend has sprung up about the ghosts of buried miners."

"Ridiculous, of course," Don Carlos added. "But we encourage the belief that it is haunted."

"Encourage it? What the devil for?" boomed Dr. Hardy.

"The mine is dangerous. The legend keeps people from entering."

"Bricking it up might do better," grumbled the doctor.

"It would take thousands upon thousands of bricks to close all the mines in the valley," said Eric. "Wouldn't it, Jaime?"

No answer. Only a curt nod. Eric continued. "Besides, most of the mines are in deserted places. The mountain Indians would knock down the bricks and carry them off in no time. It happens to fences, it happens to gates. I've wondered

143

if that might have caused that last big cave-in at the Hidden Treasure—Indians pulling down the shoring posts for fire-wood."

"You had a cave-in recently?" Dr. Hardy seized a chance to direct the conversation. "When?"

"Not recently," said Leonora. "More than two and a half years ago."

"At the time we thought it was an earthquake shock," said Padre Olivera. "Midnight Mass had just ended, and the people were going to the plaza to watch fireworks. I heard something like an explosion. For a moment I thought the fireworks maker's house had blown up. That happened once before."

"I remember the ground shaking under my feet," said Enrique Vargas.

"You were here when it happened, Señor Vargas?" I asked.

"Yes, señorita. I had come to enjoy the San Miguel fiesta."

"The night of the fiesta?" I exclaimed without thinking. "Then that was the night when . . . " I caught myself just in time, just before saying "When Veronica disappeared."

Carlos looked at me sharply. Jaime stirred in his chair. Thankfully, Eric Vanderlyn finished the remark for me. "Exactly! A night when no one would have been watching. The perfect night for the mountain people to come foraging. That's why I wondered if any of them might have been trapped in the mine."

"I said a Mass there when I learned about it the next day." Padre Olivera spoke quietly. "But I think no one was killed in the avalanche, because no relatives came to me about it. The mountain people are mostly pagan. They worship the four winds combined with a little Christianity. But when a member of a family dies, suddenly they are good Catholics for a day or two."

"The legend of the mine being haunted may have a strong basis," said Alice Hardy. "Primitive people who live close to the earth and nature often know things our science hasn't yet comprehended."

"Very likely," Leonora remarked. "The mountain people live close to the earth, all right. They're usually covered with it! Now shall we go to the *sala* for coffee and brandy?"

The shroudlike dust covers had been removed from the furniture in the enormous living room more than a week ago. It had been cleaned and aired thoroughly, yet I felt that all the mops in the world could not wash away its inherent gloom. If Miss Hardy sensed "odd currents" in the house, surely they would abound in this drafty hall with its carved mahogany paneling and rustling draperies. The candlelight—for this wing still had no electricity—was not gay as it had been in the dining room. Here its flicker seemed not to illuminate but to conceal faces and expressions, and to cast peculiar, conflicting shadows.

Dinner had been very late. Luis, too tired to protest, was sent to bed, and the elderly Señora Vargas, pleading fatigue from dancing, excused herself.

Don Carlos remained buoyant and zestful, eager for the party to continue. I did not know what news the attorney had brought him, but it had acted as a tonic. Dismissing all the servants except Nacho, who served coffee, he poured the brandy and Mexican Kahlúa himself, offering it with elaborate compliments to the women, causing young Señora Vargas to titter and blush.

I sat on a small couch, and Enrique Vargas joined me, moving much too close. An odor of rose oil assailed my nostrils from the overscented brilliantine on his hair. "I enjoy much talking English with the North American women," he confided. "They are so adventurous, filled with life, no?"

"I'm sure you find many who are in Puerto Vallarta," I said coolly, edging against the arm of the couch. "Is that why your chauffeur is armed? To protect you against them?"

"A man in my profession is bound to have enemies. And life is cheap in this country."

"I am afraid that is true," said Padre Olivera, who, seeing my situation, joined us. "How much does a *pistolero* cost these days, Enrique?"

The attorney chuckled. "Are you thinking of hiring a gunman, Padre? I can get you one from Guadalajara or Mexico City at a bargain rate. Five thousand pesos for an amateur. Ten thousand for a real professional like my driver."

"What's this?" asked Dr. Hardy, settling his bulk into an antique chair, which creaked an unheeded warning. "You mean you can have a man shot for around eight hundred dollars?"

"Oh, yes. Plus my commission, naturally." Enrique Vargas winked at me.

"This is a rather tasteless joke," I said.

"No joke, I am afraid." Padre Olivera's tone was serious. "I myself know of one such man and I have heard of many others."

"Then you will not need my help, Padre," said the attorney. "I have lost a customer!"

Giving him a withering look, Padre Olivera continued. "It is a painful burden to me that this man was born in our village, assisted at Mass here. And I failed to reach him, God forgive me. I take comfort that he was unusual. Our people here are gentle, good folk. In the great cities this is not always true."

Enrique Vargas let his arm rest on the back of the couch, so that it just touched my shoulders and neck. I rose quickly. "Excuse me. I'm curious about what Don Carlos is saying."

He was on the opposite side of the room, talking with Alice Hardy. "I find your interest in the occult fascinating, Señorita Hardy. It is delightful to meet a person who is informed in subjects about which I know nothing." His eyes flickered toward me, a quick, wry glance to include me in his ironic joke.

"I think it's fascinating, too," Ethel Evans chimed in. "I once had my fortune told and almost everything the gypsy said came true. I love fortunetelling!"

Across the room Dr. Hardy quoted ponderously, "'If ye can look into the seeds of time and say which grain will grow and which will fail, speak then to me'"

Smiling, I picked up the cue and said in a witchlike voice, "'All hail, Macbeth! Hail to thee, Thane of Glamis.'"

"The young lady knows her Shakespeare!" Dr. Hardy exclaimed, hauling himself to his feet. "You've been an actress, of course. I wondered when I first saw you."

"Not an actress," I told him, laughing. "I was much less glorified. Just a prompter. My mother did the acting."

"Classical roles?"

"For the most part. I used to give her cues when she was learning lines. I memorized so many plays that later I sailed through college literature courses hardly opening a book, as long as the subject was drama."

"What did your mother play besides Shakespeare?"

"Well, she was the star of a not very successful Ibsen festival. Hedda in *Hedda Gabler*, and Nora in *A Doll's House.*"

"Really? I was Helmer in that play years ago. Little theatre."

"Do you still remember the part?"

"Yes, with a good prompter!" He laughed loudly.

"Forgive me, Doctor," said Don Carlos, "I wish to return to the matter of foretelling the future. Your sister impresses me very much."

Dr. Hardy sank back into his chair, sighing, defeated again.

Leonora said, "I prefer to have my troubles come as surprises. Years ago we used to experiment with a ouija board. Nothing much happened. It was like a parlor game."

"Do you still have the board?" asked Miss Hardy. "I'd be happy to demonstrate its proper use."

"Really, Alice," protested Dr. Hardy. "No one is interested."

A chorus of voices drowned him out. Ethel Evans, who knew where the board was stored, hurried to fetch it.

"You referred to it as a parlor game, Doña Leonora," said Padre Olivera. "And that is my own view. Yet experiments with such boards have had unexpected consequences. Did you know that Francisco I. Madero, the liberator of modern Mexico, believed in it?"

"I think I've heard that," said Leonora.

"Yes. The planchette told him he would become the president of this country. Since that was possible only through revolution, he led a revolt. A case of man making prediction come true."

"Or the reverse," said Miss Hardy with quiet but compelling authority.

A few minutes later the ouija board was placed on a small marble table and two chairs were drawn up beside it. I had seen such boards on novelty counters but had never really examined one before. The letters of the alphabet were painted in a semicircle, and on one side of the board was the word "yes" while "no" was at the opposite. A small wooden triangle, the size and shape of an antique flatiron, stood on tiny ball bearings so it could glide easily over the surface of the board.

"Too much light for concentration," said Miss Hardy.

"Blow out some candles, Nacho," commanded Don Carlos.

I had forgotten Nacho was still in the room, he could efface himself so completely, so blend with the atmosphere as to be almost invisible.

"Dark enough," Miss Hardy announced when more than half the candles had been extinguished and the room had become a murky cavern, its somber shadows relieved only by tiny pools of wavering yellow light.

"Rest your fingers lightly on the triangle," Miss Hardy

explained to Don Carlos and Ethel Evans, who were the first to try. "Minds blank and receptive. Never move the triangle consciously, but when it wishes to move by itself, make no resistance."

To the others in the room she said, "Concentrate hard on a particular subject. What shall the subject be?"

For a moment no one could think of anything, then Dr. Hardy said, "William Shakespeare."

"Very well," agreed Miss Hardy. "All of you except the two at the board, think of a play or character by Shakespeare. Try to convey your thought to the minds of Miss Evans and Señor Romano."

I tried unsuccessfully to think about Hamlet. What had begun as a game now seemed serious, even eerie. Perhaps it was the tall, gaunt figure of Alice Hardy hovering near the table, pen and paper in hand to record letters the triangular pointer might single out. Her face was taut and ashen, while the thin lips moved unconsciously as she struggled to impose her mind on the hands of the others.

Jaime Romano sat in shadow, a brooding figure, black hair falling over the high forehead. A man withdrawn and apart, nursing some private rage or grief that burned within him.

Outside a wind had risen and I imagined it tumbling the great clouds, blotting out the moon, leaving the High Valley submerged in darkness. And my thoughts, refusing to stay in place, retraced the events of the day, returning always to an inevitable "Why?" Why had Jaime Romano told me I could not legally work here when I knew Don Carlos was sending my passport number to the governmental authorities? What deception was behind it? Why had there been an avalanche and cave-in of a mine on the same night Veronica disappeared, and on a night when Enrique Vargas happened to be in the High Valley? Now the attorney slumped on the couch, thin features in profile against the candlelight, and the shadows gave his face the lean, emaciated harshness of an El Greco portrait. According to the Padre, he had been the one who searched for Veronica. Not searched far, I thought.

"Carlos, I think you are cheating." Eric's voice brought me back to the room. "Why would the ouija call King Richard the Third *El Rey Ricardo Tercero* in Spanish?"

Carlos Romano laughed. "No, not cheating. It was my subconscious moving the pointer. I was thinking of that play, the letters seemed to spell themselves. Uncanny, no?"

"Come on, Alison," said Leonora. "It's getting late, so this will be the last attempt. Alison and I. I'm sure Alison won't cheat, and since I can't see the letters, it should be a good test."

"Really, I don't think I . . . " My objection was brushed aside by the others, and I found myself sitting opposite Leonora at the board.

"Fingertips touching lightly," said Miss Hardy. "Minds open and receptive." She lifted her arms, bare, starkly white against her dark dress, and ran long fingers through her hair, letting the iron-gray cascade over pale shoulders. "Now we will think of someone who has crossed to the Other Side."

"The dead?" whispered Miss Evans, frightened.

"Come to us now, come now. We await you . . . " Alice Hardy swayed, the white arms inscribing a great circle, her eyes were glassy and enormous. "Come now from the night . . . Come now . . . "

For a moment my hands seemed frozen on the wooden triangle. I heard the wind whisper in the vines, a shutter creaking, and the harsh, regular breathing of Alice Hardy. Then my hands moved of their own will. Or did Leonora guide the pointer? I stared at her in confusion, but she sat impassive, relaxed.

"X-L-Q-J-G—" The meaningless automatic writing ceased. Our hands rested a moment, then, frighteningly, moved again. "V-E-N-C-E—"

The others had moved close to us. Jaime Romano stared at me in a strange, probing way. Carlos leaned forward, intent, and behind him, lurking in the shadows, stood Nacho, his pockmarked features no longer impassive, but alert and wary.

"Try again. Try, try." Miss Hardy's hands fluttered near me like two white birds as she whispered insistently, "One who has gone, one passed to the Other Side, one who will speak from the grave . . . Try . . . Try . . . "

The wind had died and there was no sound but her demanding whisper and the hypnotic ticking of the ancient clock. A feeling of numbness pervaded me, my eyelids felt heavy as a slow, funereal procession moved through my mind, images, pictures beclouded in mist. A white car, a girl in a white dress, and a sheaf of roses. There were roses near me now, a vase on the mantle, and their fragrance grew overpowering, narcotic. A tortured face painted on a handkerchief. Luis' voice, faint, disembodied, repeating softly, "My mother is dead . . . My mother is dead . . . My mother . . . "

Again my hands moved, some force, not my own, commanding them.

"V-E-R-O-N-I—"

Shuddering, I jerked my fingers from the pointer. The trancelike hypnosis had vanished. The hushed room, the shadow figures in it were terrifyingly sharp and clear. I felt the eyes of the Romano brothers bore into me, Nacho's hands were clenched, and when I saw Padre Olivera cross himself, two words flashed through my mind: *He knows.*

"V-E-R-O-N-I—" Miss Hardy repeated hollowly. "Who has passed to the Other Side called—"

"Verona," I exclaimed, my voice unsteady and too loud. "I was still thinking of Shakespeare. *Two Gentlemen of Verona.* I must have given the board involuntary help. Just as Don Carlos did." My laughter rang shrill and false.

Jaime Romano suddenly turned away, but Carlos continued studying me silently, his features fixed and expressionless.

"Just proves again what I've always known," said Dr.

Hardy. "It's all in the mind, conscious or subconscious. You write what you're thinking of."

"But we were thinking of the dead," Alice Hardy answered slowly. She seemed drained of energy, bloodless.

"No, not the dead!" I protested, again too loudly. "Verona. Only the 'A' became an 'I'. You see, I hadn't thought of that play in so long—I mean, except just now." I was floundering, making matters worse, but seemed unable to stop myself.

Nacho was suddenly beside me, holding a tray. "Brandy, señorita? " The mask had returned to his face. No, not quite. The thick lips had a grimmer set and his eyes were narrow and hooded.

"Yes, thank you." Then, even as I reached for the goblet, I drew back, unwilling to touch anything he offered. "No. No, I believe not."

"I'm exhausted," Leonora remarked abruptly, rising from her chair. "Alison, would you walk up to my room with me? I'm too tired to count steps and poke about with a cane tonight."

"I must be going, too," said Padre Olivera. The old priest made his farewells quickly. When he came to me, he took my hand and a long look passed between us, an expression of silent understanding and, I thought, a warning.

Then I knew it was a warning, for although he spoke to Enrique Vargas, the words were meant for me—a reminder. "I regret I have no use for those hired gunmen you say are so cheap and available. They must look for other employers. You see, I have more powerful weapons."

"Rosary beads against bullets, Padre?" he asked. I detested the smirk on Enrique Vargas' face, the insolent manner.

"No. God against Satan," replied the priest quietly. He turned back to me. *"Vaya con Dios, señorita."*

"Thank you, Padre. Good night."

As I led Leonora up the dim stairway, her hand resting lightly on my arm, she seemed remote and puzzled.

"Twelve steps to the landing," I said automatically.

"Yes, I remember. And the fifth step is a little higher than the others. The eighth step creaks." She shook her head impatiently. "I would have enjoyed the party tonight except for that last business with the ouija board. Miss Hardy is too peculiar for my liking. What does she look like?"

I described Alice Hardy briefly, and Leonora nodded. "That's how I pictured her. So strange just before we stopped! I felt something like a cold draft. Was a window open?"

"No. I don't think so." At another landing I said, "Careful. Don't bump into St. Michael." The tall statue of the warrior saint guarded the last flight of steps leading to Leonora's room. I had never liked the sharpness of the iron sword he brandished.

At the top of the stairs she said, "I'm exhausted but not sleepy. Too much excitement. In a way, my first party," she added with a smile.

"I'm not sleepy either." In fact, I was much too wrought up to think of sleep yet. Only now were the full implications of what had happened dawning on me. Weeks ago an inner voice had warned me not to betray too much curiosity about Veronica. Instinctively I had known I must reveal no suspicions, no unusual interest. Yet tonight, against my own will and not realizing it, I had announced to everyone in the household that Veronica was not only in my thoughts, but that I believed her dead. Someone who had, as Miss Hardy expressed it, passed to the Other Side.

Would anyone believe I had been thinking of a Shakespearean comedy? No. My whole manner had given me away. I had read my own detection in Nacho's eyes, in the keen stare of Don Carlos, in Jaime Romano's abrupt turning away. And Leonora? What did she think?

"The wind's come up again," she said. "Listen to that gale! Would you fasten the shutters, Alison? I don't want to ring for a servant at this hour."

"Of course." When I opened the east window, the night air struck my face, ruffling my hair and stirring the curtains.

Leaning out, I unfastened a shutter hook, then suddenly my body stiffened as Leonora, standing behind me, touched my shoulder.

"The coolness is beautiful," she said softly. "Let the wind come in. Tell me about the night."

"The clouds are moving west. There's moonlight now." I was suddenly conscious of the weight of her hand on my shoulder. "It's a deserted world outside. The lawn and the road are silver."

"Does it make you dizzy looking down?"

"Not really." But the tower at that instant seemed higher than before, the roof of the veranda a sheer, endless drop below. Drawing back a little, I managed to reach the hook that held the shutter open against the outer wall.

"I always loved the view from this room," she said. "But I never liked being too close to the windows. I've always been afraid of heights. Nothing else really makes me nervous." Her thoughts seemed far away, as if she were debating, mulling something difficult in her mind.

"That's enough cool wind for one night. You'll catch cold," I told her.

She moved toward her chair then, touching the desk and the table as directional points, and sat, leaning back, sighing wearily.

Just as I was pulling the last shutter closed, I caught sight of a dark shape among the eucalyptus trees. "Leonora!" I exclaimed. "There's something in the drive. It's hard to see, but I'd almost swear it's the Excelentísima's carriage!"

"No doubt it is," she replied, unsurprised.

"At this hour?"

"Yes. In fact, this is the most likely hour."

Faintly I heard the neigh of a horse, the carriage moved slightly, and then I was sure. I slid the shutter bolts.

"Should I go down and see what she wants?"

"For heaven's sake, no! Sit down, Alison. She's come to

annoy Carlos or maybe she's had word about our party tonight and wants to question Nacho."

"But she told me she never sets foot in this house."

"Ha!" said Leonora contemptuously. "The servants have seen her a dozen times. Her grandsons live here. She has every right to come at any hour she chooses. Ana Luisa won't call in daylight, of course. She's afraid of meeting me. Says the very sight of me damages her heart, or maybe it's her liver. Something internal and important."

Despite Leonora's easy dismissal of the matter, the idea of the Excelentísima's nocturnal prowling alarmed me. I pictured her, black-shrouded in her mantilla, moving noiselessly through the halls, silently ascending the stairs, pausing at doorways to listen to the breathing of sleepers in their beds.

"Was she always such a . . . a . . . "

"Monster?" Leonora finished my thought. "Yes. Always. The first year I was in the valley she killed two men."

"Murdered them?" I exclaimed.

"No. It was self-defense. Some bandits came from the mountains that spring. Two of them tried to enter the Villa Plata. When they went through the door they found her standing on the stairs with a brace of dueling pistols. She shot both of them dead. I can't blame her for that, I'd have tried to do the same thing if I'd been that good a shot. But she was so proud of herself! I think she hoped they'd come to give her the chance."

We talked for nearly half an hour, Leonora telling me of the old days when the valley was often a violent and even bloodstained land. But fascinating though her stories were, my mind kept returning to the séance, the helplessness of my hands spelling out a dead woman's name, and mixed with this came the returning picture of the Excelentísima standing in the unlighted living room, crossing the veranda, watching outside the windows of the Octagon like a specter, insubstantial in the cloudy moonlight.

"Alison, stop thinking about her," said Leonora, reading my mind. "She may not be here at all. She could have sent the boy with a message."

"Of course. Now I should go. You're tired."

"Good night, Alison. Sleep well."

After closing her door, I hesitated a moment, reluctant to descend the dim stairs even though I knew them so well by now. I hoped I might hear the noise of departing carriage wheels, a horse on the cobblestone drive—but no such sound came. Foolishness, I told myself. What could Ana Luisa do to me? She was not wandering about with Spanish dueling pistols tonight. A hateful but harmless old woman savoring the conspiratorial thrill of a midnight visit. Nothing more. Yet everything tonight made me uneasy. I had not even understood my own feelings when I stood at the open window and Leonora's hand touched my shoulder. Momentarily—I hated to admit it—I had been almost afraid.

Suspicion was a contagious thing, a creature that grew and thrived by feeding on itself. Leonora Romano was my friend, a woman I trusted and admired. And yet . . .

It was the poisoned atmosphere of the house—a place where a smile masked hatred, where people blandly said "She went away" when they knew better. When they *had* to know.

I started downward, moving carefully on the steep stairs, thankful for the small bulb burning faintly on the landing. Then, just as I thought this, the light was extinguished, the stairwell lay in blackness.

Still I felt no real alarm. Temporary blackouts were not unusual in the electrified parts of the house. A generator often failed or a fuse burned out. From working with Leonora, I knew the stairs very well, just as she did. Thin moonlight shone through the high window of the landing, and I continued on, not afraid of falling.

Nine more steps to the turn, then the longest flight, sixteen steps more. Wind whistled around the gables and a sudden icy gust swept upward as though someone had just opened a door or a window. I moved cautiously across the landing, passing the dark open door of the linen closet. Next to it the life-sized statue of St. Michael towered on a pedestal, looming grotesquely human in the dimness, with his heavy sword held high to strike.

I took the next step down, my hand resting lightly on the banister.

I will never be sure of what happened next. I know there was the loud, sharp slam of a door just behind me, and as I jerked toward the sound I realized the statue was moving, leaning forward. With a cry I spun away from the descending sword, the great toppling figure, and plunged headlong down the stairs. I heard a crash of metal and plaster, my head struck something hard, then struck again, and at last blackness.

"And when you sigh, it will not be for me . . . "
                                    —Spanish poem

NINE

"A twisted ankle, some bruises, and a nasty bump that causes your headache," said Dr. Hardy the following afternoon. "No concussion. Considering how steep those stairs are, I'd say you were a lucky young woman indeed!"

"Lucky that you were here when it happened," I told him. Dr. Hardy, bearlike and gruff the night before, had turned out to be astonishingly gentle and kind. I was grateful he had barred all other visitors, even Luis, who had sent a gift of two colorful stones he had found and a note almost in English.

"We leave for Puerto Vallarta in a few minutes," Dr. Hardy said. "All you need now is rest. And stay off that ankle as much as possible. One last thing," he added, smiling. "Don't go groping in the dark and upset another statue that's bigger than you are. Very bad for your health. Especially on dangerous stairways."

"I won't," I said. So that was what had been decided. Somehow, fumbling, I had tipped the St. Michael over and then had fallen. I vaguely remembered regaining consciousness hours before and telling someone—the doctor?—about the statue moving. Now I felt too exhausted to contradict him.

"Everyone in the house is asking about you." He closed the black bag, then lifted the bedside carafe to make sure I had water at hand. "I've explained you've had a shock, that you shouldn't be bothered or disturbed until tomorrow."

"Thank you for everything, Doctor."

After he had gone, I lay against the pillows, eyes closed but unable to sleep, wishing the dull throbbing in my head and ankle would miraculously vanish. I knew I had not touched the statue, not been within a yard of it. The door of the linen room had slammed violently. I remembered clearly. The wind perhaps? The banging door could have caused the St. Michael to topple. Unlucky timing, all of it. That was the only sensible explanation, I supposed.

Leonora, the doctor told me, was the heroine of the accident. Hearing the crash and my scream, she tried to ring for the servants, and when no one answered, she at last realized that the electricity must not be working, so no bells rang in the kitchen or servants quarters. She had then descended the stairs with her cane, making her way over the fragmented statue, to find me unconscious on the second landing. When she finally reached the main hallway, her shouts aroused the servants.

The sedatives the doctor had given me were strong, for now I slipped from wakefulness into deep sleep, a slumber troubled by dreams. I was once again at the candlelit table, the guests of last night surrounding me. Miss Hardy's intense whisper "Try, try!" grew louder, resounding in my ears, deafening me. A tall window swung open and the gale made the draperies stream into the room. A pale girl, wraithlike, entered silently and, smiling, whispered, "Good evening, Alison."

Only Padre Olivera and I were aware of her presence. The priest said, "Veronica, my child, how good to see you!" But I could hardly catch his words, for now everyone was pressing in upon me, shouting, "Try, try!" My hands were paralyzed, but Veronica moved quickly to my side, and placing her weightless fingers upon mine, caused the board to spell her name not once but over and over again. Powerless, I could not stop the writing. Suddenly Jaime Romano dashed the board to the floor. Nacho's strong brown hands reached toward my throat, Eric Vanderlyn's face, a mask of rage, loomed before me, while Ethel Evans' voice, rising to a scream, cried, "She knows!" Veronica was no longer beside me, but I heard her calling as I plunged through space, "Alison, help me!"

"My lady, wake up! Please wake up!" Ramona was gently shaking my shoulder.

"What is it?" My eyes opened, and I was safely in my bed in the Octagon.

"I was on the veranda," she said. "I heard you. A very bad dream, Señorita Alison."

"Thank you for waking me." I still trembled.

"Shall I bring you tea?"

"Please, Ramona." Starched petticoats rustling, she hurried from the room.

For some minutes the reality of the nightmare would not leave me, I could not shake off the feeling that Veronica's spectral presence had actually guided my hands last night. Even as I told myself that my own mind, not another's, had chosen the letters, a faint voice inside me whispered, "Who knows?"

The best remedies proved to be the tea and the sunset. Violating Dr. Hardy's instructions, I had Ramona help me hobble to a chair on the veranda, and I sat quietly watching the western sky blaze to flaming color while the mountains darkened and purpled. Village bells chimed rosary, seeming to summon flocks of blackbirds returning to home trees for the night.

"Señorita Mallory."

I turned to see Carlos Romano approaching.

"Ramona told me you were sitting up. I hope I do not disturb you, but I wanted to see if you were better."

"Much better, thank you." The warmth, the friendly concern of his tone surprised me.

"You worry me very much," he said. "I am not at all satisfied."

"Really, Don Carlos, I'll be quite all right in a few days, Dr. Hardy said."

"*El doctor Hardy, pues!*" He gestured impatiently. "What do we know of this man? Nothing—except that he has a demented sister. No X-rays, no proper tests!"

"I'm sure there's nothing seriously wrong."

"Tomorrow you must go to Mexico City," he said. "To the hospital, where an examination can be made."

"Mexico City? I couldn't possibly go."

"The expense will be my responsibility."

I smiled. "You're very generous. But it would be quite unnecessary, and far too much trouble."

"No trouble," he answered. "In the morning I will take you in my plane. That is settled."

I had learned to recognize that Romano note of finality. In Puerto Vallarta it had left me speechless and overwhelmed. Now I had learned to stand against it.

"Thank you, but I can't do that."

"You are a very difficult girl, Alison," he said, addressing me by my first name so casually that he might have been calling me Alison for years. "You have not learned to accept things offered you. It is no inconvenience to me. I go to the capital on business in any case."

I had no intention of making such a trip, but my reasons were instinctive, impossible to explain. "I hate to admit this," I said, trying to sound sheepish, "but I'm terrified of flying. Even a huge jet airliner frightens me, and I'd panic at just the thought of a trip in a small plane. Cowardly, but I can't help it." Before he could interrupt, I continued quickly. "And with my ankle as it is, the jeep is out of the question, too. May we wait a few days and see how I am? In fact, that's all we *can* do."

Checkmate, I thought, when he fell silent.

Don Carlos shrugged his broad shoulders. "Then I can only hope for your quick recovery, Alison." Drawing up a small rattan stool, he sat beside me, quietly thoughtful. His white linen shirt, full-sleeved and open at the neck, seemed tinged with pink in the sunset light. "I have a confession to make," he said. "My reasons for wanting you to go to the capital were not entirely medical. I hoped we might get to know each other better away from here. Mexico City is a fascinating place, Alison. We could enjoy it together."

The unexpected suggestion so surprised me that for a moment I had no answer. I stared at him, confused, taken aback. During the past month he had been courteous but distant; on the rare occasions when he had shown friendliness, his attitude had resembled the geniality of a host toward an unfamiliar guest. This sudden change was incredible, yet as I saw his new smile that conveyed not just warmth but tenderness, for a moment I imagined myself in the capital with Don Carlos, a brief, glittering illusion. He was handsome, charming when he chose to be. And the idea was preposterous. Easy to see why so many women had been dazzled and fascinated by this man! Now, when he rested his hand on mine, I realized the strength of the appeal that Veronica—and who knew how many others?—must have felt. Yet I hardly knew him, had little reason to trust him, and as I tried to return his smile, wondered if I even liked Don Carlos.

"You know I can't leave here now," I said.

"I know no such thing. The work you have done has been amazing, but there are other teachers." Rising, he stood over me, leaning against my chair. "Listen to me, Alison. I have friends who own a small, beautiful house in Mexico City. They are spending a year in Spain, and you could live in this house. No, do not misunderstand! I am suggesting nothing that can offend you. In the capital I have many influential acquaintances. Finding work in your profession has no problems. I would visit you often, and I think we would become . . . friends."

"This is very kind and flattering," I said, looking away, not wanting to meet his eyes. "But my responsibility now is to Leonora. Besides, I'm not sure I'd want a position in Mexico City."

"You would find it an exciting place. Friends of mine could quickly obtain legal working papers for you. Alison, we must both think of our futures."

The mention of legal working papers suddenly shattered the spell he was trying to create. Now I could face him, sure of myself. "I can't even think of such a change until Leonora no longer needs me," I told him. "And since you've mentioned legal papers, why did you want to see my passport and visa? Your brother implied it was completely unnecessary."

He gave me a sharp, questioning look. Then, moving away, sat on the balustrade. "Jaime spoke the truth, for once. Let me explain. For a short time I thought, quite mistakenly, that you had been less than honest with me in Puerto Vallarta."

"Less than honest?"

"Yes. You had given me the impression that you did not speak Spanish, then I discovered you do."

"I'm sorry. I meant to say that my Spanish is far from perfect. And frankly, I was searching for an excuse not to take this position. I do apologize! I didn't mean to mislead you."

"It does not matter now, and would have had no importance at the time except for Veronica."

Her name had at last been spoken. And he had said it easily, casually.

"You have heard the gossip about my former wife, of course."

His saying "former" startled. me, and he must have read this in my expression, for he said, "Former at last. That was the good news Enrique Vargas brought me. I am now free of her. You have heard of quick Mexican divorces, but it is not so easy when there is a large estate and a child involved. Worse, when one has a wife who refuses to make her whereabouts known. I had to be very careful, to make sure she could not later return and have some claim. That is finished now."

Rising, he slowly paced the veranda, his voice laden with bitterness and open anger. "I do not regret Veronica's leaving me. Our marriage was a mistake." When he turned quickly toward me, the glow of a lamp Ramona had lighted in the Octagon revealed the proud, chiseled features, and the matador's scar was livid. "What was I to think when I returned from Puerto Vallarta and found the servants buzzing with news that Veronica's sister had arrived? Even Nacho, who is highly intelligent, believed it true, especially since Jaime played his unfortunate joke and put you in the Octagon. I even thought Jaime might somehow have engineered our meeting in Puerto Vallarta. Since I knew Veronica had no sister, no living relatives at all, I discounted that part of the story. Yet I had to find out if you were really what you appeared to be. Once I was certain of your identity, I made inquiries. Now I know it was foolish and unnecessary. I hope you understand and forgive me."

"You had every reason to make sure," I said. "Now I've been sitting up too long. I have to go inside."

"Let me help you."

"No, I can manage."

"Do not take alarm!" He chuckled. "I will not carry you over my shoulder. Only take my arm, then you can hop on one foot like a flamingo."

Inside, before saying good night, he asked, "You are certain you will not change your mind about Mexico City? I mean only about going to a hospital for examination. I am an excellent pilot, you would not be frightened."

"Thank you. I'm quite sure. Good night."

"*Hasta mañana, Alison.*"

Although too exhausted to understand all the implications of what Don Carlos had said, my mind kept worrying at his words, turning them over, trying to make sense of the conversation. It would be flattering to think that I had so caught Don Carlos's interest that he was ready to upset all arrangements here and whisk me away to Mexico City, where he could pursue a courtship, make the first steps toward love. But if he had some deep feeling for me—a feeling well-disguised until now—why not let it begin in the High Valley? I thought of the woman in the airport, Karen. Haughty, flamboyant, with diamond-hard glitter. She was born and bred not for the High Valley but for the night life of Paris and Rome, born to move among celebrities, accepting their admiration as the natural right of a goddess to receive tribute. Everything I was not, nothing that I wanted to be. And Carlos loved her. I had seen it plain in his face at the moment she had left him.

To myself I said, half aloud, "I don't believe him."

I awoke late the next morning with a tender, swollen bruise on my head, but the throbbing ache had vanished. A tight bandage around my ankle enabled me to hobble about the room.

At noon Luis bounded into the Octagon, demanding to know if I had received his present of the two small rocks and proudly displaying a small magnifying glass Eric had given him.

"Look, *Tía,* it makes everything so big! I can see little lines and flecks in the rocks that I didn't know were there." Because I was not in bed, he seemed to feel that my recovery was complete. "Will we ride tomorrow?"

"Not tomorrow. But very soon."

Three mornings later we were able to resume our morning routine. Luis quickly forgot my accident, and Leonora, except for expressing sympathy and worrying about my recovery, chose not to talk about it. But I could not banish that night from my memory. I would always remember that terrifying moment when the statue had seemed to move by itself.

The morning after our first ride, I escorted Leonora to her room and left her there, still not strong enough for the work of teaching. I looked down the stairs where I had fallen, seeming to see them for the first time, and caught my breath. Dr. Hardy's remark that I had been lucky now struck me as a ridiculous understatement.

My head had struck the wall, not the sharp corners of the marble newel post and not the marble base of the railing. The second landing, which had broken my fall, was little more than a narrow triangle where the steps curved—how easy to have continued plunging downward, another long flight, more sharp edges of stone. I had always known the stairs were dangerous and had worried about Leonora until I learned that she always kept her hand firmly on the banister. Now the word dangerous seemed too mild. They were a trap—one that could be fatal.

The shattered St. Michael had been removed, but the smooth-topped pedestal remained. I stared at it now, a cold feeling growing inside me. Only a whole series of the most unlikely circumstances could have caused the statue's falling at that particular moment. Ten seconds earlier I would have been above it, quite safe. Ten seconds later I would have been far enough below to have been surprised and startled, but nothing more.

The explanation everyone seemed to accept was that a servant, for reasons impossible to imagine, had moved it to the very edge of the pedestal while cleaning. It had stood there, almost teetering, until the slam of the linen-room door sent it crashing forward.

This was possible, just possible enough for those who wished to believe it. But I had noticed nothing odd about its placement when I warned Leonora not to stumble against it only half an hour before my fall.

My hand was unsteady on the knob when I opened the linen-room door and looked inside. Now it served only as storage for Leonora's linens, but was far larger than a closet, designed originally so a servant could sleep here near the tower. The sashes and shutters of the single window were now closed and bolted. Why had they been left open that night during a storm? They must have been open for the wind to have swept through, slamming the heavy door.

No moonlight, I thought suddenly. I remembered the dim glow of the glass dome at the top of the stairs, but the linen room had been shrouded in utter blackness. But if the window had been open, some illumination, however faint, would have shown through it.

Turning away quickly, I started down the stairs. For the moment my mind rebelled at thinking more about this. Impossible, I told myself; there must be some other explanation. Yet why had the lights failed at the exact moment when I left Leonora? Even I, totally ignorant of electricity, knew how easy it was to cause a fuse to burn out. One summer in Old Bridge an impish child actor plunged the playhouse into darkness simply by dropping a penny in the socket of a lamp. A child could do it—and so could an old woman, I thought, unable to force from my imagination a picture of the Excelentísima waiting unseen in the linen room, the statue already edged forward, her jeweled hands touching the back of the door ready to thrust against it with all her strength.

But why, except in some fit of insanity, would she do such a thing? Why would anyone?

I knew no answer. But passing through the living room on my way to the Octagon, I hesitated beside the small table where the séance had been held. I again remembered jerking my hands away from the board, staring at the faces around me. And I had felt at that moment a current, a force in the room—an undefinable sensing of some rage that was almost palpable.

As the days passed, everything around me seemed to belie my fear and suspicion. Afternoons were warmer now, the fields a golden brown as they awaited the coming of the great rains. Leonora, steadily gaining confidence, no longer pushed herself at such a desperate pace. Both Romano brothers were busy, Jaime pressing to complete the new dam before the rainy season, Carlos organizing an exhibition and sale of horses which was to take place in the summer.

I had little contact with either of them, and if Carlos Romano had developed a special interest in me, it appeared to have faded quickly. He continued calling me Alison and often there was a special brightness in his smile, a suggestion that we shared some secret. Once he invited me to go with him on a quick trip to the capital.

"Thank you. But no plane rides," I answered, and the matter was dropped.

One lazy afternoon during the siesta hours I sat in the patio writing a note to Margaret to say I would soon spend a weekend with her in Puerto Vallarta. Although not accustomed to afternoon naps, I was lulled by the warmth, the drone of bees in the honeysuckle, and the quiet ripple of the fountain. I let my heavy eyelids close and drowsed a moment.

A small, fierce voice shouted, "Hands up!"

I found myself staring at a dwarf bandit, Luis with a bandanna masking his face as he pointed a pistol at me.

"Don't shoot!" I exclaimed, starting to lift my hands. Then I realized that the pistol was not a toy, but a real gun. "Luis, don't point that at me," I said sharply.

The barrel was lowered, and he pulled the neckerchief from his face, grinning. "Did I scare you?"

"Yes. You're *really* scaring me still. Where did you get that pistol?"

"It's one of Uncle Jaime's." He looked uncomfortable.

"Listen to me! You must never play with such a thing. It might be loaded."

"Of course it's loaded. My uncle says nothing is as useless as an unloaded gun. But there's a tiny catch that keeps it from going off."

"Luis, give me that pistol!"

He handed it over, and I took it carefully, distrustfully. "Now we'll return this to your uncle."

"Do we have to? He's at the dam. Couldn't we just put it back in the case?"

The pleading tone was too much to resist. "All right. We'll put it back and not say anything, on one condition. You must promise never to take this or any other gun without permission."

"I promise." He said it so reluctantly that I knew his word was important to him and he would keep it.

The door of Jaime Romano's quarters stood open to catch any afternoon breeze. Entering the large whitewashed room I felt like an intruder, but told myself it was in a good cause. Unlike Don Carlos' ornate apartment, this room had no mementos, no personal objects at all except an old, much enlarged photograph of Leonora, young, happy, and dramatically mounted on a tall palomino stallion. Behind her stretched the panorama of the High Valley.

There was a single bed, an Indian rug on the floor beside it, an antique desk with a plain chair, an old-fashioned wardrobe closet, and the gun case protected by a steel screen. A Spartan sleeping room, almost as plain as the office next door. Yet compared to the cluttered, overfurnished *casa grande,* this place was attractive by its very plainness.

"Luis, the gun case is padlocked," I said, wondering if he had told me the whole truth.

Blushing, he opened the wardrobe and took out a tooled-leather boot. When he turned it upside down, a small key fell out.

"You've searched this place rather thoroughly, young man. We are now adding another promise to your first one. No more burglary. Quite clear?"

"Yes, Tía Alison."

I returned the pistol to the empty pegs in the case, then set the boot containing the key beside its mate in the wardrobe. I was not really listening to Luis when he said, "This desk is just like the one in the library. I wonder if this has a secret compartment, too."

I turned just as he pulled out a concealed drawer high in the upper paneling. Luckily, he had to reach above his head to remove it, and I took the shallow wooden box from him before he could examine its contents.

"Luis, you promised!"

"I only wanted to see if it was like the other desk," he protested, and I found myself relenting. A secret compartment was really much too great a temptation for a little boy.

"Luis! Luis!" Ethel Evans' voice called from outside. Then I heard her speak to an unseen servant. "Have you seen Luis?"

"*Cómo, señora? No hablo inglés.*"

"Luis!" she repeated loudly. "His grandmother wants to speak with him. Can't you understand anything?"

"*Cómo, señora?*"

I felt panic at the thought of discovery. Nothing could please Miss Evans more than catching us here apparently ransacking Jaime Romano's private papers. I tried to slip the drawer back in place, but it was too close-fitting—there was some trick to inserting it.

"Luis!" Ethel Evans called again.

"Go on, Luis," I told him, hoping to gain a little time. He slipped out the door, then shouted that he was coming.

Setting the drawer on the desk, I studied the open panel, soon discovering the catch that had to be pressed for release and replacement. Then, as I started to pick up the drawer, I stopped, my eyes widening. I stared down at a photograph of Veronica, a picture I'd not seen before. Veronica seated by the patio fountain, smiling dreamily, a white mantilla falling over her bare shoulders. In none of the other photos had she looked so beautiful.

A picture a lover would keep.

There were two other objects in the drawer. I saw a silver buckle with the monogram *J.R.*, and remembered the receipt in Veronica's letter file. Next to it lay a sheet of notepaper with Veronica's distinctive writing. At first I did not identify the familiar poem, because she had translated it into Spanish and it no longer rhymed. Then it came to me. *How do I love thee? let me count the ways . . .*

I read no more. I knew this sonnet by heart, and with trembling hands I replaced the compartment, then, almost stumbling, I hurried from the room into the patio. I paused near the fountain, for a moment not realizing that this was where Veronica had sat smiling. Had Jaime Romano held the camera that day? Had he inspired that look of soft loveliness in her face?

The sunlight seemed cold as I recalled the last lines of the sonnet she had so carefully translated for him. They rang in my memory like the call of the night bird, like the voice I had heard in my dream: *And if God wills, I shall but love thee better after death.*

Later that afternoon I took the mare, Rosanante, and followed a trail cutting across the valley toward the northern slopes and mountains. I needed to be away from the house, needed time to sort my thoughts and feelings.

Above all, I felt guilty. I had been a trespasser, an intruder who had violated Jaime Romano's deepest privacy, and, in a way, Veronica's. I could only console myself in the knowledge that a serious and even deadly game was being played in the High Valley, and usual rules did not apply.

Orchards and fields behind us now, Rosanante plodded along a scratched-out trail, slowly climbing, passing between great boulders, cactus, and stands of scrub timber. She circled the open pit of a mine shaft fenced off with a makeshift barrier of thorns and mesquite branches. Then passed another and yet another abandoned mine. These were not like wells, but were caverns cut into the mountain. One such, no doubt rich in its day, displayed a peeling sign above its dark entrance: *Aladdin's Cave.* There were other signs, warped and faded, announcements that this was private land and its guards were armed. Nothing remained to guard now. Only yawning stone mouths and the crumbled foundations of vanished buildings, forlorn and desolate.

The trail turned sharply, skirting the edge of a gigantic upthrust of granite and lava. Rosanante quickened her pace, and a moment later I realized that she had smelled water and grass. We were in a beautiful tiny valley where willow fronds brushed the white water of a bubbling stream. The trail now joined a rutted road, and I followed it several hundred yards to a place where the valley ended in a narrow cul-de-sac. There the stream flowed from a mine entrance, splashing over rocks to find its bed below. Two signs dangled above the tunnel's mouth, one said *The Hidden Treasure* and the other, newly painted, warned of danger: DO NOT ENTER! Nearby a shrine had been cut into the rock, where a statue of Our Lady of Guadalupe presided graciously, offerings of dried flowers at her feet.

This, then, was the haunted place frequented by ghosts of miners entombed alive a generation ago. And the place where an avalanche had cascaded down the night Veronica "went away."

The phantoms, if they emerged from the dark tunnel, would find themselves in the most beautiful spot in the High Valley. A place of ferns, emerald moss, and drooping bell-like flowers I had never seen before. Wild orchids blazed in an oak whose branches shaded a clump of calla lilies.

Dismounting, I let Rosanante drink from the stream and happily graze in the rich grass. "Perfect," I said aloud. Did young lovers from the village find their way to this spot? Did Mario and Ramona? And then I thought, Did Veronica?

Veronica and Jaime. I could not accustom myself to the idea that they had been lovers, yet I knew it was true. I remembered the Excelentísima's malicious words: "She had been meeting some man." I had dismissed this as the gossip of a spiteful old woman, but now I realized it had been true.

Veronica and Jaime. What could be more natural? Her marriage had failed, and during the last year or more she lived apart from her husband in the Octagon. Don Carlos spent little time in the High Valley, but Jaime was always here, and he, like Veronica, was alone. Now alone again. I remembered his shadow falling on the curtain as he paced the floor of his room. Haunted by grief? Or was it something more sinister than that—remorse? Perhaps Veronica had decided to end their affair. No one could know what Jaime Romano might do if enraged by injured pride and rejected love.

If Jaime Romano loved, he would love fiercely. "The devil drives him," Eric Vanderlyn had said.

The light was fading, almost sunset. Mounting Rosanante, I started back, this time taking not the trail but the road which apparently went toward the village and the *casa grande*.

Had Carlos Romano suspected or known about Veronica and his half brother? No, I decided. The old Conde had been alive then, and Carlos would have caused a public scandal that would drive an unwanted wife and the unwanted Jaime from the valley forever. No, he had not known, yet he might have suspected.

The road wound past the towering bulk of the Excelentísima's Villa Plata, its turrets rising massively against the sunset, dark, prisonlike, not one candle relieving the gloom of barred windows and deserted balconies. When near the Villa Plata it was easy for me to believe in any act of cruelty, any violence however terrible. The old woman was a merciless pagan empress. In another place, another era, she would have enjoyed decreeing torture and death with a flick of her eyelid. Ana Luisa was the grand matriarch of the Romanos, her pitiless blood flowed in their veins. I urged the horse to move faster, suddenly not wanting to be on the road alone after nightfall.

At the stable, I left Rosanante with the Tarascan Indian boy and went to the Octagon, where a note awaited me, a note I read with a rising sense of desperation. It said only: "I want to see you, Señorita Alison. Jaime R."

So my prying had been discovered already. Had Luis confessed and given me away? Now there was nothing to do but face the truth and tell exactly what had happened.

Across the patio the office was dark, but lights burned in the bedroom and through the open window I saw Jaime Romano seated at the antique desk working with a large ledger. "Come in, señorita," he said, hardly glancing up. "A moment. I am almost finished."

The two or three minutes of waiting seemed the longest of my life. There was no other chair in the room, and I stood awkwardly near the door, hoping not to look like the guilty schoolgirl I felt myself to be.

Closing the ledger, he rose. "Sit down." He pushed the chair toward me and seated himself on the desk, his shoulder just touching the carved panel covering the hidden drawer. "Señorita, how busy are you these days?" he asked.

I suspected a trap. He would soon say something about Satan finding mischief for idle hands. "Not overworked," I said carefully. "Your mother doesn't demand as much of herself as she did for a while, and Luis has other studies besides English."

"Good. I want to ask some favors of you. Favors for which you will be paid extra, naturally."

My sigh of relief was almost audible. Apparently I had not been found out. "I'll be happy to do anything possible."

"We are now arranging for the summer sale of horses. I send letters and invitations to possible buyers. Short letters, but each different from the others and many are in English. After I have written them, will you correct any mistakes in English?"

"Mistakes in English?" I was surprised. "Your English is excellent. So is Don Carlos'. I'm happy to help but I don't think you need me."

"I speak well enough and my accent is passable. But English spelling is insanity, and these letters must be perfect.

As for Carlos," he went on grimly, "he is the best-educated illiterate in the world. Even I do better, without the advantage of Swiss schools and American colleges."

"Didn't you study in the United States?"

He frowned. "An expensive foreign education is not customary for second sons in my family, although my mother wished me to go abroad. No, I attended the National University."

"Oh. Mining and agriculture?"

He gave me an amused glance. "That is how I appear to you? A farmer and a miner?"

"No. I only suppose that because of the High Valley."

"My education, Señorita Alison, was chiefly in classical literature and history. But I have other useful accomplishments such as fencing. Also, I was taught the skills of most card games and target shooting with a pistol. Do not let my whipcord trousers and my boots—which are muddy tonight— deceive you. I am a true eighteenth-century Spanish gentleman in disguise." Then he added dryly, "Perhaps my nephew will do better."

For a moment I glimpsed life in the High Valley during his childhood. Even Leonora had not been strong enough to break the chains of traditions that had continued for centuries.

"Finishing business matters," he said briskly, "I hope you will also help with arrangements for our guests at the sale of the horses. Most will not stay overnight, but a dozen will. My mother used to manage these things and now thinks she can do it again this year. She will need much help."

"That's part of my work."

"Good. You may find the horse sale interesting. There are exhibitions of riding and roping. It is very colorful."

The interview seemed to be over, but as I started to rise, he asked, "Where did you go today? I saw Rosanante was not in her stall."

"To the Hidden Treasure mine. Not inside it, of course."

"Then you saw the little valley?"

"Yes. I think heaven must look rather like that spot."

"I have not been there in a long time," he said thoughtfully. "The orchids must be in bloom now. Did you see swallows? This is the season when they come from South America."

"No swallows that I remember. But I heard a lark."

"Yes, there are larks there, and scarlet tanagers. All the High Valley is beautiful, but there it is the most—what is the English for *precioso?*"

"Precious is rather close."

"That is it. When I was a boy it was precious for mercury and some silver. Now it is precious for other things." The rugged face, whose contours might have been carved from the valley granite, softened for a moment. "The grass near the stream is matted and thick. With enough water, all the valley could be like that. Sometimes I look at the barren fields past the Villa Plata and I do not see thin grass fit only for goats. No, to me it is a garden! Green as far as my eye can travel. I will make that garden real one day."

He spoke more to himself than to me, and although he talked of a dream and his voice was far away, I felt the strength of steel behind the words. He loved this land with his whole being, yet it was not his, would never be his. The High Valley belonged to Luis alone. Surely Jaime Romano realized he was but a temporary steward! Was this part of what had embittered him, turned him into the silent, solitary man he had become?

Suddenly he ceased speaking, as though deliberately checking himself. "I have kept you too long. Thank you for the help I know you will give me."

"I'm happy to do it."

I had just reached the door when his voice halted me. "Señorita, another matter."

"Yes?"

"I recall that on the night you had your accident we danced together. "

"Rather briefly," I replied.

"May we agree that I suddenly became ill that night? What soldiers call the flare-up of an old wound?" His words and tone were edged with self-mockery, and only this morning I would have taken this odd apology as an attempt at an ironic joke. Now I knew better, and with effort I kept my eyes from moving to the hidden compartment in the desk.

"We'll agree on that," I said.

"Also, I promise you that the next time my health will be better. Good night . . . Alison."

Speaking my name seemed to be difficult for him, as though he had been forced to push through some self-imposed barrier, a man reluctant to allow the smallest crack to appear in the wall with which he surrounded himself.

Returning to the Octagon, I passed Luis' window. The young master of the High Valley sat cross-legged on the floor peering at a stone through his magnifying glass. Later I would go back to read to him a few minutes before saying good night.

At my desk I sealed and addressed my note to Margaret. In two weeks I would see her, and I found that I looked forward to her honest warmth, her candor that concealed nothing.

Standing up, I walked the length of the two rooms and back again, restless, troubled. Veronica and Jaime. The two names, newly coupled, would not leave my mind. *How do I love thee? Let me count the ways . . .* A beautiful gift to him, a poem made personal by translation into his language, a declaration of love without coquetry, open-handed as a little girl offering an apron filled with wild strawberries.

My thoughts wandered to the buckle and then to the receipt in her letter file for one silver buckle. Suddenly my pacing ceased, and I exclaimed aloud, "She *kept* things!"

Veronica had hoarded photos of the High Valley and its people. She even saved her notes as she struggled to improve her Spanish, and kept scores of pages of handwritten translations. But not one personal letter, not one contact with any friend outside the valley, not one souvenir of her life before she came here. No wedding picture, no cards, nothing whatever. All record of her earlier life had been destroyed or left behind in another place.

This was wrong, terribly wrong. Veronica's books, her pressed-flower collection, every memento of her revealed a sensitive and sentimental woman. Even if her early life had been unhappy, she would surely have preserved some record of it. Yet there was nothing. It was as though she had been born a grown woman with a husband and child at the moment she arrived in the High Valley.

I remembered the Excelentísima's words, but now they had a new meaning: "She was nobody. She came from nowhere."

> *"Even the Cross would steal*
> *if its arms were not fastened."*
> —Mexican saying

TEN

Two weeks later, as Margaret and I strolled toward the old plaza in Puerto Vallarta, the unanswered questions in the High Valley seemed a world away.

I had enjoyed three beautiful days—swimming in the clear, warm ocean, relaxing on the powdery beaches that framed the town. We talked little of my work or of the Romano family, both of us feeling that a vacation, especially a brief one, should be a complete change.

Now we were going to Margaret's rental house because the tenants, the Mexico City couple and their children, were leaving and Margaret was stopping by to refund a breakage deposit.

"When I checked the inventory, there wasn't so much as a glass broken," said Margaret. "Either those boys are born angels, or Epifania watches them day and night."

"Epifania?"

"Epifania Heiden, their mother."

"An unusual name, isn't it?" I asked.

"You seldom hear it. I think her nickname is Fani, but I don't know her that well."

Crossing the plaza, Margaret paused near the quaint bandstand. "Let's sit on a bench for a moment."

"Is the sun too hot for you?"

"No. I want to find out something." A moment later she gave me a twinkling smile. "Uh-huh! You have an admirer, Alison."

"An admirer?"

"Don't look! A man has been following us for blocks."

"Where is he?"

"Well, now he's sitting on a bench pretending to read a newspaper."

I glanced casually over my shoulder. Not far away a tall, middle-aged Mexican studied a folded copy of *Excelsior.* He was dressed in the sheer white sport shirt and light trousers which were almost a Puerto Vallarta uniform. A black sombrero with a red band and brass buckle was pulled so low on his forehead that it almost met the rims of mirrorlike sunglasses.

"I wouldn't usually pay attention to a thing like this," said Margaret. "But he's been remarkably persistent. I noticed him on the beach yesterday, and I'm almost sure he was loitering near the bookshop this morning, too. Well, let's move on and see what he does."

We continued to the far side of the square, where Margaret, pretending to check traffic, managed a quick look back. "Yes, he's passing the bandstand." She chuckled. "The amount of time he's devoting to you is what I'd call a sincere compliment, Alison."

"I can do without such compliments," I said uneasily.

Mexican men were notoriously persevering in such odd courtships, and Margaret was now telling me about a young friend of hers who had been followed for days and miles. "She got tired of it at last. She turned around, walked up to him, and said 'Stop this nonsense.' He nearly fell over his own boots trying to escape. It's usually just a game. If a man hasn't anything else to do, why not trail a pretty girl?" She glanced at me, then frowned. "Oh, for heaven's sake, Alison! Don't look so worried."

My smile was too bright. "I'm not. It's just that his glasses and that black sombrero make him look like a film gangster."

"I'm sure he isn't from Puerto Vallarta," she said. "Looks more like a city type. The town's grown, of course, but I still recognize most people who live here for any length of time."

We reached our destination, and Margaret rang the bell. Señor Black Sombrero now leaned against a shady wall near a corner.

The maid ushered us to the living room, where Epifania Heiden stood surrounded by suitcases and boxes. Her freckled, tow-headed boys were struggling to find space for fishing equipment and scuba gear.

"Thank you, Mrs. Webber," she said, accepting Margaret's check. "You have been the ideal landlady."

Her careful English had a charming lilt. An unusually attractive woman, I thought, whose fine bones and slender figure were still youthful.

"I hope you'll spend another winter here sometime," said Margaret.

"Possibly. I did not think I would ever say that. I knew Puerto Vallarta as a girl many years ago. I did not want to come back. But it seemed ideal for my husband and the boys." She shrugged helplessly.

"Yes," Margaret agreed. "Old-timers like to remember a sleepy fishing village and they want to keep that memory unchanged."

"I suppose so," said Epifania Heiden doubtfully. Her own reasons for not wanting to return here seemed to have nothing to do with nostalgia, but she did not explain.

Wishing them a safe journey to Mexico City, we left. Outside, there was no sign of Black Sombrero, but within a block he had picked up our trail again, always staying about fifty yards behind.

183

"True devotion," said Margaret.

I doubted it. What was the point in following me, if I remained unaware of it? He took pains not to be noticed, and although I knew nothing about this Mexican game of follow-the-señoritas, it appeared obvious that a man playing it would be sure the woman was aware of him.

We lost Black Sombrero when we took a taxi to Margaret's house, but his presence stayed in my mind, arousing doubts and suspicions I had suppressed and diminishing the pleasure of my last night at Margaret's.

When Primitivo arrived to pick me up the next morning, there was no sign of Black Sombrero lurking behind a jacaranda or hiding in the bougainvillaea. It was easy to tell myself that Margaret had been right, that he had been nothing more than an idle man playing a game that was harmless, if annoying.

Familiarity made the road less frightening, and part of the way I was able to concentrate on the newspapers Primitivo was delivering to the valley. The front pages of all three were splashed with bold headlines about the kidnapping of a rich industrialist on a highway not far from here. "A brutal act by radical terrorists," said one paper. Another noted that it was the second such abduction in recent months.

Primitivo pointed to the paper and, in excited tones, said something intelligible. He could not read, of course, but knew about the crime from some other source. Pointing again, he exclaimed, "Not far," and made a sweeping gesture indicating the mountain fastness around us, peak after peak stretching on for miles. "Hiding," he said, and I realized that this was another of his cheerful thoughts for the road. The terrorist kidnappers and their victim might well be concealed in this rocky, almost uninhabited wasteland. It seemed probable enough, and reading further, I found that one newspaper shared Primitivo's suspicion. The Mexican army and air force, it said, were scouring the mountain fastness.

A difficult search, I thought. A thousand kidnappers or bandits could vanish without a trace in these endless canyons.

Primitivo accelerated the jeep, gesturing again, but not to the mountains. Small dark clouds hung low in the northeastern sky. I understood the word "rain," and clung to the seat as the vehicle careened around bends and curves, wondering which was more perilous, our speed or being caught on this road in a thunder shower.

Minute by minute the clouds grew larger and more threatening, and as a wind rose they stampeded across the sky. We were almost to the valley's mine-tunnel entrance, when the deluge struck like a cannonade, torrents cascading from dark skies while the canyons reverberated with thunder and bolts of lightning zigzagged among the peaks. Then, like a swimmer surfacing, we were in the tunnel, leaving the downpour behind. This time there were no pedestrians to be picked up. We drove silently through the stone caverns, past yawning side passages. Passing one of these, I asked Primitivo, "Where does it lead?"

He understood my question, and with one finger traced a pattern of circles and twists in the air. "Far," he said. "Far, far!"

Rain again pelted the jeep as we emerged, but in the valley the downpour was not a blinding flood, although at the *casa grande,* the gargoyle rain spouts shot out streams of water like huge fountains. As the jeep halted, Luis darted from the door and down the steps, carrying a huge umbrella. "*Tía Alison!*" He must have been waiting in the hall, watching for me.

In the Octagon, he never left my side while I unpacked my bag, and he demanded every detail of my stay in Puerto Vallarta. "Look what I picked for you!" he exclaimed proudly. The bud vase was crammed with wild strawflowers from the fields.

"What a beautiful bouquet, Luis!"

"Tonight we are all going to have supper together in the dining room," he said.

"Are there visitors?"

He shook his head. "Grandmother said that at least once we must eat supper together like a civilized family. I do not quite understand."

Ramona came to welcome me, and to remind Luis that although the driving rain would keep him from lessons with Padre Olivera, he still had studying to do. He went to his room, muttering complaints about arithmetic.

"How sweet of him to have picked these flowers for me," I said, touching the small, graceful vase. "By the way, Ramona, when did you change the vase?"

"I changed nothing, my lady. It has always been in this room."

"No, the other one was silver. This looks very much like it, the same size and shape, but is made of . . . " I did not know the Spanish word for "pewter," and had to say, " . . . a different metal."

Ramona was bewildered. "This vase is silver, no?"

I realized that she did not know the difference between silver and polished pewter. Actually, the two vases were so alike that I would not have noticed the change had I not touched this one.

I asked, "Has another girl been cleaning the room?"

"No, my lady. And the vase has never been taken from here." Then she broke off, smiling. "Ah, how stupid I am! The Señorita Evans polished all the silver things. I had forgotten, it was weeks ago."

I vaguely remembered Miss Evans complaining about the way the servants cleaned silver. And yes, she had said she was going to polish everything herself.

"She returned this to the Octagon, my lady," said Ramona with a twinkle. "Perhaps the señorita is as ignorant as I am and does not know one metal from another."

"A good joke on her," I agreed.

Ramona's own honesty was so complete that the notion of a deliberate substitution did not cross her mind. The vase formerly in this room, I felt sure, was now incorporated into Miss Evans' décor of "lovely things," sitting on a what-not or a shelf with the thousand other objects with which she surrounded herself.

I did not care, the two objects, although different in value, were equally beautiful. Nevertheless, I remembered too well that Señora Castro, my predecessor here, had been accused of theft, and I was determined to set the record straight as soon as possible. I pictured Jaime Romano, an inventory list in hand, demanding, "Where is that silver vase, Señorita Mallory?"

At suppertime, when we gathered in the dining room "like a civilized family," it was still raining. Jaime, as drinks were served, stood near a tall window scowling blackly at the drizzle.

"Rain brings new life to the grazing lands and settles the dust," remarked Carlos, sardonically amused at his brother's displeasure.

Jaime turned from the window, slapping his thigh in frustration. "This early rain will delay work on the dam at least a week!" He muttered Spanish words I didn't understand.

"Watch your language, Jaime," said Leonora.

Eric Vanderlyn, who had come down from the construction site, adroitly changed the subject to a technical discussion of irrigation, and everyone was grateful although no one really listened.

We were called to the table then, but a change of locale did not make Leonora's "civilized" dinner any more successful. The Romano brothers reminded me of two lions crouched to spring. Luis, always awed by his father's presence, kept his eyes averted and ate almost nothing. Miss Evans rambled on about her own poor digestion.

Eric, trying valiantly to fill the conversational vacuum, asked, "What did you do in Puerto Vallarta?"

"Nothing, and it was glorious. Swimming, a little shopping. I bought some books."

"What are you reading?"

"I've just started a remarkable novel. *One Hundred Years of Solitude.*"

"A depressing title," murmured Miss Evans.

Jaime frowned at her. "One of the great modern novels in the Spanish language."

"I really love one character," I said. "José Arcadio. The man who invents things."

Eric smiled. "Yes, José Arcadio. You know, my father was so much like him it's uncanny."

"Did he construct machines with pendulums?" I asked.

"He certainly did," said Leonora. "Christian, Eric's father, was a superb engineer. There wasn't anything mechanical he couldn't repair and keep running. But some of those mad inventions!"

"Remember the day when the perpetual-motion machine escaped?" said Eric, laughing.

"It was on wheels, with all sorts of springs and pendulums," Leonora explained. "He worked on it upstairs in the rooms Carlos has now. One day it rolled through the door and straight down the stairs. You never heard so much screaming by servants!"

"That ended perpetual motion," Eric said. "Then he turned to lenses and optics, like José Arcadio in the book."

"Well, the telescopes didn't escape," Leonora added with a chuckle. "But it was a sad day when he took up solar energy."

"What happened?" I asked, pleased that the conversation now flowed smoothly.

"He rigged this device with mirrors and tubing and lenses. It looked rather like a telescope," Leonora told me. "It was supposed to concentrate the sun's rays. One day Christian left it near a sunny window and it burned a hole the size of a dinner plate in a carpet I'd just bought. Oh, I was furious! But Christian was delighted. He kept shouting 'It works! It works' and danced around the room."

"Where are the telescopes now, Grandmother?" Luis asked. "I'd like to look through them."

"Christian's telescopes? I really don't remember."

"I have them in a closet," said Don Carlos. "I was interested in learning a little about astronomy. They belong to Eric, of course."

"I appreciate your keeping them for me," Eric said. "Along with the remains of perpetual motion, the pendulum butter churn, and everything else."

"When you're older, Luis," said Don Carlos, "you may ask Señor Vanderlyn to let you use a telescope."

Luis murmured, "Thank you," but his face clouded at the forbidding, familiar phrase "when you are a little older."

Leonora rose from her chair. "I've ordered coffee and Kahlúa served in the sitting room. Shall we go there? No, Ethel, don't guide me. I have my cane and know the way, thank you. Carlos and Jaime, please don't excuse yourselves. I want to talk about the stock sale and which horses we'll show. We have to make plans."

Over coffee, Leonora kept all talk confined to business, and it was astonishing that the warring brothers could declare a truce when it came to matters affecting the ranch.

Miss Evans and I were to help with arrangements for housing the guests and to supervise the servants who would be feeding at least eighty people who would be here only during the day. I had already taken care of the letters Jaime asked me to check, and there had been almost no errors in English, which was as I expected.

After an hour Luis began to yawn and rub sleepy eyes, but Jaime said, "No, Luis. You must listen. This will be your work some day."

While the others discussed horses, cattle, and prices, Miss Evans and I sat a little apart, and now I had a chance to clear up the question of silver changing to pewter.

"By the way, Miss Evans," I said, keeping my voice low so I would not interrupt the Romanos' business session, "when you polished the silver, you returned a different vase to the Octagon."

For an instant her face blanched, turned ashen, but she concealed her alarm quickly. "Different? I'm sure not."

"The first one was silver, and the one I have now is polished pewter."

"I hate to contradict you, Miss Mallory," she answered stiffly. "But the Octagon vase was always pewter. I remember clearly."

"My mistake, then," I said. The point was established, I had no reason to argue.

But she seemed compelled to press the matter. "I recall how remarkable it was that the vase hadn't been scratched. Pewter is so soft, and these servants use scouring powder on it. Really, Miss Mallory, I'm quite positive!"

Leonora interrupted us. "What's this? What vase?"

"We were talking about a pewter vase I mistakenly thought was silver," I said.

"A large bud vase with a leaf design?" she asked.

"Yes."

"There are two such vases. I was so fond of the pewter one that my husband had a copy made in silver mined in the High Valley. Does that settle the mystery?"

"I think it does." I avoided looking at Ethel Evans, not wanting to see her mortification. She had done just what I suspected: switched vases to add the more expensive one to her already cluttered room.

"Bedtime for Luis and me," Leonora announced.

"For all of us," agreed Eric. "Tomorrow's an early working day, if the rain lets up at all."

"Coming, Luis?" I asked.

"I'll walk Grandmother to her room," he said.

I went to the Octagon. There were still no electric lights in the rooms and corridors leading to it, but I had solved the difficulty of making a long detour through lighted areas by always carrying a small pocket flashlight attached to my key ring. Its beam was tiny, but enough. My fall on the stairs had taught me to be prepared for darkness anywhere in the house.

After preparing for the night and changing into a warm robe and slippers, I stepped onto the veranda going toward Luis' room. Late though it was, I wanted to say good night to him and perhaps read aloud a page or two of *The Wind in The Willows,* our current bedtime book.

The rain had slackened, yet torrents still gushed from the eaves. Luis' window, the draperies open, cast a blurred light on the veranda floor and balustrade. But when I reached the window, I saw that his room was empty. Had he lingered to talk with Leonora? A picture of those steep, hazardous stairs flashed through my mind, then I dismissed it. There would not be another "accident" there. The next one would take place somewhere else, in some unexpected place at a moment when no one was prepared for it.

Then his door opened and he came into the room. When I tapped on the glass, he ran eagerly to the window and unlocked it.

"I was worried," I said. "Were you with your grandmother?"

"Only for a moment, *Tía.* Then I went to look for the telescope."

"The telescope? But your father said to wait."

"I wasn't going to touch it. Just look. I thought maybe it was in the hall closet outside my father's room. But it isn't."

"All right, Luis. But don't make a habit of prowling about the house after bedtime, young man."

He sat on the high bed, his legs dangling over the side.

"Are we going to read about Mr. Toad?" he asked.

"Just a little."

"I like the story. But I don't know some of the English words."

I drew up a chair and was opening the book when he said, quite casually, "The Señorita Evans is very angry. She was having an argument with somebody."

"How do you know that?"

"When I went past her door, I heard her voice. She was speaking fast English. *Tía,* what does the word 'geridov' mean?"

After several false starts, I realized he was saying "Get rid of."

"It means to make something or someone go away. In Spanish, *eliminar* or *tirar.*"

He nodded. "I thought maybe it was that. Maybe Señorita Evans was talking about a servant she does not like. She said, 'Geridov her.'" Luis frowned, trying to puzzle something out. "Does not the English word 'medals' mean *medallas?*"

"Yes."

"And I know a prize is a *premio.* Why would a servant have medals and prizes?" He sighed over the impossibility of English. "The señorita talked about these things—very loud and angry, but too fast for me."

"Medals and prizes?" I asked. "Who was she talking to?"

Luis shrugged. "I do not know. My father or my uncle. Maybe Señor Vanderlyn. No one else speaks English except my grandmother, and she was in her own room."

There were others, I thought. Nacho understood English even though he never spoke it to me. And the Excelentísima might be somewhere in the house even now.

"It does not matter how angry Señorita Evans is," Luis added firmly. "My grandmother would not permit her to make any of the servants go away. Neither would I."

Luis untied his shoelaces. "Please, *Tía,* read before it is too late."

I managed three pages, stopping twice when he asked the meaning of words. But my mind was not on Mr. Toad of Toad Hall. I thought of the silver vase, of how the blood had drained from Miss Evans' face when I mentioned it. And I knew that she had not been speaking of a servant when in the heat of anger she said to an unknown listener, *"Get rid of her. She meddles and pries!"*

"The land awakens with the rains.
Does your love awaken, too?
Or are you a desert with no flowers for me?"
—Song for serenades

ELEVEN

The one great storm, which lasted three days, transformed the
High Valley. The slopes, as by a miracle, were suddenly green,
cactus flowers, violet, blue, and magenta, burst into bloom,
and poppies turned the hillsides golden. Now I understood
why Jaime Romano at times spoke so desperately of water.

The approaching summer rains were often in Leonora's
thoughts, too. During our morning rides, which were much
longer now, she frequently asked, "Alison, are there clouds in
the northeast?"

I usually answered, "No." Or sometimes, "A few mare's
tails." Then she would sigh and grumble.

One day, looking at the beautiful land around me, I said,
"Are early rains so important?"

"Important?" She was astonished. "They mean life. For
the village people early rain is the difference between comfort
and poverty. The men work for the ranch, of course. But the
women have corn patches and gardens. A dry year spells
disaster. I've seen the people so desperate for rain that they

took the statue of the Virgin from the church and stood it in the hottest, driest field."

"Really? What did Padre Olivera say?"

She chuckled. "When he learned it was going to happen, he took a quick trip away. It's pagan, of course. In some villages they take all the statues out of the churches and beat them with sticks when there's a long drought."

I learned no more about Miss Evans and the unknown person she had spoken to, nor did she make any apparent attempt to force me from the High Valley. Yet I knew that if wishing could make a thing happen, I would have been sent packing long ago. As Leonora's accomplishments grew, so did Ethel Evans' resentment of me. Now Leonora tied her own shoes, filed her nails, did well at the table, and selected her clothing from the closets, confident that her outfit would match the accessories she chose. Ethel Evans was no longer essential, and I read bitterness in every look she gave me.

Yet I had little reason to think about her until one morning when we were not riding but having a lesson in Braille, which was proving difficult because Leonora had small interest in it. Her mind wandered, she seized any excuse to avoid work, and this particular morning the diversionary tactic was to talk about her jewelry.

"You haven't noticed my necklace."

"Who could miss it? I was going to compliment you on it later. I didn't want to get off the subject." The necklace, an elaborate piece designed to go with a ball gown, could hardly have been less appropriate for Leonora's dotted cotton dress.

Unclasping it—with no difficulty, I was pleased to see—she held it out for inspection. "Columbian emeralds. They were a wildly extravagant gift to me. And you know, I'm not very fond of jewelry. I haven't taken this out of its case for ages. Today it was a whim."

The necklace was made of finely wrought silver links with seven large stones. "Magnificent," I said.

"Magnificent?" Leonora smiled. "What a tactful way of saying 'ostentatious.'"

By now I had learned not to contradict her with flattery when she was absolutely right. "The stone in the center is beautiful, though," she added. "Hold it up to the light. It has real fire, and you almost never find that in an emerald."

"Yes, I see." But I didn't. The stone was attractive, yet the inner prisms had no light at all. Glass, I thought suddenly. Or paste. Imitations good enough to deceive most people at first glance, but unconvincing when one looked closely.

Leonora was talking of the occasion when the necklace had been given to her. I did not listen, for too many unpleasant memories assailed me. I recalled sweet old Mrs. Parker who studied at Bradford Center. The supposedly loyal maid who'd been with her for years substituted dime-store figurines for costly old Dresden, replaced a Viennese mirror with a cheap copy, and since Mrs. Parker had no close friends or relatives, would have continued stripping the expensive apartment had she not made the error of pawning a silver bell and putting a steel one in its place. Mrs. Parker's trained ears detected the difference at once, she appealed to the Center, and the police were called.

Then there was poor Mr. Henderson whose greedy niece had carried off family heirlooms. Vicious, and so easily done. Who would say to Leonora, "Aren't your emeralds fake?" No one would be that blunt and tactless, no one would risk giving offense, just as I could say nothing now. For I was not positive. To voice my suspicions would be tantamount to accusing someone—perhaps falsely.

"I've often thought I should sell it," she said. "There are certainly enough things to spend the money on. Is my keeping it foolish sentimentality, Alison?"

"Well, if you don't really like the necklace, and never wear it . . . " This was the way to find out, I thought. One glance by an appraiser would give the answer.

I looked at my watch. "Time's up. You avoided work very subtly today. But don't think I've given up. You'll be literate one of these days."

Confused and troubled, I left her. The emeralds had changed everything. Now the substitution of a pewter vase seemed no longer a harmless pride in objects that led Ethel Evans to furnish her room as a museum. What eventually became of all those objects she collected? The house was huge, so many closets and cabinets and shelves. Could the servants keep track of all the hundreds, even thousands, of things stored here? Nor would they know which things were valuable and which were not. Don Carlos and Jaime had no interest. There was only Leonora—and she was blind.

Any theft, however small, was serious enough. But a bud vase, even an expensive one, seemed nothing compared to emeralds that must be worth a small fortune. What could I do about it? Nothing but be alert, and for the time being, keep suspicions to myself.

I walked toward the village early that afternoon, Padre Olivera having invited me to lunch. I was only a few hundred yards from the house when Luis came running to overtake me, dressed in the absurd Fauntleroy attire the Excelentísima demanded.

"You're supposed to go to the Villa Plata today," I said. "Won't you be late?"

"It does not matter, *Tía*. She will be cross anyway." Luis seemed quite undisturbed by this. He pointed ahead, toward the carillon which rose majestically tall and slender. "Barn swallows have built nests at the very top of the bell tower. Have you been in the tower, *Tía*?"

"No."

"Then I will show it to you."

"We'll have to look quickly or we'll both be late," I warned him.

We entered through a door so low that I had to duck my head. Inside was a round room with stone walls and floors. Dust motes danced in beams of sunshine that shone through slitlike windows. The great shaft soared above us, empty except for thick beams supporting bells of all shapes and sizes. In one corner dangled more than a dozen heavy ropes.

"When you pull those," said Luis in awe, "iron hammers strike the bells. You can play a tune if you know which ones to pull."

"Do you know how?"

"No. Old Mateo, the bell ringer, says he will teach me next year. I will have to have plugs for my ears! Come, *Tía*." He started up the stairs circling the inside of the tower. They were dangerously steep and had no railings.

"Careful, Luis."

"It is all right."

Soon I was breathless. We reached more bells, different in design, suspended near arched windows. "These do not play songs," Luis explained. "They are *esquilas*. You ring them by turning them over and over." For a second his small hands rested on the wooden top of an *esquila*, longing to push it, a powerful temptation.

"Higher up we can see the nests." Luis scampered ahead, ignoring my warnings.

I followed slowly, glancing down once and promptly regretting it. The height made my head spin, and now I dreaded going back down.

We were almost at the platform where a huge bell dominated the tower. "It is called St. Michael and came from Spain," Luis shouted back to me. "Four hundred years old, my grandmother says."

I rounded a corner of the stairs and gasped. The stone steps ended abruptly where a platform must have crumbled and fallen long ago. Now there was only a narrow, rotted-looking plank spanning a gap to the balcony where Luis stood.

Another bell, not so large as St. Michael, but huge and heavy, hung above the break in the stairs where it could be rung from either side.

"That bell is rung only when there is danger. It means a brush fire has broken out or other terrible news. Everyone comes running when it rings."

"Luis, did you just walk across that plank?" My voice trembled a little.

"Yes, *Tía*. There is no other way to get to the nests. It is very strong. See?" Before I could stop him, he moved across it again, coming quickly toward me. The plank was nearly three yards long, and I held my breath as he passed the center, where with a faint creak it sagged under his weight. Then he was beside me. "It is safe. I have gone over it many times."

Well, this was the last time, I thought grimly. "Luis, the wood is very old and you're growing bigger and heavier all the time. One day it will break."

"I am careful."

"Being careful won't help. Don't ever walk across it again until we can have it changed. I mean it!"

Our descent seemed interminable, and every step of the way I kept thinking of Luis hurtling from the broken plank to the stone floor below. Before we parted, I made him promise solemnly not to visit the tower until it was made safe.

Made safe? As I walked on toward the village, I realized this was impossible. No railings, the precipitous steps uneven and winding. Exactly the place for an accident . . .

Too many accidents. The refrain kept haunting me as I passed smiling villagers on the road. A fire, a broken swing, a runaway horse, my fall the night of the fiesta. *Too many accidents.*

Yet everything around me seemed to contradict my own fears. The High Valley breathed tranquil beauty. Irises and primavera, newly blossoming, fringed the road and hidden birds with songs like those of bobolinks warbled in the oaks and lime trees. Nothing, it seemed, could slash or mar this landscape.

Then I became aware that the birds had suddenly fallen silent. A tiny shadow flashed past me, and looking up I saw one of the Excelentísima's hawks inscribe a circle in the sky, skimming the treetops. The steel-taloned predator always nearby, always waiting and watching . . .

With the coming of summer rains, spirits lifted, voices acquired new cheerfulness, and laughter filled the kitchen and the servants' quarters. Mornings remained clear and sunny, but in the late afternoon, almost daily, clouds spilled across the northeastern rim of the mountains to roll across the sky, watering and nourishing the land. Sometimes I awoke in the night to the sound of thunder and the patter of a shower on the veranda roof.

Even the horses sensed the promise of an abundant year. Old Rosanante turned coltish and Leonora kept a firm rein on Estrella.

"She's frisky these days," said Leonora, enjoying a challenge now that she felt secure.

We rode farther and farther afield, and Jaime Romano made no attempt to stop us, nor were we constantly trailed by Mario.

Leonora made only one further attempt at a family dinner, and this time she invited Padre Olivera, whose benevolent presence, she hoped, would have a calming effect.

I met him at the door that night, and he entered loaded down with rather crude earthen pots he had brought from the village. "For the Señorita Evans," he told me. "The potter had promised them to her, but is ill. Tonight I am his delivery boy."

"Miss Evans bought these?"

"Yes. She has become a good customer for them. I understand she sends them to friends as gifts."

Incredible, I thought. In this house we were surrounded

by exquisite pieces of folk art, Mexican crafts incomparably better than any village work, and she had never praised any of it. On the contrary, she was contemptuous of the earth-warm Mexican pitchers and plates I found lovely.

Luis was excused from the late meal that evening and sent to bed to recover from a summer cold. Dinner conversation moved along easily, until Leonora suddenly said, "Do you remember my Colombian emeralds? I've decided to sell them. Money from that necklace can be put to good use."

She spoke, I thought, to Jaime and Carlos, but Miss Evans instantly protested. "Oh, you couldn't part with anything so beautiful!"

"It would pay for finishing the new dam and more," said Jaime.

Miss Evans started to chatter about "sentimental reasons," when Carlos interrupted her, his voice cold. "The necklace was a gift to you from my father."

"That's why this decision has been difficult." she replied.

"Not difficult—ill-advised," he answered, shooting an accusing look at Jaime, whose face turned hard as stone. "The necklace belongs to all the family. One day Luis' wife will wear it, and later his son's wife."

"There's a limit to heirlooms," said Leonora calmly. "I have other things, too many perhaps. Luis' bride will not seem naked for lack of jewelry."

"Finish the dam and build more catchpools," Jaime told her, "and Luis can one day buy this unknown bride half a dozen emerald baubles, if he's that foolish."

Carlos' eyes flashed, color blazed in his cheeks. "You would use your father's gift in your attempt to make my son into a farmer?"

Both men were halfway out of their chairs, when Padre Olivera interrupted, a surprising note of command in his quiet voice. "May I propose a better gift for Luis' future wife? I suggest you give her an educated husband."

"What's that, Padre?" Leonora asked.

"Luis cannot continue studying with me much longer." He turned to Don Carlos. "It would not insult your father's memory if the money were set aside for Luis' education. In the fall he must go to a good school, nearby perhaps. Later he must go abroad, just as you yourself did, Carlos."

Leonora said wryly, "With less disturbing results, I trust."

To my astonishment, Carlos chuckled. "Luis is to follow my orders, not my example."

Jaime sat silently, arms folded across his chest as he leaned back in his chair. I saw a fleeting expression of calculation, then a suppressed smile. As executor of the estate, he had no doubt already planned the financing of Luis' education. Now that money could go into the High Valley. He had won an unexpected victory.

"Very well, Padre," said Carlos. "It will be a gift to Luis from his grandfather. That is honorable, I think. Tomorrow I go to Mexico City to bring back three guests for the stock show this weekend. I will also make arrangements about the necklace."

"Why not let Señor Ramos in Puerto Vallarta take care of that?" Jaime asked.

Again Carlos' eyes flashed. "I will not have a small-town jeweler gossiping about our affairs!"

Jaime shrugged. Town talk was obviously beneath his contempt.

I studied Ethel Evans' tense face. If, as I suspected, there had been a substitution of the emeralds, it would be exposed tomorrow. Her features now were drawn and she nervously twisted and untwisted her lace handkerchief. But her expression was not one of fright. Strangely, it was more like triumph.

On Friday evening the house had a gala atmosphere of anticipation. Tomorrow would see the culmination of weeks of work and planning. A bus had been chartered to meet prospective buyers at the Puerto Vallarta airport, and other guests, Leonora told me, would arrive by car, truck, and jeep.

Despite her handicap, Leonora showed she was still a

tireless organizer. "Take the village band off the list, Alison," she said. "I've made a bargain with the musicians. Nacho is in charge of liquor service, and Eric will check on him. Nacho is dependable unless he notices something like mud on Carlos' boots. Then he'd drop anything to clean them. Anything else on the list?"

"No. All taken care of. If you'd work a little harder on Braille, you wouldn't have to ask me. You'd keep your own lists."

"The first sensible reason I've heard for bothering with all those dots! Maybe I'll reform."

Carlos with his three guests arrived in the plane about eight o'clock. The newcomers appeared to be a trio of unsociable and doubtless rich businessmen who despite their swagger felt ill-at-ease in the home of Spanish aristocrats. They quickly retreated upstairs to play poker and dominoes.

The moment they left the living room, I braced myself for an explosion over the emerald necklace. None came. Smiling, Carlos said something to Leonora, and she nodded happily, exclaiming, "Good! You got a better price than I thought. And putting it into telephone stock is exactly right."

So I had been mistaken. Yet, curiously, I did not feel relieved. It was no use trying to tell myself that I should wait for more evidence. In my mind I had built a damning case against Ethel Evans, and my misjudging the emeralds did not change it. She was up to mischief and my suspicions remained unshaken.

Jaime Romano and Eric Vanderlyn arrived a few minutes later, having completed arrangements at the exhibition ring near the Villa Plata and after moving thirty horses down from the upper valley.

Leonora suddenly said, "I hear trucks on the road! And are there horses?"

Then we all caught the noise of motors, and Carlos moved to a window. "*Dios!* It is the army! At least a hundred federal troops."

"What the devil!" exclaimed Jaime, starting toward the hall and the front door. A moment later he returned, accompanied by a tall Mexican officer in a dusty uniform.

Smiling, Carlos extended his hand. "Captain Montez, I believe? We met months ago at a *charreada* in Puerto Vallarta."

"Yes, of course. Good evening."

"You seem to have brought a rather large escort."

He glanced around the room, surprise on his rough face. "Has no one heard the news?"

Jaime asked, "What news?"

"Don Ramón Santos has been kidnapped."

The room was instantly filled with excited, shocked voices. A servant who had followed the captain in now slipped out to carry the report to the kitchen.

"Who's been kidnapped?" I asked Eric.

"Ramón Santos. One of the most prominent men in this state."

The captain gave us the facts briefly. The millionaire's car had been halted by two men disguised in the blue uniforms of policemen. Then he had been abducted at pistol point, a chauffeur left behind, bound and gagged.

"Like the other kidnappings," said Jaime. "Political terrorists again?"

"So it appears," the captain replied. "It follows the pattern of earlier crimes. This time, however, we have a witness—the chauffeur."

"He described the men?" Carlos asked.

"Vaguely. There were three. Two wore uniforms. A third, who followed in a Buick station wagon, wore a red-checked shirt. They covered their faces with scarves the second they had stopped Don Ramón's car."

"Quite a description," said Jaime, raising an eyebrow. "All about clothing which has no doubt been burned by now."

Leonora had been listening intently, and now she spoke. "We are all shocked by this terrible thing, Captain. But I do not understand why you have come here. Surely not to tell us the news!"

"We are searching, señora. The kidnappers may have taken cover in the mountains. They have done so before."

She shook her head. "Not here. The valley people would report strangers instantly."

"I have heard the area is dotted with abandoned mines," he answered. "Perfect hiding places, no?"

"Not at all," said Jaime. "You would have to enter and leave a mine. You would be seen. Besides, most of the tunnels are too dangerous for the kidnappers themselves. There are avalanches, and now, in the rainy season, flash floods. These criminals are not such fools, Captain Montez."

The officer stood up. "I have my orders. We will bivouac near the village tonight. At dawn we begin combing the hills."

"A moment, Captain," said Leonora. "We cannot accommodate all your men, but for yourself and your officers, our house is yours."

"You are gracious, señora. I must stay with my men."

After he had gone, there was a moment of silence as each of us considered the news. Then Leonora said, "Kidnappers hiding in the High Valley? Rubbish!"

Carlos had moved to the window. "I see my Mexico City guests are outside talking with the captain. They may lose sleep over this. Each will wonder if he is next."

"Are they that rich?" Leonora asked.

"Yes," he replied, a touch of bitterness in his voice. "That rich." Then he turned to me. "Until this is over, I do not want Luis to wander off by himself. He must not even walk to the village alone."

"Carlos, he's a child," Leonora objected. "These gangs have never taken a child. They know it would infuriate the people. All the cases in the last two years have involved grown men."

"There is always a first time," said Carlos grimly.

Ramona came quickly in to report that Luis was wide-awake and demanding to know about the soldiers. "What shall I tell him, please?"

"The exact truth," said Leonora. "He'll learn it all anyway. Also tell him his grandmother sends her love, and he's to go to sleep at once. And, Ramona, please bring two cups of chocolate to my room. Will you see me upstairs and chat a moment, Alison? I have a surprise for you."

Once in her own room, Leonora moved with no hesitation, going to a carved chest, opening the top drawer, and producing a large package gaily wrapped in china paper. "For you, my dear!"

"Leonora!" I exclaimed when I opened it. "How beautiful!"

"It's a China Poblana costume I ordered from Mexico City. Traditional for women riders," she told me. "But I had them make a split skirt. *Charra* girls always ride sidesaddle. More modest, they think. It's very ladylike and pretty to watch, but I didn't suppose you'd enjoy riding that way any more than I ever did."

The blue-green garment with its gay red yoke was cut from fine cotton flannel and fell long and richly full. A white shirt had been decorated with delicate embroidery and its sleeves were clasped by four silver cuff links.

"Boots and a sombrero are in the closet," she said. "And to be traditional, wear red ribbons in your hair."

"Leonora, I love this, but . . . "

"Don't say I shouldn't have done it. It's a present because of an anniversary I forgot."

"What anniversary?"

"Losing my sight," she told me quietly. "I used to wonder how I'd ever get through the first year. Jaime kept insisting we hire a teacher for me, but it seemed useless."

"Jaime insisted on a teacher?" I asked.

"Oh, yes. He hired Señora Castro and brought her here. She tried hard. I think I was just too discouraged to make an effort. I wanted to let her go, but Jaime kept saying I would have to have a teacher and if I discharged one, he'd simply hire another." She smiled suddenly. "He said I'd give up before he did!"

Don Carlos had told me nothing of this in Puerto Vallarta, I thought. Helping Leonora had been presented as entirely *his* plan.

"Anyway, I kept believing that if I could survive the first year of blindness, the second one would be easy. Childish, I know. Yet I kept looking forward to that anniversary when everything was supposed to change. Well, the important day came and went weeks ago, but I was so busy that I didn't notice. I forgot it completely until days afterwards. That's because of you, Alison."

There was a gentle tap on the door, then Ramona entered with our chocolate. Putting it down, she said, "Will that be all, my lady?"

"Yes, thank you, Ramona," Leonora replied, then tilted her head. "Something's wrong. I can tell by your voice."

"No . . . nothing."

But her eyes were red-rimmed and I was sure Ramona had been crying.

"Only a small matter in the kitchen," she said, swallowing hard. "Nacho used some harsh words. I always weep when I am angry. It is so foolish! I cannot help it."

Sighing, Leonora murmured, "Nacho again!"

"It is not important, my lady," Ramona added quickly. "Nacho becomes angry because he is such an unhappy man. How can a man be contented when he has no children, no sons? We all understand this and are patient, but tonight everyone is nervous because of the people coming tomorrow. It is natural."

"You are a kind girl, Ramona," said Leonora. "If there is more trouble, I will speak to him. Now good night." When Ramona had closed the door, Leonora remarked, "Unhappiness doesn't excuse everything."

"I've never felt easy when Nacho was near," I said. "Yet I don't know why."

"He pussyfoots!" snapped Leonora. "Slithers!" Then her voice softened. "He was born the year the plague swept through the valley. We thought he recovered completely, but long afterwards, when he was grown and married, he asked my husband to send him to doctors in Mexico City. You see, he fathered no children. That's a shameful thing here, a disgrace for a man."

"Did the Conde send him?"

"Yes. The doctors took tests, and the news must have been a terrible blow to Nacho. There would never be children. I'll never know how the people in the valley learned this, but they seem to have heard someway. Most of them pity him; others make sour jokes about it. Probably that's turned Nacho into what he is—bitter, solitary. He cares for no one except Carlos." She paused, and added, "I suppose he's devoted to Ana Luisa, too. Some people are like the worst kind of dogs. The more they're kicked, the more they return for abuse. Of course, Nacho grew up with Carlos. That may explain some blind worship."

"Grew up with him? But Nacho must be ten years older!"

"Ten years?" Leonora shook her head. "About two months is more like it. As boys they were inseparable, but it was always the master and the slave."

It was late, and we finished our chocolate quickly. "Will you go to the *charreada* tomorrow?" I inquired.

"No. I'll stay here to entertain wives who don't like the sun and are bored with watching riders. Besides, my dear mother-in-law will attend. I'll not give her the pleasure of enjoying my difficulties."

"She might be astonished at how well you do."

Leonora chuckled. "Wouldn't that disappoint her? No, I'll wait another year."

Leaving her room, I started downstairs, automatically

checking to make sure the small flashlight on my key chain worked and, as always, moving cautiously past the door of the linen room.

A lamp burned in the entrance hall and the front door stood ajar. I was about to close it, when a voice outside said, "Alison?"

"Yes." I stepped onto the veranda. Jaime Romano sat on the steps alone, his back resting against one of the tall wooden pillars.

"You are awake late," he said.

"So are you."

"I know. But such a night as this, all of it should not be slept away. Sit down, Alison."

The warm darkness was drowsy with the jasmine fragrance of sweet-by-night. Crickets and cicadas trilled in the *copa de oro* vines, and toward the village lanterns twinkled and fires burned with yellower flame where Captain Montez and his men had pitched their tents.

"The soldiers are not sleeping either," he said. "Listen."

Very faintly, carried by the breeze which rustled the foliage, I heard a guitar and voices singing softly. "I know the melody," I said. "It's lovely, haunting. I can't hear the words."

He whispered, "'Oh, dear one, if I should die o'er the ocean's foam, softly a white dove on a fair eve would come . . . Open thy casement, dearest, for it shall be . . . My faithful spirit that loving comes back to thee . . . '"

Jaime smiled quietly. "No doves will come tonight. Only the owl who has been calling in the orchard. He is lonely, I think. Are you ever lonely, Alison?"

I looked away. "Lonely? I have so many things to do. No hours for loneliness."

"You do not need to find such hours. Loneliness comes of itself. No matter how hard one works, no matter how filled the hours are. Is it not true, Alison?"

"Yes. It is true too often." I thought of my own life, and I imagined his, realizing for the first time that there was a bond between us: loneliness.

He gazed upward, past the arches and pillars of the house to the sky and the great stars, incredibly brilliant in the thin air. "'The silence of space frightens me . . . I am engulfed in infinity and afraid . . . '"

"Are those also the words of a song?"

"No. Words from a book I read long ago, a book by the Frenchman, Pascal. They have stayed with me."

I looked at his strong, unyielding face, the dark forelock, eyes that even in the night were a cold, hard blue. Yet I remembered his countenance at other times, in other moods. I would never forget my glimpse of his grief-stricken vulnerability when he had stood in the Octagon gazing at Veronica's framed handkerchief. He was not the man of steel he pretended to be. Pretended? No, that was not the right word. Jaime Romano pretended nothing, but he concealed much of himself, turning his hardest face to the world.

"I can't imagine your being afraid," I said. "Not even frightened by space or silence."

He smiled then, the rocky features softening. "No? Then you do not yet know me as well as I thought you did. Let us say that at times I am afraid of myself." He rose quickly, seeming to tower over me. "Also, sometimes I am afraid of you."

"Of me?" I exclaimed. "Why should you be?"

"Why not?" The smile altered, became faintly mocking. "For me you are a dangerous woman. We will talk of that another time. Good night, Alison."

"Ride, horseman, proud and swift,
The prize is yours today . . . "
—Rodeo song

TWELVE

I awoke early, but others were up and stirring long before me.
From the stable came whistles, singing, and shouts of men as
they groomed horses, and I had hardly finished dressing in my
new costume when Luis skipped in, aglow with excitement.

"*Tía*, we are both in *charro* clothing!" he exclaimed. He
wore a new embroidered shirt and fancy trousers with silver
buttons—a miniature of his father's riding outfit. "My grandmother gave me this. And look! A present from Uncle Jaime!"

Proudly he pointed to a silver belt buckle much too large
for him. "It has my initials on it. L.R."

I looked at the buckle in astonishment. It was, I thought,
an exact duplicate of the one I had seen in the compartment of
Jaime Romano's desk.

"How handsome, Luis," I said, kneeling down to examine
it closely. No, this was not a duplicate, but the same buckle. A
silversmith, in changing the "J" to an "L," had done his work
carefully, but the etching had been so deep that one could see
where something had been ground and polished away.

"Uncle Jaime says this is the most valuable buckle I will ever own, and I must always keep it."

"He is right, Luis." Rising, I touched his thin shoulder. How could Jaime Romano part with this gift after keeping it so long? It was a beautiful thing he had done, a present to Luis from his mother, even though he might never know. "Take good care of it. Be proud of it."

"Oh, I am!"

Cars that must have left Puerto Vallarta at dawn began to arrive an hour after breakfast. Guests were greeted at the *casa grande,* offered drinks or coffee, then sent to the exhibition rings. They were an exuberant, happy crowd looking forward to a day's entertainment, yet at times the good cheer died at mention of the kidnapping. Some were friends of the victim, and they buzzed with rumors and vague reports.

"Ransom is ten million pesos!"

"No, no. Only five million."

Another disagreed. "I heard there was no ransom note at all. A crime of vengeance!"

Meanwhile, a *mariachi* group played lively folk tunes and servants presented orchids to female guests. Leonora remained poised and patient, although I was sure she wanted to snap at some old acquaintances who went on and on with commiserations and sympathy, dramatizing her misfortune as well-meaning but insensitive people will.

The chartered bus from the airport brought a chattering throng dressed in everything from glittering *charro* outfits and Puerto Vallarta sportswear to dark business suits. Several women wore China Poblana costumes like mine, and some others, too well-fed, bulged in hot pants.

When the crowd started for the exhibition rings, Luis tugged at my arm, demanding we ride together.

The bullring behind the Villa Plata resembled a miniature of the Colosseum in Rome, built of heavy granite slabs and decorated with stone sculpture. Although the arena was ample, only one tier of seats surrounded it. This building was an extravagant family toy constructed long ago for the Romano family, their friends, and distant neighbors.

Nearby, a curving stone grandstand accommodated spectators watching equestrian events. The festivities began there with a simple but beautiful parade of horses ridden by Mario and other valley boys, joined by several dazzlingly costumed guests. I thought of the animals entering Noah's Ark in pairs as I watched two tall palominos, two Arabians, two English hunters.

Then came saddle horses bred in the High Valley, smaller mounts, only fourteen hands high but spirited and intelligent. They wore flowers, ribbons and pompons in their manes and almost danced when the village band played a gay polka.

Two pretty, flashing-eyed girls gave an exciting demonstration of sidesaddle riding, and the crowd cheered them.

Luis sat beside me, and today I, not he, was the pupil, as he astonished me with all he knew about horses, riding, and even the superstitions of the riders.

"*Charros* say it is lucky to ride horses of certain colors," he told me. "See the one Mario has? That is a good-luck color. *Alazán-tostado.* The golden brown."

"That black stallion is beautiful," I commented.

"Yes, but most *charros* will not buy black horses unless they have white spots. Black horses go crazy in the full moon. We have two black colts we hope to sell to *gringos.*"

Next the ranch boys and some visitors performed a startling exhibition of lassoing, and the other spectators, although they had seen such shows hundreds of times, were as excited as I was. Then men hurried in front of the stands carrying two tall posts with a crossbar lashed between them at the top. "The ribbon race!" cried Luis, clapping his hands. "*Tía,* they are going to run the rings!"

"What does that mean?" Just then someone tapped my shoulder, and turning, I saw an old man, a horse trainer on the ranch, smiling at me.

"Señorita, will you give us a ribbon for the race?"

"A ribbon?"

"You have to, *Tía!*" exclaimed Luis. "That makes you a queen of the fiesta. One of its godmothers!"

I untied the long red ribbon, letting my hair fall loose. "Here you are."

The two girl riders were also giving ribbons, and below on the track a wire was strung between the two posts near the crossbar.

"What are they going to do?" I asked.

"Run the rings! The ribbons go over the wire and a small ring is tied to each one. You will see. The riders will try to do something very difficult."

When the first attempt was made, I understood what "running the rings" meant. A young *charro*, his horse racing at full speed, charged toward the three dangling rings, a machete in his hand. The goal was to spear one of the rings with the tip of the machete and carry it off with the attached ribbon. Hard to do at any time, and especially so today when a breeze moved the rings.

The first three riders failed. The fourth succeeded, but won little applause because his mount had not raced fast enough. Still, he displayed the ribbon boastfully, and the band struck up a lusty tune as he rode to the old man who seemed to be the judge. Some words were exchanged between them, then the victor rode to where the two pretty girls sat. Leaping into the stand, he doffed his sombrero grandly and knelt before one of them. He gave her the ribbon, and she returned it as a gift. Now everyone cheered while the girl blushed, turning her face away.

After four more unsuccessful tries, the second ring was retrieved and the presentation performance repeated. "That rider cheated a little," said Luis. "He reined his horse at the last second. That is why some of the other riders whistled at him."

Luis looked again at the track. "*Tía,* only your ribbon is left! Who will win it?"

Then scattered applause rippled through the crowd. At the edge of the field I saw Carlos Romano mounted on a superb gray horse with markings like charcoal streaks. "My father is going to ride now," said Luis, disappointed. "He will take the ribbon and it will all be over."

"He never misses?" I asked.

"Never."

Carlos Romano's gray stallion leaped into motion, the rider and his mount seeming to be a single being as they charged forward, gathering speed by the second.

"Ay, what a horseman!" exclaimed a man near me. "Beautiful! Magnificent!"

They flashed past us, I saw the machete slowly lifting, pointing like a sword. But at the last instant the wind fluttered the ring and ribbon. It swung away from the knife tip and Don Carlos missed it by a hair's breadth.

Although he had failed to gain the prize, the crowd had not forgotten the dramatic beauty of his charge. Shouts of "Bravo!" rang in the stands, and cries of "Again! Once again!"

The noise around me drowned the pounding hoofs of another horse, and I did not realize what was happening until Luis shouted, "Look! My uncle!"

Jaime Romano's great roan stallion, Yaqui, was flying past the stands, his rider crouched low. A sudden silence fell. Then, as the speeding horse neared the posts, Jaime Romano rose in the saddle, standing upright in the stirrups, lifting not a machete but a simple stick as the horse plunged on.

"He took it! He took it!" The shout was everywhere, and the band burst into *Dianas*, the music of applause.

Returning slowly, Jaime held the ring high in the air, letting the ribbon float gaily in the breeze. He was not in *charro* dress, but wore whipcord trousers and a plain white shirt open at the throat. "No spurs," whispered Luis in awe. "He did not intend to ride today!" And it was true he carried no machete but had picked up a stick somewhere.

Without bothering to ask the judge whose ribbon had

been won, he approached Luis and me, removed his sombrero, and vaulted the railing.

"I return your ribbon, señorita," he said, dropping to one knee. I had expected an ironic smile, some quick, wry remark. But his dark face was grave and the startling eyes, gazing into mine, were intent and serious.

"It is yours, señor," I said, giving it back, awkward, unsure of myself.

"*Mil gracias.*" He rose, lifting the ribbon and displaying it to the crowd in a strangely solemn manner. They were still cheering when he rode away.

If Jaime Romano was the hero of running the rings, the late afternoon belonged entirely to Don Carlos. After an elaborate picnic lunch, most people moved to the bullring to see men work with what Luis called "the brave herd."

"Will a bull be killed?" I asked, holding back a little.

"No, no. This is a demonstration only. And they will not be bulls. Only cows are used."

"A cow fight?" It seemed ridiculous.

"A bull must never fight twice," Luis explained. "He becomes too wise and dangerous. The cows will show the bravery of the herd today."

The black, squat beasts I soon saw certainly bore no resemblance to any cow I had been near in New England! Snorting, ill-tempered, and razor-horned, they pawed the ground, charging this way and that, amazingly rapid thrusts backed by half a ton of muscle rippling beneath coarse hides. The nimble men and boys who engaged them in mock combat needed true courage.

Don Carlos showed his skill for only a few minutes, but no more was needed to prove his ability and cool nerve. The other men had merely moved. Carlos glided, danced, spun the cape with dexterity beautiful to watch. Anticipating every move of his animal opponent, he toyed with it, working so close to the horns that I found myself gasping. Incredibly brave—or incredibly foolhardy. I could not decide which. When he was near enough for me to see his face, it was transformed, ecstatic in the joy of battle, eyes enormous, a muscle in his cheek twitching, making the jagged scar move.

"My father is brave, no?" asked Luis.

I agreed, but studying the boy's expression, I felt he was more frightened than admiring.

Even though Don Carlos had dressed himself in the traditional "suit of lights" that flashed in the sun. he did not bother to remain long in the ring. His saunter, the tilt of his head as he left suggested that he was above such poor competition, and he hardly acknowledged the applause. One shrill, harsh voice kept screaming, *"Ole, ole!"* and I glanced across the ring just as Luis said, "My great-grandmother is here, *Tía.*"

I had not seen the Excelentísima's entrance, but it must have been memorable. The outrageous wig and much-dyed black dress were unchanged, but she had added a billowing red mantilla with sequin embroidery, and the coachboy, kneeling beside her, waved a great fan of vermilion plumes. Ana Luisa had also decided upon another touch to guarantee attention. A brown cigar smoldered in a pearl holder, and she sat wreathed in smoke.

"She wants me to join her," said Luis glumly, when he saw her gesturing toward him. "I will come back in a moment, *Tía.*"

I was happy enough not to go with him, having no wish for another encounter with the Excelentísima.

Over a loudspeaker someone announced, "Magnificent brave bulls, typical of this herd! Exhibition only." Static drowned out the rest. Then the gate on the far side of the arena swung open and a huge black bull thundered into the circle, head lowered, nostrils distended as he snorted in fury. He was alone in the ring, to be seen, not fought.

Glancing toward Luis, who was listening intently to Ana Luisa, I saw Ramona standing just behind them. Smiling, I waved to her, but she shook her head and made a beckoning gesture. Rising, I made my way through the crowd and a moment later was standing beside her. "The Excelentísima," she whispered. "Listen to her, señorita."

Kneeling quietly, so neither Luis nor the old lady became aware of my presence, I heard her speaking in a tense, almost hypnotic voice. " . . . and sometimes boys, even small ones, jump over the barrier to work with the bulls. A brave thing, no? Your father once did that when even younger than you are, Luis."

The child seemed spellbound. "Did he have a cape? A sword?"

"No, nothing! Only a woman's mantilla, red, like the one I am wearing now." She slowly removed the shawl from her shoulders.

Below in the ring, the bull, horns still lowered, paced angrily, searching for an opponent, the black tail slashing back and forth.

"Everyone cheered your father that day," she continued hoarsely. "How courageous he was! Armed only with a mantilla like this one." She pressed the scarlet cloth toward him. "See, Luis! The bull is on the other side now. The barrier is not very high. Luis . . . Luis . . . " The Excelentísima's eyes burned with frenzy and her painted features contorted.

Just as the boy's hands touched the low railing in front of him, I seized his shoulders. "Luis! Give back the mantilla. We have to go home at once!"

For a second his expression was trancelike, then he seemed to awaken. "Yes," he murmured. "I want to go."

"Luis will remain with me! Leave at once, Señorita Mallory!" Ana Luisa seethed with fury, the great head trembling on her narrow shoulders.

"Luis and I are both leaving," I told her, an anger as fierce as her own blazing up in me. "I listened, I know exactly what you were trying to do. And don't think you've heard the last of this!"

She rose to face me, fists clenched as though to strike at

my face. "I will have you out of the High Valley before sunset! Do you think I will be insulted by a *gringa* she-goat?"

She spat then, but I did not flinch. "Come, Luis," I said, holding his arm firmly. "Your great-grandmother is ill. We must ignore her behavior."

I led him quickly away, through the whispering, murmuring people who had witnessed the scene. Behind us Ana Luisa screamed curses and imprecations, but I paid no attention.

Outside, Luis, his lips quivering, said, "*Tía*, I did not know what to do. I was afraid of the bull."

"You should have been. I'm proud of you again, Luis. Proud of your good sense."

Primitivo leaned against the jeep, waiting for passengers. "Have someone bring our horses back to the stable," I told him. "We will ride with you."

Rain pattered lightly on the jeep as it halted at the *casa grande.* Most of the visitors, except those spending the night, were departing now, but avoiding the front part of the house, I took Luis straight to his room. He sat quietly on his bed, tense and confused. There was no need for us to talk about what had happened. He knew his great-grandmother had tried to goad him into doing a dangerous thing. That he could not understand why, did not matter. Luis had no ties of affection with her. Except physically, he was beyond her reach, she could not hurt him.

We talked for a few minutes about the horses, about the magnificent riding of both his father and his uncle, and before long Luis became sleepy, ready for a nap.

I did not feel like joining the guests having cocktails in the living room, but knew Leonora would question my absence. This was a day of triumph for her. I would not spoil it by telling her what had almost happened. Tomorrow was soon enough.

When I greeted her, she smiled knowingly. "I hear you lost a ribbon today, Alison."

"Yes. I think your son collects them."

"Carlos does. Not Jaime."

"Have you managed all right here?"

"Apart from spilling a glass of lemonade on old Señora Gonzalez, I've done beautifully," she said. "But you sound tired. All the talk will be business now, so go and rest if you like."

Night had fallen and the Octagon's lamps burned brightly when I heard a quick, heavy stride on the veranda. Jaime Romano knocked, then entered without waiting for me to admit him. Flinging himself into a chair, he said, "Ramona just told me what my saintly grandmother tried to do today. Thank God, you were there!"

"I'm not sure I was needed," I answered. "Luis might not have jumped into the ring to show off. But she tried her best to make him do it. I heard every word. It was horrible! Impossible to believe she could have said such things. Yet she did!"

"I know. She grows worse each year. And what can I do?"

"Keep Luis away from her, for one thing!"

"Luis is not my son. How far can I interfere? Yet I must do whatever is possible." He smiled ruefully. "At any moment we shall receive a royal order for your banishment. Perhaps even a visit to the house tonight."

"And what will you do?"

"I think my mother will answer any such requests. And I think she will express herself quite clearly."

Broodingly he stared at the floor, his hands clenched. "I must tell you something that is not easy for me to say. If you had been with Luis a few months ago and he had leaped into the ring, I would have thought you had caused it. That you had urged him, taunted him perhaps."

My eyes widened. "You thought I'd endanger a child? Why should you think that of me?"

"I did not know what to believe when you first came here!" Rising, he strode to the window and stood gazing into the night. "I could not understand why Señora Castro had been sent away when I was not here or why he had arranged for you to come in her place. Maybe he was your lover."

"My lover?"

He shrugged. "Why not? Women have always found him

attractive. If you were his lover, you might find the presence of a son by a former marriage inconvenient. How could I trust you?"

Suddenly he slammed his fist into his open palm. "There was another possibility. You were not lovers, but he had brought you here to torment me with memories of Veronica. He could do that. It would be like him."

"Memories of Veronica?" I asked.

He turned quickly toward me, his body taut. "I have never spoken of this before. I thought I never would. Veronica and I loved each other. We did not intend that this should happen, but she was very much alone, and I—I, too, was lonely. It happened. We could not help it."

Looking away from the intensity of those eyes, I said, "I think I understand."

"This was no cheap or ugly thing!" The words, so long held in, now broke forth. "Yet we felt guilty. And that is why she left the High Valley. For my sake."

"She left—for you?"

"Yes. One night I told her I could endure this no longer. The High Valley is my home, but it was unbearable for me. I remember how she looked at me that night, looked at me with eyes like yours. She said she had done me a terrible wrong, she could not forgive herself for it. But this was not true! She never tried to make me love her. It was a thing that happened. I told her this, but she would not listen. She only said I must wait a few days before going away. So I waited. Waited through the fiesta of St. Michael. And then it was too late." He sank into the chair, his strong shoulders suddenly weak, and with a helpless gesture he brushed the lock from his forehead.

After a moment he continued, his voice far away, as though he spoke of events that had happened to a stranger. "I stayed on here, hoping she would return. Then my father died, and I found myself trapped, responsible for the valley."

"You didn't expect this?" I asked softly.

He shook his head. "No. I should have. My father said often that he would do such a thing. I thought he was saying this to punish Carlos, as a threat, no more. The High Valley has always gone to the eldest son, always. But my father had not forgiven Carlos. Besides, he knew I would protect the valley, that it is in my body and my blood. How Carlos must hate him for it!"

Jaime gazed at me, his stare hard and penetrating. In the silence the clock on the bedside table ticked with unnatural loudness. "Yes, Carlos hates," he said at last. "Just as I hated him for bringing you here to replace Veronica—I thought. And I hated you for reminding me of things I had to forget. I watched you, the way you suddenly lifted your head, how you stood near the lime tree and let the wind ruffle your hair. For a time I believed I was seeing Veronica again. Then, slowly, I knew I was not. It was you I watched, Alison.

"The night we danced together, I suddenly felt I was hurting Veronica, letting her memory die. And I felt in danger. It was better to be lonely than to take risks of suffering again. Nor could I fall in love with an illusion, as Veronica once did."

"An illusion? Do you mean Carlos?"

"Yes, Carlos. She told me once that she had been desperate and lonely when they met. 'No one to turn to,' she said. And so she married an illusion—a promise of love and security she had never known. It is hard for me to forgive Carlos for that. No, it is impossible."

I hesitated, then said what I had to say, dreading the answer. "You still love Veronica, don't you?"

"No. I remember her with kindness, with affection. She deserves no less from me. But it is over, finished. Even after I knew this, I was afraid to speak with you. Who could tell for sure? You might be Carlos' woman." Frowning, he asked roughly, "Are you?"

Color rushed to my cheeks. "I am no one's woman!"

He was close, so close that my pulse was pounding, and I gazed into his face, longing to believe what he said, yet frightened. "No one's woman? Not even mine?" His hands clasped my arms. "I think I love you, Alison," he said softly. "I think it so often that I have become sure."

"Love . . . me?" My breath seemed to choke me. I knew so little of him, yet I wanted him to hold me closer, wanted to lose myself in his strength. Yet, afraid and bewildered, I drew back.

His hands fell from my arms. "You are afraid. You do not trust me."

"No, not that. I—I'm not ready for this," I stammered. "I hadn't imagined that you felt this way." No, I had not known. Yet, while not admitting it to myself, I must have hoped he might care for me, to have unconsciously been telling myself it could lead to nothing but unhappiness.

He shook his head. "You are afraid. So we must wait until you have no fear, until you are sure of me and of yourself." Reaching into his pocket, he drew forth the red ribbon I had given him that afternoon. "Señorita Alison," he said, his lips but not his eyes smiling. "I return this. One day it will again be mine. It will be your gift to me when you are ready."

Numbly I accepted the long, bright strip of grosgrain.

"I have waited long," he said. "I can wait longer." Then, leaning close to me, he whispered. "Goodnight now. Sleep well, *querida!*"

As he left, I nearly called to him to come back, but I stood helpless, unable to speak. Again words from the past seemed to clamor inside me. Donald's words: *If I could see, you'd run from me, hide yourself.*

Donald had been right. I knew this now. And I could not hide from Jaime Romano, could not run away. To say that I loved him would be to commit my life to Jaime, to the High Valley. I knew from the way he had spoken of Veronica that this was a man who, touched by love, would give himself completely, demanding all in return, my whole being, my whole life.

I felt my lips silently forming the words "I love you." Yet I was still unready and afraid.

"Some jaguars stalk in daylight . . . "

THIRTEEN

Three days later the soldiers left the valley, their search unfinished, for word arrived that the kidnapped millionaire had been ransomed and released. He had been blindfolded and held captive in mountainous country, he told police and reporters.

"Why not in these mountains?" asked Don Carlos gloomily. "Perhaps in our own valley."

"Nonsense," said Leonora, no longer sounding so positive.

Such a worry was quickly forgotten in the atmosphere of new security the valley suddenly enjoyed. The sale of horses had been highly successful, and now trucks loaded with cement and steel rolled toward the construction site of the dam. Leonora announced that there would soon be a new electrical generator in the south wing of the house.

I saw little of Jaime Romano after our talk in the Octagon. When we met, there were always others present, and each time he gave me a quizzical, half-amused smile that seemed to ask, "Do you have something to say to me, Alison?"

I had no doubt about what he had told me of himself and Veronica. Yet there came a few terrible moments when I could not help wondering if the story had ended exactly as he claimed. Could a love so fierce have changed into consuming hatred? I did not want to belive this—desperately I did not. Jaime, I was sure, was a man of profound goodness, often difficult, always bluntly honest, and he wore his outward gruffness and coldness like armor against a world which had made him suffer. Inconceivable that he could have harmed Veronica. Yet sometimes when I saw him riding toward the orchards, erect in the saddle, determined and proud, the doubt assailed me against my will. Could he have somehow been driven beyond control? No, I told myself. Not Jaime!

One night I was awakened by the music of guitars and a violin outside the Octagon. From the window I saw four young boys from the village grouped on the lawn, wearing tall flowers in their sombreros, and one sang in a pure, clear tenor the haunting melody of *"Las Mañanitas,"* the song of birthdays and serenades.

The next day I saw Jaime, who had just mounted Yaqui, near the stable. "Did you hear the serenade last night?" I asked, not liking the awkwardness in my voice. "It was lovely."

"I know nothing of serenades. I do not hire musicians to play for selfish girls."

"Selfish!" I exclaimed.

Leaning down, he said softly, "A girl who will not give away even a ribbon is miserly indeed, no?" He touched Yaqui's flanks and rode away.

I did not see him again until several days later when Leonora called a family counsel to decide about Luis' schooling, and I was asked to give an opinion.

"Margaret Webber mentioned a small school in Puerto

Vallarta," I said. "Luis could come home every weekend, so it wouldn't be a total break."

"Good," said Carlos. "But let him enter a few days late, after the fiestas here. I remember how I was shipped away every year just before San Miguel Day. Missing the fiesta was one of the worst things about growing up."

"I seem to recall one fiesta you didn't miss," said Leonora grimly. She turned to me. "He ran away from a school in Mexico City one year and came back here for San Miguel Day. He hid in the bell tower."

"How beautiful it was!" said Carlos. "I watched the Roman candles and star showers from high in the tower. Glorious!"

"It must have been," I exclaimed, imagining the panorama of the valley illuminated by green, red, and yellow flares ablaze in the sky. "I'd love to see that."

"Sometime you will," Jaime said softly.

"You know, Carlos," Leonora remarked, "I never thought the fiestas were important to you."

"Many things were important that no one thought about!" he replied with unexpected anger. For an instant I glimpsed a rebellious child hating the domination of his father. And hating his stepmother, too? Had Leonora's iron will been another chain to bind him? "My son will enjoy freedom I was never given!"

"You took it just the same," said Leonora lightly, smiling.

"'Take what you want, and pay for it,'" he retorted. "I've done both."

"Yes," agreed Jaime lazily. "Usually at discount prices."

Carlos said nothing, but his aristocratic features had never before struck me as so sharp, so hawklike. Yes, a hawk. As though some ghost conjured by the Excelentísima had stolen into the room and taken possession of her grandson. Then he smiled and the ghost was exorcised. "Our Alison has, as usual, come up with the correct solution. What would we do without her?"

"I hope never to find out," said Jaime, and once more I read a question in his eyes.

To distract Luis from his worries about school, I planned a picnic. "Not on the lawn or in the patio," I told him. "A special one. You, your grandmother, and I. We'll start early and go to the most beautiful place in the valley."

"Which place?"

"My favorite spot is the bank of the stream near the Hidden Treasure."

"Oh, yes, *Tía!* And I could find different rocks for my collection." Then his face clouded. "Could my grandmother ride so far?"

"I'm sure she can. It's an easy ride if we follow the road past the Villa Plata."

When I mentioned the idea to Leonora, she was enthusiastic. "That would be a real outing! I haven't been up to the Treasure in over two years. What day shall it be?"

"I thought next Saturday. That wouldn't interrupt Luis' lessons with Padre Olivera, and it can't be later because the fiesta's next week." I hesitated, then added, "Does he visit the Excelentísima that day?"

"Luis now goes to the Villa Plata only when accompanied by his father," she said. "And Carlos is quite busy these days."

It was unnecessary for her to explain. The flat tone of her voice told everything. She knew what had happened at the bullring, and she was taking no risks. I was also sure that whatever complaints Ana Luisa had made about me, Leonora had answered.

Jaime must have learned of our plans from Luis, who was bubbling with excitement and told everyone in the house. On Friday morning, when Leonora and I were working with a page of Braille, he entered the tower room. "I have come to invite myself to a picnic," he said.

"You'll go with us?" Leonora was astonished.

"Why not? I look forward to escorting two lovely ladies to a lovely place."

"But tomorrow's Saturday. The pay roll! You never go away on Saturday."

"You dislike my company," he told her gravely. "You offend me by finding excuses."

Leonora laughed. "Wonderful, Jaime! Like the old days!"

Smiling with unusual gentleness, he said, "No, *madre mía*. Better than that. *Hasta mañana, Alison.*"

When he was gone. Leonora said, "I wouldn't have believed it!" She pursed her lips thoughtfully and her sightless eyes seemed to study and analyze me. Then she nodded, but made no comment.

That afternoon I found myself humming, almost singing aloud, *"These are the songs of the pretty little mornings,"* the words of *"Las Mañanitas."*

Tomorrow would be beautiful—a day I had planned for Luis and Leonora suddenly belonged to me. I would be with Jaime in a place that was clean and open, away from the shadows of the *casa grande*. It was like a new beginning.

Don Carlos had said he was flying to Puerto Vallarta that evening, so I wrote a quick note to Margaret telling her to expect me in a week, that I would accompany Luis the day he enrolled in school. Outgoing mail was always left on a table in the entrance hall, and I had just placed my letter there when Ethel Evans' angry voice cried out at the head of the stairs, "Be careful with those things! Don't carry them by the cord, it might snap!"

Startled, I looked up to see Primitivo midway on the steps, a large paper-wrapped parcel in each hand. Miss Evans, standing above him, repeated shrilly, "Not by the cord!" Then she started forward so rapidly that Primitivo must have thought she was falling, for he reached out to help her, dropping one of the packages. I heard a crash of shattering earthenware, and rushing to it, I retrieved the parcel, which had rolled down several steps.

"No, I'll get it!" shouted Miss Evans.

But she was too late. The strings had loosened and the paper gaped open. As I lifted it, smashed fragments of a native jar fell at my feet, along with several small figures of beautifully carved ivory and ebony—an antique set of chessmen had been concealed inside the pottery.

Ethel Evans halted a few steps above me, petrified. Minutes seemed to pass before she recovered the power of speech. "I was sending to town some pottery and a little imitation ivory chess set I'd bought."

"It won't do, Miss Evans," I said quietly. Kneeling, I gathered the chessmen—lovely Oriental pieces, their ivory yellowing with age. "Give me the other parcel," I told Primitivo in Spanish. "Then we won't need you any more."

We went in silence to Miss Evans' room, and her lips were a thin slashed line as I unwrapped the second package. A cheap earthen bowl, worth only a few pesos. Inside it, concealed by newspaper, I found a small book bound in calfskin, a hand-illuminated edition of the poems of Sor Juana de la Cruz.

"Prove it!" she said, the sharp chin jutting out defiantly. "*You* put those things there! You or that filthy servant. Don't think you can get away with this nasty trick!"

She was not even embarrassed, much less frightened. What did Leonora really know of this childhood acquaintance, of what had happened during the years when they had no contact? Miss Evans was apparently not new to the business of thievery.

"It's just your word against mine," she went on, jeering at me. "And if you're smart, you'll keep your mouth shut."

The affectations of gentility and helplessness she affected so skillfully had vanished. I no longer saw the delicate lady of the sitting room, but the beast from the basement, a hard, unscrupulous fighter who was not softness, but claws.

"Stop this nonsense, Miss Evans," I said sharply. "There's no difficulty at all in proving it. My only concern is for Leonora. I want to spare her as much pain as possible. Don Jaime is executor of the estate you've been robbing. I intend to tell him. That's the end of my responsibility."

"Yes, tell him," she sneered. "And when Leonora knows what I've found out about you, how you've behaved with both Jaime and Carlos . . . "

"Cheap lies won't work, Miss Evans. Don't bother trying them!"

I strode angrily from the room, carrying the ceramic bowl with both the book and the chess set in it.

Jaime, I was told, would not return to the *casa grande* until late that night. There was nothing to do but wait until tomorrow and then talk privately with him after our picnic. Miss Evans was not going to flee the country, and I saw no point in ruining our long-awaited outing. Time enough afterwards. I gave the chessmen and the poems to Ramona, telling her to put them in a safe place.

A few minutes later, as I walked through the patio on my way to the Octagon, I heard the engine of Carlos Romano's plane. Pausing, I watched it climb higher, a metallic flash in the fading sunlight. The plane gradually became a dark speck in the sky, but my eyes followed it as it made a wide turn, circling, then disappearing not in the direction of the coast and Puerto Vallarta, but flying inland toward the great cities, the capital and Guadalajara.

In the morning Ramona came to my door earlier than usual. "I have bad news, my lady," she said. "There has been an accident at the dam."

"An accident?" Fear flashed through me. "What happened?"

233

"Some sort of door—is it called a floodgate?—came open in the night. No one was hurt, but Don Jaime had to go there before dawn. He said he was sorry, but you must have your picnic another day."

"No one was hurt," I said. "That's the important thing."

But it did not prove to be the only important thing to Luis and Leonora.

"Why not have *two* picnics?" Luis demanded. "Our own today and another with Uncle Jaime?"

"I knew something would prevent his going," said Leonora. "We'll go without him."

I felt unsure. "He said we should go another day."

Her head inclined. "I'm quite capable of deciding what I want to do. Luis, tell the boy to saddle our horses. We're having our picnic, Jaime or not."

That ended the matter. Half an hour later the three of us, with a heaped basket, rode slowly toward the Villa Plata on our way to the Hidden Treasure. I tried to put aside my disappointment that Jaime was not with us and thoughts of what I had learned about Ethel Evans. I would have the burden of this unshared knowledge longer than I had hoped.

We were less than a mile from the *casa grande* when I heard someone shouting, and looking back, saw Ramona, mounted on a burro, frantically pursuing us.

"What is it?" I asked anxiously when she was within earshot. "News from the dam?"

"No, my lady." Ramona panted from her struggle with the burro and her battle to straighten her long, full skirts that bunched around her thighs. "I came to help. See? I have brought my own tortillas."

"Help with what?" Leonora demanded. But she was in too good a humor to be annoyed. "Well, come along and enjoy yourself. You can gather herbs for the kitchen."

"Yes, my lady. I will be very useful."

Ramona's uneasiness and flushed face gave her away. She had come, I decided, to watch over us, since no one else was available. It was sweet of her, even though useless and unnecessary. We followed a familiar way, and on such a glorious morning as this the notion of harm or danger seemed impossible. The sky was a cloudless cobalt-blue, while fields and orchards, washed by the night rain, gleamed in the sun, the long, lazy leaves of pepper trees shining.

Luis began to sing, and soon Leonora joined in, and then Ramona.

> *"I gave my love two apples*
> *I gave two ears of corn,*
> *I gave my love a ribbon*
> *To deck his saddle horn."*

Laughing, I touched the ribbon that tied back my own hair. Not a red one—this was black to match my sombrero and dotted shirt. A pretty ribbon, but on a saddle horn it would have been the color of mourning . . .

"Luis, where are you?" Leonora called sharply.

"Right here. I am inspecting rocks with my magnifying glass."

"Good. You were so quiet I thought you might have gone inside the mine."

"I'm watching, Leonora," I said. "And Luis wouldn't do that anyway."

"Hum," she said, expressing little faith in the promises of small boys.

It was midafternoon now. We sat on the ground only a few yards from the dark mouth of the mine in the coolest, shadiest spot in the cul-de-sac of boulders and cliffs where we had picnicked. The brook I had discovered only a few months before had turned into a foaming torrent fed by the rains and by swollen, hidden reservoirs lying deep within the mountain.

"I love the sound of flowing water," said Leonora. "You know this stream once disappeared for months."

"How did that happen?"

"The cave-in. The night the whole north wing of the mine collapsed. Three years ago next week. The night Veronica . . . " She checked herself, conscious of Luis.

I remembered then, remembered Eric talking of it. Like an explosion, he'd said. Then like an earthquake.

Looking down the road we'd followed, I tried to imagine that night. Everyone at the village fiesta, shouting and bells and fireworks. Now in my mind I pictured Veronica's small white car moving quietly in the darkness without headlights. If she herself had been in the car at all, it was not as its driver. Living or dead, Veronica had been only a passenger, a helpless one, being transported to a final place. Of that I now felt sure.

Jaime had told me that Veronica left the High Valley for his sake, but I could not believe it. Perhaps that had been her intention, but even so, it left every question unanswered. Why did she not take Luis with her? There had been a note for Carlos; later a note for her father- in-law. But not a word to Jaime himself. The events surrounding her departure were no less mysterious and disturbing because of what she had said to Jaime.

Now I imagined her car following the road across the Bridge of the Gospels, rounding the Villa Plata. Was the Excelentísima watching from a balcony? Had she given orders? Did she know what was taking place? The car would have rolled past the spot where we were now sitting and entered the mine. Later, night rain would have washed away all trace of its tire marks.

Was it still there inside the mine? Crushed, buried forever beneath tons upon tons of stone and shale?

"Cave-ins are strange," Leonora mused. "The miners say you can bring down a mountain with a whistle. It's almost true, you know. A shout, someone touching one loose beam. Maybe just one small stone falling. Then an avalanche."

"You said the stream vanished, then came back. How? Did the village men dig in the mine?"

"No! No one was fool enough to try that. Other parts of

the mine would have fallen in at the first stroke of a pickax. The stream found its own way out."

Luis slipped his magnifying glass into its leather case, put it in his pocket, and came over to us. "A rain cloud," he said, pointing to the northeastern sky.

"I suppose it's time to go home," I told him. "Where's Ramona?"

"Gathering mint."

I thought I caught sight of someone moving among the willows a little more than a hundred yards away, where our horses and Ramona's burro were tethered. Luis' sharp eyes had seen the same thing, but he said in a low tone, "That is not Ramona."

"Someone from the village, then." I began to pack leftovers in the basket, covertly watching the place where I had noticed the figure concealed among the trees. Estrella, the most sensitive of the horses, suddenly whinnied and moved aside. A man in a black sombrero stepped quickly backward, vanishing behind the trunk of a tree. I had only a glimpse of him—an impression of the black hat, a checked shirt, and something cradled in his arms. A stick? Surely it couldn't have been a rifle!

Luis, also pretending not to watch, had noticed something else. "His neckerchief is tied around his face, *Tía*," he whispered. "Like a bandit's."

"What's that? asked Leonora.

"Someone, a man, is hiding among the trees near the horses," I told her quietly. "I think he has a rifle. Luis says his face is masked."

"Are you sure, Luis?" She was uneasy but not alarmed. "With all this wild talk about kidnappers, one might imagine anything."

A soft whistle came, so like the call of a cardinal that I would have mistaken it, had not Luis said, "Ramona."

I saw her then on the cliff above, kneeling behind a dark pinnacle of rock where she was hidden from any watcher in the trees at the mouth of the cul-de-sac. She must have climbed the far slope of the granite wall and circled back.

She raised her hand, holding out three fingers, then pointed in the direction of the willows. When she repeated the gesture, I understood its meaning: not one man but three were lurking there. She indicated a rifle, another rifle, then put her hands to her face, showing masks. After one more quick gesture she slipped away, going for help, I supposed.

I reported the pantomimed conversation to Leonora, trying to keep my voice from betraying fear.

"If they mean trouble, they won't wait until Ramona gets back with men," she said flatly. "Can you and Luis scramble up the cliffs? Maybe pretend you're playing a game?"

"No. There's no way out except to go toward them."

"The mine." Luis, white-faced, struggled not to tremble. "We could hide in the mine."

"We don't want to make a mistake, Luis," she told him. Leonora rose, stretching her arms, the most careless and natural gesture possible, revealing no sign of knowledge or alarm to the watchers.

But the faint breeze freshened, a gust of wind swept through the willow fronds. Three men stood there, and when I saw the blue uniform coats two of them wore, my heart hammered. Two uniforms, one checkered shirt. Exactly as Captain Montez had described the kidnappers.

They knew I had seen them, there could be no more pretending. As they stepped boldly from cover, I saw a glint of sun on a buckle worn on a dark hat, a hat of a peculiar shape. In that instant it flashed through my mind that I had encountered this man before. He had followed me in Puerto Vallarta, and I had called him Black Sombrero . . .

"Is it true that one lives only on earth?
Not forever on earth: only a short while here."
—Aztec poem

FOURTEEN

Black Sombrero raised his rifle. I heard a sharp *crack,* then the whine of a bullet as it hit the granite cliff inches from Luis, then ricocheted, plowing into the ground near my feet.

"Grandmother!" Luis screamed. "Run!"

He seized Leonora's hand, and she stumbled after him into the yawning entrance of the mine. As I raced to follow them, splinters struck my cheek when another bullet hit the wooden post of the entry. Dimly I saw Luis and Leonora just ahead of me, and in a few steps I had caught up with them, taking her left arm while Luis held the right.

"Smooth here," she gasped. "No pits . . . passage left . . . very near."

An arched door leading to a black tunnel loomed in the wall beside us. "Turn?" I asked.

"Yes, turn."

Before we plunged into the utter darkness beyond, I glanced back and saw three figures silhouetted against the flooding light of the entrance.

"Slowly," Leonora whispered. "Quiet. Maybe ten steps." She was the leader now, and as we inched along, Leonora's fingers read the walls like Braille. Slow, funbling, yet not on unfamiliar ground.

A guttural voice shouted in Spanish, "Halt or we'll fire!" And a hundred echoes cried, "Fire . . . Fire . . . Fire . . . "

"Those men are afraid, Luis," she whispered. "They're afraid of the mine. But we're not!"

He did not answer, but his hand, now holding mine, squeezed more tightly in a frightened attempt to reassure me.

"Low, narrow door near us." Leonora spoke no louder than breathing. "Somewhere . . . yes."

Stooping low, we moved through another arch, this one, my fingers told me, framed not by wood but with blocks of cut stone. Once inside the next passage, she said, "Now we wait." And pray, I thought.

Another shouted threat rang through the darkness— nearer, I believed—and the echoes answered. Then rifle shots, a hundred, a thousand it seemed, ringing in every direction, multiplied as they reechoed and resounded in the stony hollowness of the mountain. "The fools!" whispered Leonora. "They'll bring the roof down on themselves!"

And on us? I felt Luis shudder, and I held him close to me.

Now heavy footfalls rang in a nearby corridor, certain, confident steps. A flashlight, I thought desperately. They carried a flashlight or had made a torch. Leonora must have realized the same thing at the same instant, for I heard a faint, helpless sigh. Only a matter of time and they would find us. A few minutes more. And then what? Even in the panic of flight I had realized these men were not ordinary kidnappers. The shots fired first at Luis, then at me, had been meant not to frighten but to kill.

"Halt!" a man yelled. "I see you!"

He must have fired then at some shadow, for the echoes were farther away. But before they died another sound, more ominous, had begun, a low, grinding rumble like faraway thunder. Slowly it grew, increased, became a deafening roar. The men searching for us screamed, then the screams were blotted out by the avalanche.

The rock wall trembled against my back and I choked on dust as Luis hurled himself into my arms. I felt the floor shake and shudder, and beyond the narrow door of our refuge iron girders shrieked as they were twisted and crushed.

Then the crashing of rock, the shattering of beams and shoring slowly died away. "Don't move," whispered Leonora. "Don't speak!"

An eternity seemed to pass while we waited, silent and motionless, terrified that the least sound or reverberation might bring the ceilings above us tumbling down. At last she said, "I think we're as safe as we will be. We'll try to go back."

"The men!" said Luis. "The men with rifles!"

"I don't think they can hurt us now, dear," she told him gently.

Fumbling in my pocket, I found the key chain with its tiny light. When I pressed the switch, I gasped to see the figure of a woman in white standing near us, her arms outstretched.

"The Blessed Virgin," Luis murmured. Leonora had led us to a shrine, a small chapel built long ago by the men who labored and often perished in these tunnels. Unlike the rest of the mine, here a vaulted roof was mortared and braced with hand-hewn pillars of stone.

"I'll go first," I said. "I can see a little with this light. You two hold hands and follow me."

Outside the low door, the corridor lay strewn with rubble, fallen rock and broken beams made of warped tree trunks. We moved cautiously ahead, then, when we reached the main entrance passage, I gasped to see huge blocks of stone sealing the tunnel.

"*Tía?*" asked Luis, his voice faint.

"Closed off, I suppose?" Leonora spoke wearily. She had expected this. "Any opening at all?"

"None." I forced despair out of my tone. "Maybe I could pry some stones loose."

"No! You might bring the rest of it down on us."

"Ramona will bring help," said Luis, making a show of confidence. "She wouldn't let anything happen to us."

"Of course not," Leonora agreed. "But we'd better not wait for Ramona. Do you hear the water? We'll find a drier place."

Listening, I caught a faint. gurgling sound of the stream. Leonora then spoke to me in rapid English, so fast that Luis could not understand. "This passage must have collapsed all the way to the entrance. The stream's blocked. It'll flood in a few minutes. We have to go on!"

"Speak Spanish, *Abuela!*" Luis cried out, his taut nerves breaking at last. "Please speak Spanish!"

As if in answer, a faraway voice shouted, "*José? Juan? Dónde están, por Dios?*"

The three of us froze, huddling together. I switched off the flashlight, and we waited, hardly breathing. Farther down the main tunnel a strong white beam appeared, moving slowly from the floor over the walls, upward to the ceiling.

"Are you here?" he called. "I'm lost!" The echoes mocked him, "*Lost . . . lost . . .* " I could not distinguish anything about him until he lowered the flashlight and a second later a match flared as he lighted a cigarette.

"Black Sombrero," I whispered in Leonora's ear. I did not tell her that he still carried a rifle. He must have been deep enough in the mine, searching for us, to have escaped the avalanche.

There was a sudden rushing of water as somewhere nearby a hidden pool overflowed, and using the noise to conceal our stumbling footsteps, we retreated the way we had come. Instinctively I moved toward the refuge of the chapel, but Leonora murmured, "No. It will flood soon."

We made our way slowly, deeper into the mountain, turning and circling, winding through corridors and vast galleries, through an endless maze where the air was dank and stale, every few steps bringing us to another trickle of water dripping from the ceiling, running down slimy walls to form rivulets at our feet. I tried to keep the tiny flashlight shielded, but we were forced to use it, even though its faint ray might guide Black Sombrero to us.

"Do these corridors connect?" I asked Leonora softly.

"Yes. They crisscross everywhere."

"Then we might meet him," whispered Luis. "He might even be ahead of us."

Ahead—behind us—moving swiftly through a parallel passage, his way speeded by the powerful light he carried. Against this we posed the small advantage that Leonora had once known the mine well.

"There should be an altar just ahead," Leonora told me, keeping her voice low. "Tunnels on either side of it. We go right." A map of the Hidden Treasure seemed to be implanted in her mind.

"Look!" exclaimed Luis. "Light!" He started to rush forward, but I caught his arm, then, before he would speak again, clapped my hand over his mouth.

"Ssh! Luis, be quiet." I took my hand away. The light he had mistaken for an exit was moving now, crossing the corridor ahead where two passages intersected. I switched off the flashlight, and we cowered against the wall. My hand touched wood, not rough shoring but smoother planks. An adjoining passage or room had been boarded up.

Leonora realized where we were standing, and her keen hearing caught the first warning of danger. Without speaking, she gently pushed Luis and me to one side of the closed entry and I heard her step very quietly to the other. Close to us came the sound of a steel spur scraping on rock, then a muttered oath. The chinks between the planking became narrow streaks of light as a white beam played over them.

I heard Black Sombrero's heavy breathing as he paused, leaning against the wooden barrier. He cleared his throat, then there was a creaking sound as he pressed his hands against the planks, testing their strength. Then he kicked the lower boards hard, bringing down a cloud of grit and dust.

It was then Luis coughed. He tried to choke it off, but the sound was unmistakable.

"*Ay!*" The man's exclamation of surprise and discovery seemed shouted in my ear. He kicked the planks furiously, then a rifle butt crashed against them.

I flicked on our light, seized Luis' hand, and gave my arm to Leonora. Flight, no matter how noisy, was our only hope. Shots reverberated in the caverns as he fired at the barrier. As we ran awkwardly on, I heard him kicking and hammering at the boards, hurling his strength and weight against them. How quickly could he batter them down? A few minutes, surely not more than a few minutes.

The passage curved, opened into a room where I saw in the dimness the altar Leonora had described. "Left or right?"

"Right," she said.

Passing through a narrow entrance, we came into a vast, cavernous gallery whose broken floor was strewn with split boulders and rubble. My light seemed smaller than ever, lost in this huge cavern where the farthest walls lay beyond its feeble reach. There was a sudden fluttering, swishing sound in the air above us, and when I shone the beam upward, Luis stifled a cry of terror. Bats swarmed against the ceiling, clung to the giant stone columns the miners had left as supports. Aroused by the light or the sound of our steps, they swirled in clouds, hundreds upon hundreds, uncountable, swooping and flapping across the ray of light.

"Keep going, Alison," said Leonora quietly. "Hurry. Straight ahead. Cave bats, Luis. Don't be afraid."

I flinched as one sailed past my face. The servants mentioned vampire bats that attacked cattle. Could this be the hiding place of the swarm? Shuddering, I pressed on as quickly as I dared. Then Luis let go my hand, and crying out, struck this way and that, flailing his arms, trying to ward off the creatures skimming around him in the darkness.

"Give me your hand!" I said sharply. "Luis!"

When we reached another winding corridor, I looked back. No light, no sign of pursuit.

But only moments later I heard wild shouts and rifle shots. We had not lost him. He had trailed us to the bat-infested gallery. But how? We had passed a dozen intersecting passages, yet he had known our route. Then I realized the truth. Our muddy footprints marked the way clearly.

"Leonora," I said. "We're leaving a trail. Footprints."

"Oh Lord," she breathed. "I didn't think of that." She hesitated only a second. "Then we'll have to detour. Watch for a corridor to the left, one that slopes down."

A moment later I found it, and as we descended the slope, clinging together, the roar of an underground torrent raged nearby. Then cold brown water swirled around our ankles. We turned twice, staying always in flooded passages, shivering, and I thanked God for Leonora, who kept saying, "Only a little farther. Only a little way . . . "

It was perhaps an hour later when we halted for rest, exhausted, unable to move another step. I had suffered the only serious mishap so far, losing my footing at a slippery spot and falling into a shallow but icy pool. Now, soaked to the skin, my teeth chattered and I trembled with cold.

The corridor we were now in was broad and dry. Luis curled up on the floor while Leonora and I sat near him, resting our backs against the uneven stone wall. I turned off the little flashlight, whose beam was becoming weaker and weaker.

In a few minutes, as soon as Luis's regular breathing revealed he was sleeping, I asked, "Where are we going?"

"Toward an old air shaft, I hope. *If* I've remembered the way, *if* it's still there. When we find it, we'll pray that you or Luis can climb out."

"And if we can't?"

She spoke quietly in the darkness. "Then we make other plans." After a moment she said, "Alison, I'm going to describe the way to get there, as well as I can remember it. I want you to memorize the directions."

"Why? If you know the way?"

"I hope we've lost the man who was following us, but there's no counting on it. And now we can't even be sure what happened to his two friends. For all we know, they're wandering around near us right now. If they find us, we part company."

"Part company? But . . . "

"Yes. You take Luis and follow the way to the air shaft. I'll turn another way and shout and make enough noise to draw them away for a while at least."

"Leave you behind?" I exclaimed. "I couldn't do that. You know I couldn't."

"That is exactly what I am ordering you to do, Alison! I don't matter. Luis must survive, not just for his own sake but for the valley."

"What does it matter if . . . "

"Three hundred families live in the village. Their future depends on the ranch. I don't trust that future to Carlos."

"To Carlos? I don't understand."

"If anything happened to Luis, his father would inherit the High Valley. There are no other heirs. I know Carlos very well. In a year the ranch would be bankrupt. He'd sell it piece by piece to live in Mexico City or Madrid or Paris. What about the people who were born here—as their fathers and grand-fathers were! This is their land, too."

I had never looked at it this way before. Of course, Don Carlos was his son's only heir. A monstrous, impossible notion crossed my mind. Carlos had everything to gain if one of Luis' accidents proved fatal. Surely no man could be so cruel and unnatural as to destroy his own son! Such horrible things did happen, of course, and I could picture the Excelentísima, Medea-like, acting in cold blood. But she was a madwoman.

"Tell me about the men hiding in the willows," said Leonora. "You said two wore uniforms?"

"Yes. They dressed exactly as Captain Montez described the kidnappers."

"Strange, isn't it?" she murmured thoughtfully. "Here in the valley uniforms would attract attention."

"Leonora, I saw the third man, the one not in uniform, before. He followed me in Puerto Vallarta."

"Are you certain?"

"Yes." An alarming certainty formed like ice in my mind. I had known from the closeness of the shots outside the mine that these were not usual kidnappers. Now another fact was added. These men had *wanted* to be identified by distinctive clothing, had *wanted* to be connected with the abduction of the millionaire. These were not kidnappers at all, but hired gunmen such as Padre Olivera had mentioned, paid killers of the sort Carlos' attorney had practically boasted of knowing.

"You're trembling, Alison."

"It's the cold. Getting soaked didn't help." My teeth began to chatter, and I stood up, rubbing my hands together, moving my shoulders and arms in a futile effort to warm myself.

Leonora, in a low voice, carefully explained the route to the air shaft, then said, "Remember, if there's trouble or I delay you, I'm to be left behind. You must not hesitate, Alison. Now wake up Luis. We have to go on."

Murky, labyrinthine passages wound on and on, as gradually my flashlight began to waver and fade. Twice we found ourselves at dead ends, and painfully retraced our steps, always listening, straining to hear any footfall of the man who stalked us.

Then Leonora, with quiet excitement, said, "Air! I can smell fresh air! I can feel it!"

At almost the same instant Luis whispered, "A light. I see light."

Ahead of us in the blackness was a faint, ghostly luminescence—dim moonlight shining through an opening in the rock above. Staggering, stumbling over shale heaps and for a moment too joyful to be silent, we made our way to the shaft. As I stepped into the pale radiance, my heart hammered and my head spun giddily with relief.

Then, as I gazed upward, despair overcame me. The shaft was broad, more than a dozen feet across, and far above I saw a half-moon ringed by white cloud. Even in the dimness I knew the walls were smooth and slick as wet marble. The remains of an old ladder, broken and rotted, lay in pieces at my feet.

"*Hola!*" shouted Luis. "Can anyone hear me?"

"Luis, be quiet," said Leonora tensely. "We don't dare shout."

"Where are we?" I asked her.

"Far up the valley. The edge of the slope. It's an out-of-the-way place." Then she brightened. "Someone in the village must remember this opening. They'll come for us."

Who would remember? I wondered. The Excelentísima? Nacho? Black Sombrero—who might well be the man Padre Olivera had said was born in this valley?

Luis soon slept again while Leonora and I kept watch. "He has to come through this safely," she said, speaking as always in low tones. "He's had too much tragedy. Life has been cruel to Luis."

"I know. Leonora, how could his mother have deserted him? Never written to him?"

"I've lain awake nights wondering. I think something happened to her soon after she left here. A fatal accident and no one identified the body, maybe. Or something worse."

"Worse?"

Leonora hesitated. "She might have taken her own life. The note she mailed to my husband almost suggested it."

"What did it say?"

"It was peculiar. She wrote it in Spanish and made a lot of mistakes. Only one sentence. Veronica told the Conde it was better that he forget her and smile than remember her with sadness."

"Did she write the same kind of note to Carlos?"

Leonora shifted her position uneasily. "No. It was an unforgiving note, and as in the other one, words and even sentences were scratched out. I think she wrote it under terrible strain. There were more mistakes in Spanish than she usually made. She said, *'Tengo que estar absolutamente sóla, si voy a me entender . . . '"*

As she went on quoting the Spanish words, I translated them in my mind. Veronica had told Carlos that she must be absolutely alone if she was going to understand herself. She said she could not stay with him any longer and was leaving immediately. Also, she would take nothing from him, now or later.

Jaime must have told me she had written this, for I vaguely remembered the words.

"Carlos hasn't been very fortunate in his marriages, and it's probably his own fault," she said. "Veronica. Before that, Fani."

"Fani? Was that his first wife's name?"

"Yes. That's the nickname for Epifania. I felt sorry for her. Childless marriages are usually unhappy here. There's so much social pressure."

"Epifania . . . " I repeated. "What became of her later?" Even before Leonora replied, I guessed the answer.

"I heard she remarried. A Dutchman or a German in Mexico City. I'm not sure." Leonora's head was nodding, and a moment later she sank into a fitful sleep.

I sat staring upward through the long shaft at the cloudy stars, thoughts racing in my mind, as I remembered the first day I met Carlos Romano. The party Margaret's friends had given and Carlos halting at the head of the steps, then turning back, not wanting to cross the sun deck, avoiding a meeting with someone. Epifania Heiden, now wife of a German businessman in Mexico City. Carlos' wife long ago. He had wanted no connection to be made between them, no memories to be aroused. But why? And suddenly I knew the answer.

"You are dead, do not return to this house.
Touch not our hands, touch not our lips!
Return no more . . . "
—Tarahumara funeral chant

FIFTEEN

"What time is it?" Leonora had whispered this question three times in the last hour.

"Just after eleven." My throat and my head throbbed, my voice was nearly gone. The effects of my falling in the pool of icy water had now shown themselves. During the night, trying to keep watch while the others slept, I had alternately felt myself burning and freezing.

"People should have come for us long ago! Doesn't anyone remember?"

For hours, ever since dawn, we had stared at that taunting patch of sky, an empty, bright symbol of unattainable freedom. And each hour that passed gave more time for the hunter in the black sombrero to find his way through the maze of passages.

"I dreamed they were ringing the alarm bell in the tower," said Luis faintly. "I dreamed everyone came to find us."

I pressed a hand against my burning forehead, as though I

could somehow rub away the fever. At moments the outlines and shapes around me seemed to blur and fuse together.

"If we had some matches, we could build a fire," Leonora said. "Someone might see the smoke."

Matches, I thought numbly. Fire. There was the wood of the broken ladder, pieces of fallen shoring. Was any of the loose stone flint? Could we strike a spark? I looked up where the globe of the sun, yellow and blazing, had reached the rim of the shaft, and then turned to Luis. "Do you have your magnifying glass?" Even whispering was painful.

"Yes, *Tía*." He drew it from his pocket.

"We'll gather wood. Start a fire."

"How?"

"I'll show you."

In a moment we had collected the driest splinters and small bits we could find and placed them in a pile. I managed to show Luis how to hold the glass to catch the sun's rays and focus them into a sharp, hot beam. There was so little time. The direct sun would shine into the shaft only for minutes.

Luis said, "Look! A little smoke. It's starting."

No longer able to help, I watched dully, my breath coming heavily, a sensation that I was choking, smothering. I lay back, letting my eyes close, and although not fully asleep, a fevered dream took possession of me. I sat on the prompter's stool in the wings of the Old Bridge playhouse. Helene, in a sweeping dress of maroon velvet with puffed Victorian sleeves, stood on stage only a few steps from me, bathed in the spotlights. She spoke, but I could hear no words, and the print of the prompt book in my lap blurred and swam. Helene's slender figure shimmered and flashed, a spray of light, then the features dissolved, changed. Veronica stood in her place, uttering the same lines, moving, gesturing, but still soundlessly. Then I heard the sharp slam of a door, and the stage darkened.

"*Tía, Tía!* Wake up!" Luis was shaking my shoulder. When I forced my eyes open, I saw he was smiling.

"Has Jaime come?" I asked, the words forming themselves painfully. Jaime had to be here. Somehow that was all that mattered now.

"Not Uncle Jaime. An old man who saw the smoke. He has gone to bring help."

I sank once more into a half-conscious state, aware only that Jaime would be here soon.

Leonora was gently wiping my brow with her handkerchief when I lost all sense of time. Minutes or hours passed, I could not tell. Then I heard voices, felt strong hands lifting me from the floor, and a strange disembodied sensation of rising weightlessly and flying.

My eyes opened again, and I found myself gazing into Jaime's face. He carried me in his arms, gently, as easily as if I had been a child. When I tried to speak, he said. "Hush, *querida*. You are safe now."

I knew there was something important, terribly important, I must do, and I knew tears ran down my cheeks. What had I planned in the night? Something important . . .

"Jaime," I whispered, at last remembering. "I want . . . I . . ."

"What do you want, little one?"

"To give you . . . " Weakly I struggled to loosen the ribbon that bound my hair.

He held me closer, yet his voice seemed to come from a great distance. "No. You cannot give me what is already mine."

I knew daylight and I knew when darkness came. I knew I lay in my own bed in the Octagon and the nightmare of Veronica dressed in Helene's costume returned often. Once, half awakened, I realized that Jaime was sitting quietly beside my bed, and at other times there was a strange man, who I thought must be a doctor, with me. I felt the sting of a needle, an injection, and then slept again.

Ramona helped me drink warm soup, steadying my hand, but shaking her head when I tried to speak.

My first real awakening, after the fever and delirium had passed, came suddenly. Explosions and gunfire penetrated my sleep, and I sat up quickly in bed and said aloud, "What is it? What's happening?"

"You are awake, señorita?" said a soft voice. "You called?" Mario had entered from the hall and stood near me. The bedroom was dim, illuminated only by a lamp burning on the desk in the adjoining sitting room and by a pale nightlight. "I heard explosions. There—again."

"It is fireworks in the village, señorita. This is the night of San Miguel."

"San Miguel? Then I have slept . . . "

"Two days and two nights. You were very ill. Don Jaime brought a doctor from Puerto Vallarta. He said you would be well as soon as the fever ended. And it has ended, no?"

"I think so." My voice was hoarse, I felt weak and tired, but the fever had vanished. My throat no longer pained me. and for the first time my mind was again clear of ghosts and delirium.

Mario switched on a lamp, and opening a thermos on the bedside table, poured me a cup of chocolate.

"Where is Don Jaime?" I asked. "I want to speak with him."

"Everyone is in the village at the fiesta. He wanted to stay with you, but is expected at the church. The *patrón* must attend the celebration and the Mass. All people from the *casa grande* are there. But Doña Leonora is in her room sleeping. Shall I awaken her?"

"No. What I must say is for Don Jaime." A chilling memory swept through me. "Mario, what of the men who fired at us? The man who pursued us in the mine?"

"Forget them, señorita. Not one escaped. The shaft was guarded until last night, when another avalanche closed it forever. No one in the mine could have survived. Forget them! They deserved what . . . " He broke off, and lowering his eyes, crossed himself quickly, believing—as all the village folk did—that it was a sin to speak evil of the dead.

"If you are sleepless, señorita, the doctor left these for you." He indicated a saucer with four red capsules. "Take only one."

"I won't need any, thank you."

He smiled, a warm, kind smile that brought light to his brown eyes. "We will watch over you until Don Jaime returns. Now drink the chocolate. I am just outside the door if you call."

He started to leave, then turned back, his smile now mischievous. "Don Jaime asked me to tell you two things if you awakened."

"Yes?"

"He now has the correct ribbon, the red one, and it decorates his saddle tonight. Also, do not worry about anything taken from your doll's house." When I looked puzzled, he said, "In your fever they say you kept repeating that something was taken from the doll's house. You spoke the words in English many times, I think."

"I don't remember."

"Don Jaime said you must have dreamed you were a little girl again. Whatever has been taken, he promises to replace. Rest well, señorita. "

I sipped the chocolate, grateful for its warmth and nourishment. Apparently during my fever I had spoken my dream aloud—shouted it perhaps. No one had understood what I was trying to say. To the people in the High Valley, a doll's house was a toy, not the name of a drama by Henrik Ibsen, the story of a wife who leaves her husband. I rose from the bed, a little wobbly, dizzy for a second or two. Moving slowly, I went to the closet and found my warm robe and slippers.

A familiar book had been removed from the bookcase— *Six Plays by Henrik Ibsen.* I remembered seeing it there only a week before. Yet I did not really need to examine *A Doll's House* again. Now that my memory had been stirred, the lines of Nora, the wife, came back to me as clearly as if I could again hear Helene speaking them as she swept across the stage in a maroon velvet costume: "I must stand quite alone if I am to understand myself and everything about me. It is for that reason that I cannot remain with you any longer . . . I am going away from here now, at once . . . "

These were the words of one of the plays Veronica had struggled to translate into Spanish. For she had never written a letter of farewell to Don Carlos. The note that disguised her real fate had been nothing more than an exercise, only one of the scores of translations she had done, bits of poetry, speeches from Shakespeare, and for Jaime a famous sonnet. Leonora had said that words and phrases had been scratched out of the letter. Of course. Things in Nora's scene with her husband that did not quite fit, replies, names would be obliterated.

I thought of the note the Conde Luis later received from Mexico City—a message about forgetting her and being able to smile. It, too, was surely a stolen exercise. Some poem whose lines I could not quite remember, but it would be found among Veronica's books, not in Spanish but in English.

How simple it had been, how easy! Veronica had handwritten passages to apply to almost anything, and there was little chance anyone would identify the original. Veronica was not a very accurate or inspired translator, and no one here, not even Leonora, knew literature in English. Spanish would have been another matter. Jaime and probably his father would instantly have recognized a passage from *Don Quixote* or *Blood Wedding* or *One Hundred Years of Solitude*—

"The fire!" I said aloud. We had talked about that novel, even mentioned the character who, like Eric Vanderlyn's father, had invented a powerful burning glass. Ramona, speaking of the time the barn caught fire, had said, "The sun was so bright that day."

Luis' tiny magnifying glass had set wood aflame in only a few minutes in the cave. I pictured the device Christian Vanderlyn had built, with its double lenses and powerful reflectors, standing on the balcony of Don Carlos' apartment, harmless-looking, probably mistaken for a telescope if anyone happened to notice it. And its beam did not have to ignite wood, but dry, almost explosive straw in the nearby barn.

I could not bear to think about it longer. I needed rest now, sleep, until Jaime returned after the midnight Mass. Then I would tell him all I knew, rid myself of this burden.

Moving toward the bed, I glanced in the mirror and saw myself, pale, drawn, unsteady. The Excelentísima's spiteful words came back to me. Carlos had told her that I was a shy, awkward woman. "Probably not very intelligent. Spineless." Now I knew she had spoken the truth. This was exactly the way he must have described me. That was how I had impressed him in Puerto Vallarta during an interview when I felt uncertain, afraid of him, and had given no hint that I spoke Spanish. That was why he had hired me—to replace the suspicious Señora Castro and to prevent Jaime's bringing another capable woman into the house, a woman who could understand the servants' gossip and in time, like Señora Castro, would begin to ask questions.

Lying down, I covered myself with the sheet. As I reached to turn off the lamp, my hand brushed the saucer of sleeping pills and two of them rolled across the table, falling to the floor. I felt too weary to pick them up. Drifting into sleep, I heard Mario speaking softly to someone in the hall outside. He had said, "We will watch over you." I supposed he meant himself and Ramona, and felt grateful and secure knowing they were nearby.

The far-off clanging of village church bells awakened me again. I lay still, refreshed and much stronger. Lights burned cheerfully in the sitting room.

The night wind had come, and now the house seemed uneasy on its ancient foundations. The wooden pillars of the veranda creaked beneath the weight of the roof and somewhere a loose shutter complained of unoiled hinges.

I heard footsteps beyond the colonnaded partition, and was about to call to Ramona, to tell her I was much better and wide awake, when a pacing figure crossed the archway. It was not Ramona—it was Ethel Evans. I stifled a gasp. How could they have left me with her? I thought wildly. It was impossible! Surely they knew . . .

But they did *not* know. There had been no chance to talk with Jaime, and I had deliberately not spoken to Leonora about her old acquaintance. If Miss Evans volunteered to miss the fiesta to keep watch with Mario, it would seem an act of kindness.

She looked at the watch pinned to her gray dress, then rubbed her hands together nervously. When she stepped just inside the arch to make sure I was still sleeping, I lowered my eyelids and kept my breathing regular and heavy, all the time watching closely.

Ethel Evans was a frightened woman. Her eyes looked wide with desperation and the thin fingers trembled as they moved from her hair to her mouth to the brooch at her high collar. She glanced again at her watch, as though the hour had not registered on her mind before.

Moving from view, she walked toward the window and I heard her unfastening the lock. I quietly put on my slippers and stood beside the bed, apprehensive yet not really afraid, knowing I had only to call and Mario would come.

A heavier step sounded on the veranda, a man passed my closed draperies, then entered the sitting room.

"You're here at last!" exclaimed Miss Evans, tense and whispery.

"I was delayed. It does not matter."

My heart seemed to stop beating and my hands were icy as they touched my cheeks. Carlos Romano had returned.

"She is still sleeping?" he asked.

"Yes. Even the bells didn't awaken her. I counted the capsules. She'd taken two."

"So much the better. If she is groggy it will be easier to . . ."

"I don't want to know!" Ethel Evans verged on hysteria. "This is none of my doing! I know nothing about it."

"Naturally," he said, soothing her. "You were kind enough to forgo the fiesta for Miss Mallory's sake. Now you are afraid of falling asleep, so you will go to the kitchen to make a cup of tea. When you return, you sit in this chair and read a magazine. There is no reason for you to look in on Miss Mallory. You know how peacefully she was sleeping." Then the gentle, persuasive tone shifted to a threat. "You understand, Miss Evans? You will make no mistakes!"

"I understand," she answered weakly.

"I think you know that a Mexican prison is a most uncomfortable place for such a lady as yourself."

"You're a fine one to talk!" Her attempt to sound defiant gave way to trembling. "I've never touched anything really valuable. I kept still about the necklace when I knew you'd changed the stones. I say we're even."

"We will be even after you have gone to make your tea."

So the emeralds had been substituted, and later, when threatened with discovery, Carlos had carried the imitations to Mexico City. Not to sell—there was no need for that. Luis, according to the plan, would not survive to have an education. And who would question the records of the new master of the High Valley?

"Now go to the kitchen," he said. "Hot tea will cheer you up."

I heard the sound of the veranda window opening, then closing behind her. For a moment I stood paralyzed, unable to stir. Surely Don Carlos did not know that Mario was just outside. The boy's strength was no match for Carlos, but that did not matter. Mario would be a witness. His presence alone would prevent Carlos from harming me.

A footfall in the sitting room aroused me to action. I had to be nearer the hall door when I faced him, nearer Mario and safety. Rubbing my eyes as though I had only that moment awakened, I moved to the archway, calling sleepily, "Hello? Is someone here?"

We almost collided. "Don Carlos! I thought I heard someone."

"You are awake, Alison. Good!" He stepped aside to let me pass. "I hope you are feeling better?"

"Much. I'm practically myself again." I moved nearer the door.

"Excellent. But you seem to be trembling. A chill, perhaps?"

"Slight. Nothing really." I forced myself to meet his eyes and managed a smile. He was dressed in dark leather, and wore black riding gloves which, with a pistol strapped to his hip, gave him the appearance of an executioner. He seemed at ease, but the scar slashed on his face was livid tonight and pulsed faintly.

"I have a message from Doña Leonora," he said. "She would like you to join the family for a special celebration after the Mass."

"How thoughtful of her," I murmured. His vanity astonished me. Could he think I would believe such a story—that Leonora, knowing I was ill, would summon me to a fiesta at such an hour? "I thought she was still here sleeping," I said.

"She felt better after a rest and went to the village." He had lied so successfully and so often that now he felt anything he said, no matter how preposterous, would be believed.

"She wants me to come to the village?"

"No. We gather each year at the bell tower. The bells are blessed by Padre Olivera. You will find it interesting."

The bell tower. I thought of those steep, winding stairs spiraling floor after floor. The bell tower at night—deserted, isolated.

"You're trembling again," he said. "Another chill?"

"Yes. I don't think I'm able to go out. Please tell Leonora."

He stepped toward me, his face darkening. "We cannot disappoint her."

"Very well, then. But I must tell Mario." Whirling, I flung open the hall door, then gasped. Mario lay on a straw mat sleeping heavily, a half-empty bottle of tequila beside him. "Mario!"

As I knelt to shake him, a powerful hand gripped my shoulder. "No, señorita. He will not awaken for hours. Earlier he accepted a small drink from Nacho. Why not? It is the night of the fiesta."

Drugged, I thought. Tomorrow no one would believe Mario's protests. The bottle, the odor of tequila spilled on the mat, would tell against him.

Carlos pulled me to my feet. "We waste time, Alison. We will be late."

Time . . . if only I could delay him. How long did the High Mass go on? An hour? "I'll change to something warmer," I said.

"No need. Your robe is warm enough. And do not worry about its informality. This will be a very small, intimate gathering." He was toying with me now, mocking me. I would go with him, he felt, not only because I had no choice, but also because I would want so desperately to believe he was telling the truth.

Taking my arm, he propelled me toward the veranda. "We can walk there in a few minutes," he said. "The moonlight is lovely. Perfect for a stroll. You will enjoy it. We are going to follow the lane through the orchard, much prettier than the road."

How had he discovered what I knew? I wondered dully. How had I given myself away? Then I remembered the words I had repeated over and over in my delirium. *"Taken from a doll's house."* Even Mario had learned of it. But Carlos was the only one who would understand the meaning. And now what was my life to him? Nothing. Less than the lives of the bulls into whose hearts he had plunged a sword.

He was mad—the madness so apparent in the Excelentísima lay concealed in her grandson. Yet as we left the *casa grande* and moved toward the lane which shimmered in the moonlight, I found myself almost believing that I would really find Leonora and Jaime and Luis waiting for me at the bell tower.

I forced the illusion, the false hope from my mind. That

was what he wanted me to think, to go on hoping until the last second. Although he no longer gripped my arm, it was useless to attempt flight. I knew how easily he could overtake me. Think, I told myself. There had to be a way—some way.

Stopping abruptly, I looked up at him. "You still have a chance, you know," I said as calmly as I could.

"A chance? What does that mean?"

"Everyone's at the fiesta. With your plane you could be in South America before anyone can prove what you've done." The words came too rapidly, too jerkily, but I raced ahead, improvising frantically. "It may take weeks for Margaret Webber to get answers from the attorneys who are checking the records of Luis' birth."

"What do you mean, Alison?" He leaned close to me, and I forced myself not to draw back.

"It was so obvious to Margaret and me after we spoke to Mrs. Heiden. Your father believed you divorced her because she gave you no children. Now she has two fine sons. So the lack was yours, not hers, wasn't it? I suppose it all happened because of the plague that swept through the valley at the time you were born. A terrible, tragic thing for you as well as for Nacho."

"Go on, Alison," he said, his eyes narrow.

I knew I had hit upon the truth, but had touched a matter so dangerous I could not pursue it. Something else, I thought desperately, another tactic. "Eric Vanderlyn and I talked about the fire in the barn," I said quickly. "We were quite sure how it started, but couldn't believe the truth, because we still thought Luis was your son. But he isn't, of course. Veronica's child, yes. Not yours. Soon everyone will know."

"How will they know, Alison?" He rested his hand on my shoulder, gently this time but too near my throat. "Tell me how?"

"Margaret's attorney will find out." Silently I prayed for strength not to panic. "When you wrote that you had a wife and a baby boy, everyone here accepted it. Why wouldn't they? You *had* to have a son. That was the only reason your father welcomed you back. Veronica joined in the pretense. She must have loved you very much, or else Jaime is right and she was desperate for security for herself and her baby."

He frowned, uncertain for the first time. "So you've talked with Jaime, too?" he asked.

"Of course. And with Padre Olivera. He thinks Veronica felt guilty because she helped deceive your father. She really cheated Jaime of his inheritance and was going to confess it. You couldn't let that happen. So you had to get rid of her."

"You interest me, Alison, but we must not be late for the celebration," he said. "We can talk on the way. Come, now. Arm in arm. More friendly, no?"

In the brilliance of the moon, the lime trees seemed frozen, their leaves icy, unreal. I glanced furtively backward, hoping to see anyone walking in the night. The lane stretched deserted. Had it been this way when Veronica—I didn't dare let myself finish the thought.

"There's still time to get away," I told him, trying to control my trembling. "Everyone knows. They just haven't enough proof yet."

"You are a very imaginative woman, Alison," he said. "I misjudged you when we met. I thought you were a rather stupid girl—shy, easy for me to manage. A great improvement over Señora Castro."

"Yes, I know. That's why you hired me."

"Of course. I thought it best that I myself make the selection, not Jaime." He laughed, a dry, mirthless chuckle. "I could not have done worse."

The bell tower loomed ahead of us, tall and stark against the sky. No candles flickered in its dark arches, no sign of a celebration. I felt my throat constricting with fear.

"You're intelligent enough to know when the game is over," I said. "No one can prove any serious crime yet. Fraud, of course. Miss Evans is bound to talk about the theft of the emeralds. But no one can prove that you"—I forced out the words—"that you killed Veronica." His grip on my arm tightened. "Why not get away now?"

"You are the one who fails to know when the game ends," he said sharply. "The Señora Webber has contacted no attorneys. I have had a man watching her."

"Yes, she's been aware of that. The man in the black sombrero. One of the three you hired to ambush us on our picnic. Did you arrange the accident at the dam to make sure Jaime wouldn't be with us?" I asked without thinking, although I knew I must not put questions to him, that I must pretend I had learned everything and told others of it. We were approaching the tower now. I had two minutes, three minutes more. What had he planned for me? Another accident? That I had wandered out, delirious with fever, climbed the steps of the bell tower and fallen? That must be what he intended. I stifled a gasp as I remembered the day when we had talked about seeing the fireworks from the bell tower. "How beautiful!" I'd said. "I'd love to see that." Carlos had heard me; so had Jaime and Leonora. I had innocently provided evidence to cover up my own murder! I was not sure anyone would believe the story of another accident—but what would that matter? Carlos, in his madness, must now feel that my death in the bell tower would be accepted just as Veronica's disappearance had been.

"You are lagging!" He jerked me forward, showing his strength. "Señora Webber knows nothing. I have opened and read every letter you have exchanged. Also, I have talked with the people you claim to have confided in. Do you think I would not sense a change in them? All useless lies, Alison."

At the edge of the lane, only a few yards ahead, I saw a movement in the shadows. A surge of hope coursed through me and I drew in my breath, ready to scream. Then, calmly, a burro ambled from the trees, paused to munch a bit of grass, then went his way.

"You condemned yourself, Alison," he said, "the night when Dr. Hardy and his sister came to the house."

"At the séance?" I asked. "When I spelled Veronica's name to test you? Others saw your reaction, you know."

His lips twisted in something like a smile. "You understand nothing! What do I care for such nonsense as spirits talking through boards? But what you told Dr. Hardy at the dinner table made me realize I had to get rid of you, one way or another."

"Dr. Hardy?"

"The daughter of an actress who helped her mother learn lines. Learn by heart the plays of Ibsen! In time someone would tell you the words of Veronica's letter, and you would recognize them. I had to act, and I did. It was simple to arrange your fall on the stairs. You had your chance then, since you survived. If you had gone to Mexico City with me, in a few days I could have told you we no longer needed you here. Or I might have managed in other ways."

Seizing both my arms, he forced me to face him. "In Mexico City I could have handled you easily, because you have always found me attractive, no?" When I did not answer, he shook me. "Admit the truth, Alison!"

I made myself look into the half-insane eyes, the features contorted by a terrifying, exultant madness. "Yes, Carlos," I whispered. "Yes. That's why I would never tell anyone."

"Do not tell me foolish lies. I will destroy whatever stands between me and what is rightfully mine!"

"A child! A helpless child!" The words choked me.

"What is this child to me? The spawn of a half-breed *torero* who died on the horns in Buenos Aires. His son—not mine! And the child of a stupid, passionless woman who aroused contempt in me. I used her as I needed, and the fool thought I loved her. Then she tried to defy me, threatened me. But the valley is mine! Mine! And I will win it back as the first Romanos did—not by weakness but by blood."

His eyes blazed and the steel fingers bit into my arms as I clenched my teeth, holding back a cry of pain. For a moment his breath came heavily, in gasps, then he was in control of himself again. "Come. We have an appointment to keep," he said.

I struggled against him, but he held me easily with one arm, while his other hand moved suddenly to his side and drew the pistol from its holster. "No more fighting. No cries. You will walk ahead quietly."

Now we were on the path to the door of the tower. He no longer bothered to hold me, and I stumbled a few steps ahead of him, knowing the pistol was trained on my back. The door stood agape as though awaiting me. Just as I reached the threshold, it flashed through my mind that Carlos would not fire the pistol. Maddened though he might be, my fate was to appear accidental. Lunging forward, I slammed the door behind me, searching frantically for a bolt or bar—and finding none. I threw my body against it, trying to hold it shut against the relentless pressure of his strength, knowing it was useless.

Moonlight streamed through the windows above. I saw the stairs clearly, and not thinking, spurred only by terror, I let the door give way and darted toward the steps, panting, choking for breath as I climbed, passing the loft with the chime ropes, running wildly on. I heard him following me, slowly, inexorably. For him there was no hurry. For me, no escape except to throw myself from the high windows.

The plank Luis had once crossed gleamed in the dimness. I did not hesitate, did not pause to consider whether it would bear my weight, but fled across it, feeling it creak and buckle beneath my feet. Then I was on the other side, the top of the tower, the end of all retreat. Far below Don Carlos followed without haste.

Kneeling, I tore at the plank. If I could pull it loose, send it crashing down . . . Splinters pierced my fingers, but the heavy nails held fast. Only a moment left now, as I reached above my head and pushed the huge bell that hung from the highest beam, the alarm bell. It swung only a little, and summoning all my strength, I tried once more. The bell moved, a long, tolling note rang through the tower, across the fields and orchards. Then a second stroke, deafening, a booming voice in the night.

Cursing, Don Carlos charged forward, up the last flight of stairs, as I threw my weight against the bell once more, and it responded, telling the village, the *casa grande,* the vast valley that there was danger and that someone was in the tower.

Carlos loomed before me, a dark silhouette against the arches. He had to stop me, dared not lose a second. Perhaps he, like Luis, had crossed this same plank a hundred times in childhood, for now, with no thought except reaching me, he rushed forward.

A sudden cracking of wood, sharp and loud as a rifle report, a startled cry as it gave way—then a long scream that ebbed in the darkness as he plummeted downward, hurtling through empty space, his fall unbroken until he struck the floor at the foot of the stairs.

I sank to my knees, sobbing, holding my head in my hands, weeping for myself, for Veronica—and for the demented man whose body lay far below. At last able to stand, I staggered to the window that overlooked the road, clinging to its bars, waiting.

I heard hoofbeats approaching at a gallop, saw a cloud of dust in the road, and a moment later Jaime and three other riders reined their horses at the tower.

"Who's there? What is it?" he shouted.

"Jaime!" I called. "Jaime, I'm here!"

"Alison?" He swung from the horse and ran toward the tower door, vanishing from my view. I did not let go the bars, did not look down into the darkness when I heard him exclaim, *"Carlos! Madre de dios!"* He was on the stairs now. "Alison! Are you all right?"

"I am . . . all right."

Still I could not turn from the window. Better for the moment not to think, not to feel, not to remember. I stood still, my eyes moving from the panorama of the High Valley to the courtyard of the tower where Yaqui awaited his master, proud in the moonlight, a long red ribbon fluttering from his saddle horn.

Jaime was shouting to the men below. "*Una reata!* Or cut a bell rope. I must cross!"

I could not understand their answers or the sounds behind me. I understood nothing until I felt Jaime lifting me gently to my feet, holding me close in his arms. "*Querida!*" he whispered. "Thank God. Oh, thank God!"

"He is gone, Jaime. No more fear, no more shadows." I looked into his face, gentle, caring. "I love you."

"We love each other. We will go away, we will forget this. Then we will come home."

I clung to him, drawing strength from his strength, love from his love, knowing that I would not again hide myself, not run away, and that home was where Jaime was.